W9-CCE-804

ASHES, ASHES

JO TREGGIA

ASAS

ASAS

ES,
ES

SCHOLASTIC PRESS ■ NEW YORK

Library of Congress Cataloging-in-Publication Data

Treggiari, Jo.
Ashes, ashes / by Jo Treggiari. — 1st ed.
p. cm.
Summary: In a future Manhattan, devastated by environmental catastrophes and epidemics, sixteen-year-old Lucy survives alone until vicious hounds target her and force her to join Aidan and his band, but soon they learn that she is the target of Sweepers, who kidnap and infect people with plague.
ISBN 978-0-545-25563-9 (alk. paper)
[1. Science fiction. 2. Survival — Fiction. 3. Epidemics — Fiction. 4. Environmental disasters — Fiction. 5. Dogs — Fiction. 6. New York (N.Y.) — Fiction.] I. Title.
PZ7.T717Ash 2011
[Fic] — dc22
2010032398

10 9 8 7 6 5 4 3 11 12 13 14 15

Printed in the U.S.A. 23 Reinforced Binding for Library Use
First edition, June 2011 Book design by Elizabeth B. Parisi

FOR BETTY FRANKLIN,

SUSAN TREGGIARI,

AND MY FEARLESS, INTREPID LUCY PARRIS

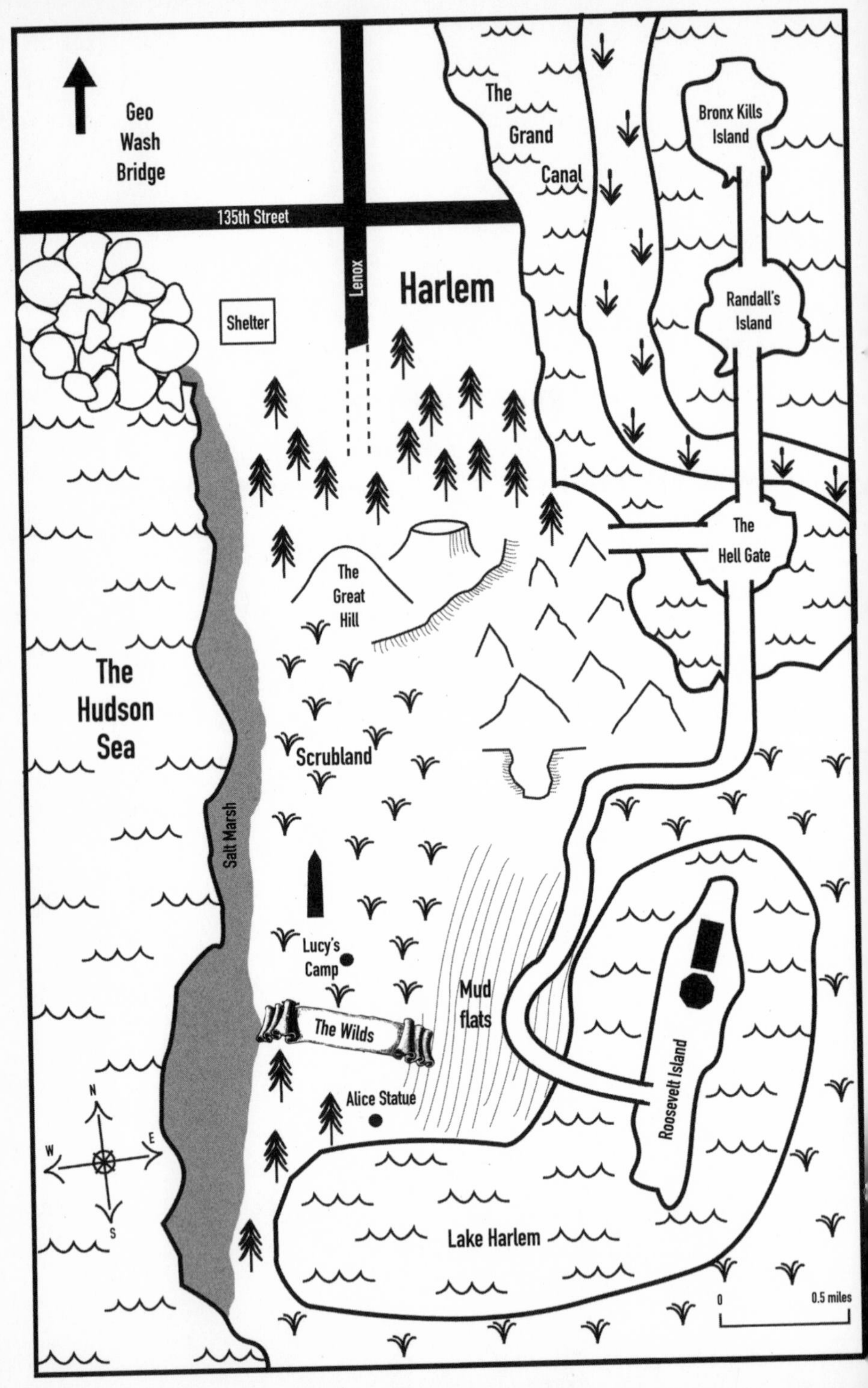

Geo
Wash
Bridge
135th Street
Lenox
Harlem
Shelter
The
Grand
Canal
Bronx Kills
Island
Randall's
Island
The
Hell Gate
The
Great
Hill
The
Hudson
Sea
Salt Marsh
Scrubland
Lucy's
Camp
Mud
flats
The Wilds
Alice Statue
Roosevelt Island
Lake Harlem
N
E
W
S
0
0.5 miles

Ring around the roses
A pocketful of posies
Ashes, ashes
We all fall down.

CHAPTER ONE

TURTLE

Lucy hunched over the corpse and felt a tiny bubble of hysterical laughter gurgle up. But as she stared at the lifeless turtle stretched out on the rough plank, the laughter died abruptly. The tang of fresh blood was unpleasant. She should have butchered it outside, by the shore, but the hour was getting late and she'd felt exposed on the sand. Besides, she had never actually done a turtle before, never noticed how the wizened face and papery eyelids made it look like a very old person.

She positioned the knife edge along the thinnest section of gray, wrinkled neck and pushed down, fixing her gaze steadily in front of her. The knife stuck. She tried to stop her brain from screaming thoughts of sinew and bone, and leaned her weight on her hand. The flesh resisted, then suddenly gave way. The knife slammed into the hard wood underneath, and the head rolled off onto the ground with an audible *thump*.

Her stomach heaved. Fortunately, it was empty. Lucy put her knife down and dragged the woven screen away from the entry hole to her shelter, letting a breeze sweep in and clear the stench from her nose.

She closed her eyes and breathed in deeply, sinking to her knees. She could smell the scent of impending rain. She wondered whether she could survive it for another year. Two days of steady rain had already turned the ground outside her camp into a series of muddy pools threaded by soggy grassland, and since her shelter lay in a hollow, there was now what amounted to a narrow moat right outside the front entrance.

The floods had first come about five years ago, when she was eleven years old. Melting polar caps; rising sea levels; increased rainfall; a steady battering of hurricanes, tornadoes, and earthquakes weakening the land: everything the scientists had warned them about. And the world mapped in her geography books had changed with a frightening rapidity;

continents shifting shape, coastlines altered. San Francisco, Los Angeles, Venice, Thailand, Spain, her beloved Coney Island, Japan, had all but vanished beneath the waves. Australia was half the size it had been, shrinking like an ice cube in a warm drink, and New York City had become a clump of six or seven scattered islands connected to the mainland by a few big bridges — the Geo Wash, the RFK, the Will Burg. Some were only accessible during the Long Dry.

Small but fast-moving canals flowed over the same routes as the old roads. Lexington Avenue, Fifth Avenue, 42nd Street, were all underwater now. But people had rallied and rebuilt. They'd stretched suspension bridges strong enough to hold a dozen people and a few bicycles at a time across the swollen canals that now ran in a crisscrossing grid over what had been Manhattan. Thousands of sandbags shored up the dikes along the smaller waterways, and a massive wall of masonry and detonated high-rises had been built in an attempt to keep the inland sea back from the edges of Harlem and Washington Heights. Cheap plywood houses sprang up on stilts, altering the cityscape. Deep, wide gutters were cut into the ground, and cars were banned from the city, except on the outskirts and the few roads that had survived the earthquakes.

They'd called it "New Venice" jokingly, and it had seemed okay then. Lucy, living in the solidity of northern New Jersey, miles away from the shores of the sea, had felt safe, and she'd kept on taking the train into the city or hitching, kept on cruising the vintage stores for cool clothes. It rained frequently, making whole neighborhoods inaccessible for months out of the year, and the summers were more sweltering than ever, but the streets were still packed with people buying and selling or just hanging out. And then, as if all that had been just a dress rehearsal for some disaster movie, four years later the plague had arrived.

She could almost hear the newspeople again, like something out of one of those cheesy old sci-fi television shows: the warnings to stay inside; the rising panic; the video of gaunt, red-eyed survivors, their skin seemingly charred; the doomsayers with their sandwich boards, black robes, and crazy talk about disease-carrying birds and God's wrath. Seeing anchorwomen, who normally looked like airbrushed mannequins, seriously freaking out was scary. Lucy still had nightmares. She still woke up certain that her skin was covered in scabs and she was bleeding to death from the inside out.

Instead of globe-eyed aliens or a gigantic meteorite headed straight for Earth, it was the resurgence of a killer disease that had reduced the global population to less than 1 percent of what it had been within three short months. Eating healthy, exercising, living in a big house, driving a fancy car—none of that mattered at all. The pox took almost everybody, and it seemed that people between the ages of thirty and sixty died faster and harder than anyone.

And who would have guessed that Lucy would have turned out to be luckier than her entire family?

Lucy "Lucky" Holloway. She used to hate her nickname, but now—now it was different.

It was weird to think that her younger brother, Rob, had started calling her that as a joke. He'd also nicknamed the dog, Rex, "Tex Mex" after it had been discovered that the golden retriever could scarf down a dozen frozen burritos without vomiting, and he'd renamed their older sister, Susan, "Maggie" (short for "Maggot") because she liked to eat rice pudding while bundled up on the couch in an old blanket.

Maybe Lucy had gotten off easy. *Lucky* instead of *Lucy* wasn't too bad, and most people didn't realize it was meant sarcastically because of her ability to trip over her own two feet, break dishes, and knock books off of shelves merely by walking past them. As a preteen, she'd managed to run through the glass French doors that led into the kitchen from the pool, not once, but twice, necessitating visits to the emergency room and eleven stitches in her calf the first time and then, six under her chin.

She knew her clumsiness annoyed her parents. She'd always felt as if she were a changeling dumped into their magazine-perfect midst. She didn't even look like them, having inherited some recessive gene from an ancient Welsh ancestor. She was slim and gray-eyed, with wildly curly black hair—shocking compared to their pink and blond athletic good looks. She was awkward and she was ugly. And worse than that, she wasn't a superjock like her brother or a brainiac like her sister. She was something her happy-homemaker mom and her big-lawyer dad just couldn't understand: good at nothing in particular.

In her journal she'd written long, angry, tearful diatribes about feeling out of step and alone at home and at school, where the cliques were ruled by people just like her brother and sister, until she'd convinced herself she didn't care, forced herself to tune out when Rob's latest game score or Maggie's newest scholarship was being discussed over the dinner table. At least she hadn't been nicknamed after something that pulsed and wriggled on rotten food.

Poor Maggie. Gone, and her old blanket gone, too, burned in a useless attempt to get rid of the sickness. Together with the quilts Grandma Ferris had painstakingly pieced together and Lucy's threadbare teddy bear and the embroidered sofa cushions and everything else it seemed had made life soft and comfortable. Great piles of sheets and bedspreads, mattresses and pillows were piled sky-high in every neighborhood, then doused in gasoline and coaxed into infernos that burned for weeks. When the wind was coming from the east, Lucy imagined she could still smell the acrid fumes like burnt hair, could still see the towers of black smoke billowing against the blazing blue sky. It was not until the Long Dry was over and the Long Wet began again that the fires were finally quenched by the pelting rains. The parched dirt liquefied into slow-moving rivers of sludge and covered everything in mud, including the pits—the deep trenches used once the cemeteries were full, where bodies were stacked in rows like cut logs and scattered with quick lime to hurry the decay in an attempt to prevent reinfection. Then the controlled bombings began, turning high-rises into massive concrete cairns over the sites where thousands had died within days of one another. The skeletal bodies, the livid marks on blackened skin, were buried under tons of rock, and all the crushing details of life as it used to be were erased.

The memories she tried to preserve were of her life before the plague descended, and in her mind it was like those times were lit by a gentler sun, all Technicolor blurry and beautiful. She remembered the smallest things: her mother's buttermilk pancakes and homemade blackberry jam, the smell of fabric softener, the feel of socks without holes. Now, looking at her grimy fingernails and dirt-encrusted skin, she was amazed at how much she had changed. How things like homework, a daily shower, and a hot breakfast on the table seemed so unimaginable to her now.

She was certainly not lucky. She was Lucy, plain and simple.

She leaned back on her heels, staring at the flattened pile of dry grasses where she slept, her sleeping bag with her vintage leather motorcycle jacket scrunched up for a pillow; the crooked shelf she'd hung from a couple of branches holding a dented tin plate and bowl; a camping knife, fork, and spoon strung on a piece of string so she wouldn't lose them; her backpack with the essentials; a change of clothing. All she had left in the world besides her knife, the survival manual she'd scooped off the floor of a bookshop with all the windows smashed out, and a few other personal items. The book was battered and stained, pages escaping from the cracked binding, but it was precious.

She scraped her hair back off her sweaty forehead. It was too short to stay tucked behind her ears and just long enough to fall into her eyes constantly. She felt an oozing wetness on her cheek and looked at her hands. Mud, blood, and who knew what else. Tears? Lucy didn't cry too often. She figured she'd used them all up by now. She bit her lip hard between her teeth and stood up clumsily. She'd been crouched over for so long that her right foot had gone to sleep. She dragged the screen back over the doorway, then limped over to the bucket she kept filled with rainwater and rinsed her hands, drying them roughly on the legs of her jeans.

The turtle wasn't getting any deader, and she had a lot to do before she lost the last of the daylight. She walked back over to the rough table she'd made out of a few pallets and peered down at the manual, held flat under a couple of rocks. The instructions had seemed simple enough. The capture had been easier than she had expected: sneaking up on the creature while it sunbathed on a mud bar on the shore of the Hudson Sea, grabbing it by the thin leather whip of a tail, and holding it well away from her body until she could shove a stick between the snapping jaws. And she hadn't felt much sympathy, not after it tried to bite her; hadn't felt so much as a twinge, even though before everything that had happened she'd been a strict vegetarian. No, she'd held it flat against the ground with the pressure of her knee, waggled another stick in front of the cruel, predatory-bird mouth until the neck was stretched taut, and then bopped it hard on its little old lady head with a handy rock.

She checked the book again. There was a page missing; there must be. She flipped backward and forward, looking for the sequence of actions that would yield four slabs of pink meat, as pristine and antiseptic as anything you could have bought off a refrigerated shelf in a grocery store. If there had still been any around. She stabbed at the creature in a sudden fury. The knife turned on the shell. She yelped and tossed it from her in disgust. She'd gouged her left palm—a long, wide gash that instantly welled blood. She sucked on her hand, not really enjoying the coppery taste. She pulled her bandanna from her neck and wrapped it around the wound, pulling the ends tight in a knot with her teeth. Then she kneeled down and picked up the knife, rubbing the dirt from it and checking the blade for damage. She heaved a sigh of relief. It seemed okay. She ran her thumb over the edge, feeling a burr of roughness, the smallest of nicks. It would need to be re-honed before she could continue.

"Stupid, stupid, stupid," she told herself.

At the bottom of her backpack was a narrow rectangle of gray stone. It felt like fine sandpaper. Five sweeps of the blade against it and the edge was sharp enough to draw a thin line of blood across the fleshy part of her thumb. She turned the knife over to sharpen the other side.

Lucy walked back over to the book and pushed her hair back behind her ears again with force. The gory remains of the turtle were laid out on some broad leaves. It looked nothing like the neat illustration. The vibrantly colored picture showed tidy quarters of pale rosy meat—not this mutilated lumpy mass leaking muddy water and blood. The shell was the problem. Bony, hard as granite, it just wouldn't come off. She'd followed the instructions, tossing the corpse into a saucepan of water over the fire. She'd even left the turtle in the pot for longer than the ten minutes specified, but now she had to wonder if perhaps the water hadn't been hot enough.

The words danced in front of her eyes. She stared so long that they stopped making any kind of sense. The sun was setting, and the light leaking through the willow screens was dim. Lucy inserted the knife between the shell and the carcass and jimmied it around. There was a snap and the tip of the blade broke off. She stared at the knife for a moment, disbelieving, and then with a cry of rage, she picked up and threw the book with all her strength, sending it skidding across the dirt floor.

"Crap!" she yelled, and instantly was aware of the frustration welling up in her throat and the hot tears coming. She bit down hard on her lower lip until the pain pushed back the angry sobs catching in her throat. *Deep breath.* You did not waste food. Not when it was so scarce. Not when the birds were poison and squirrels were skittish. Carefully she checked over the knife. The main part of the blade, about six inches, was still good. She could use it for most jobs. With a sigh, Lucy bent down and picked up the book, shuffling the pages back into the binding and smoothing the cover.

She leaned over the body, poked at it with her finger. The turtle's legs flopped like a rag doll. She couldn't imagine anything less appetizing, but there was no way she was going to give up now. She hadn't eaten anything since that morning, and then it had only been a scoop of porridge and a handful of dried, shriveled raspberries, which had tasted moldy. She took a couple of pieces of wood from the scanty pile stacked beside her and added them to the fire. She held her hand over the mouth of the cooking pot. It was hardly steaming. The wood was too green, the fire still not hot enough; the cooking stones barely sizzled when she aimed a gobbet of spit at them, and the dented saucepan of water refused to boil.

She sighed. Her fists were clenched and she could feel the pinch of her nails against her palms. It was already too late in the day to build up a good fire. The turtle's mottled skin, the ragged ruin of its neck, were taking on an unhealthy gray appearance. And she could smell something swampy and briny, like stagnant water. It was already cooler than it had been for the last six months, but still warm enough to turn meat bad fast. If the last four hours weren't going to be a complete waste of time, she'd have to do something. Lucy hefted one of the heavy, river-smoothed rocks she kept nearby and smashed it into the shell, which broke into irregular pieces, some large enough to dig out with her fingers, some small bits, like yellow pottery shards, embedded into the leathery skin of the turtle's underside. She went to work picking out the pieces until she could make a long incision in the belly. She shoved her hand in under the tough hide and scooped out the stomach and intestines, careful to breathe through her mouth. She'd gutted plenty of fish in the last year, and the looping entrails didn't bother her too much anymore. They were neat little parcels as long as she was careful not to puncture them. She piled them on a few broad dock leaves and covered them up against the flies. Later she'd bait her fishing lines with them and see if the catfish and eels liked innards better than the night crawlers she normally used. She flipped the turtle over, smashed the upper plate with the rock, and picked out as much of the shell as she could. After consulting the book again, she made four slits down the inside of each leg and cut away the skin. It slipped back easily, sort of like peeling a banana, and with only a little bit more cutting she was able to pull it free from the turtle's feet.

Lucy ran her finger over the hide, wondering if it was tough enough to patch the many holes in her boots. *Nothing wasted,* she thought, putting it aside to deal with later. She'd cured a rabbit pelt and a couple of squirrel skins before and ended up with serviceable but stinky leather, too stiff to work with easily but good enough to mend holes. She looked down at the oozing carcass, casting her mind back to tenth-grade biology, trying to remember anything useful. That had been frogs, in any case. Rubbery, fake-looking, and smelling overwhelmingly of formaldehyde. If she had a frog in front of her now, she'd have been able to skin and fillet it in two minutes flat, like one of those Japanese chefs.

She had a wild impulse to just dump the turtle and eat acorn porridge and dried berries for the fourth day in a row, but her acorn flour store was getting low, fresh meat was rare, and she needed the protein. She suspected, too, that there was more squirming weevil than powdered acorn at the bottom of the old coffee can. Perhaps if she just shoved the meat back into the saucepan, put the lid on, and left it to sit for a while over the bedded embers, the flesh would fall from the bones and she'd have turtle soup or turtle tea. There were a couple of shriveled wild onions left, some woody mushrooms she could toss in. She'd eaten far worse.

Lucy stuck the turtle in the pot and covered it, piling the

smoking wood around it. She rinsed her right hand in the bucket of water, getting most of the blood off, though not the dark matter stuck deep under her nails, and wiped it dry on her jeans. Her left hand throbbed, and she wondered if the bandage was on too tight. Her skin felt greasy with sweat. She stripped off her thick sweatshirt. Underneath she wore a tank top. Lucy sniffed at her armpits, wrinkling her nose, and then quickly sluiced her upper body. Now that the waters were rising, she'd be able to bathe again. It had been far too long. Weird how she hadn't noticed the odor of stale sweat and grime that permeated the shelter. Time to change the bedding grasses and air out the rush mats she had pieced together during the long nights. Lucy had ended up with cuts striping her palms and fingers and looking as if she'd lost a fight with a bramble bush. She would light some sage bundles later to clear out the musty stink and the smell of dead turtle.

She pulled her sweatshirt back on. Her neck felt tight, her hands shaky, and the wound beat in time with her heart. She wrapped a shawl and then her sleeping bag around her shoulders and sat as close as she could to her small fire. The smoke burned her eyes. She was procrastinating. There were things to do before nightfall, but she had checked the calendar notches she had cut into the bark of one of the four support trees and knew the moon would be full, which would give her more light than usual. She could get a later start, and a few minutes' rest would do her good.

Beyond the cracks in the interlaced willow screens she had made to disguise the small clearing where she lived, she could see the huge, red sun setting above waters that looked as thick and black as molasses.

Lucy dreaded this time of day, when there was a pause and her thoughts rose up and threatened to submerge her. As long as she was busy doing, she could keep the loneliness at bay. She drew the edge of the sleeping bag up around her ears, the shawl over her head, and nuzzled into them, smelling the nose-tickling mustiness of leaf mold, ground-in dirt, and the dried grasses she slept on. Her mind buzzed at her like an annoying mosquito.

She needed to walk the circumference of her camp, check the snares she'd set, the trip wires, the bundles of grass she had laid down on the ground that would show her if anyone heavy-footed had come near. Lucy groaned. She was so tired. Her days were always long, but sometimes it seemed as if it didn't matter how early a start she got.

She thrust the sleeping bag aside, bundled up the shawl, and got to her feet, popping her neck and shrugging her shoulders up and down a few times to work out the tightness. She checked a few more things off her mental list: She needed drinking water, so she'd have to make a wide arc and pass by the lake, and she needed as much wood as she could carry, now that the rains were gathering force. There'd been two torrential downpours lasting ten or twelve hours already, and it was only the beginning of June by her rough monthly calendar. She'd been less than careful about keeping track of the days and nights. The Long Wet brought monsoons, riptides, flash floods, and sudden lightning fires—the worst of them falling roughly in the middle of the cycle, but if anything was true these days, it was that the weather was erratic.

She'd check her snares, of course, hoping for a ground squirrel or rat, and her fishing lines, although during the Long Dry the lake waters had receded, leaving about twenty feet of dry, cracking mud before the first dribbles accumulated in shallow pools. A mudskipper maybe, a newt, or a salamander, though she didn't like the gluey taste much. It was too dark to go digging for shellfish by the sea. She'd plan on doing that tomorrow.

First she listened. But there were no noises except for the rhythmic hum of insects. Next she peered through a hole in the mesh of supple willow limbs that screened the front entrance to her camp. Lucy knew every tree, every bush, every grassy hump silhouetted in the gathering dusk. It was a landscape she had peered at and studied night after night. She had counted the weird hummocks carved out of the earth after the last quake—there were twenty-three of them standing guard like silent sentinels.

Nothing seemed different, but lately she'd had the unsettling feeling of eyes on her. She checked for movement. The air was so still, the grasses didn't stir. She pulled up the black sweatshirt hood. Then she picked up a couple of plastic gallon jugs for the water, looping a length of rope through the handles, slung a woven grass bag over her shoulder, checked that her knife was snug against her hip, and lifted the front door screen out of the way.

A long puddle of water lapped against the piled sticks and brush she'd stacked against the outer walls to keep the rainwater from seeping in. She splashed through, feeling the cold wetness through the thick leather of her boots and a double layer of socks, ducked her head slightly, and replaced the screen. She backed up about five feet, making sure her small fire pit was invisible from the outside. It was. *Good.* She'd spent a lot of time stuffing most of the larger chinks with moss and dried grass recently. Plus, now that the rains were coming, the willow sticks she'd shoved into the ground to make thicker walls would begin to grow and leaf-out. Willow was amazing! A cut stick would take root easily. The four slender, flexible trees she had bent down and bound together at the top to make the sloping roof were already bushy with new growth.

If you didn't know the camp was there, it was almost invisible against the surrounding foliage and shrubs, like the snug, domed nests the field mice made themselves out of grass stalks. She glanced at the sky. The moon was beginning its rise, full as she had hoped. Purple clouds boiled; the wind had suddenly picked up and the scent of rain was heavy. It would mask the smells of smoke and cooking turtle, she thought. Taking one last look around, she set off toward the lake, her nerves stretched tight and jumping.

The terrain was already changing. There were splashes of green leaves within the dusty gold. And the ground was spongy underfoot, treacherous with puddles and sinkholes. There were pretty much only two seasons now—drought and flood.

Her boots squelched a bit, but so far they were not leaking too badly. It was so quiet—save for the scritch of small claws scrabbling up tree trunks and the angry, explosive noises of disturbed squirrels. She always thought they sounded as if they were cussing her out. On the way, she inspected various snares she'd concealed under bushes and by likely holes, crossing back and forth along the narrow spit of land, her senses in hyperdrive. They were all empty. One showed signs that a predator had gotten there first. Tufts of silver fur snagged in the branches, a few driblets of blood. She kneeled down, touched the soft, downy clumps. Rabbit, she thought, rather than squirrel. Too bad. Rabbit was a delicacy these days, but she couldn't help but be glad that there were still foxes and coyotes around. So many animal species had been wiped out in the plague.

As if to echo her thoughts, a howl rent the air. She stiffened. She knew the clear belling and crystal sharp barks of the foxes and coyotes as they called to one another. This was deeper, urgent—the sound of a hunting pack of dogs. Her head swiveled in the direction of the baying. She thought it was at some distance yet. But behind her. She shuddered, fighting the urge to break into a panicked run. Not just behind her, but between her and her camp. Most predators were still scared around humans; her smell was enough to keep them at a distance. But the packs of feral dogs were large and hungry, and they had no fear of people.

She considered. She'd work her way to the lake and circle around, giving them wide berth. The land rose slightly just beyond the water's edge, and she'd be able to get a better look. And she could check the water levels at the same time. There was the tarnished bronze statue of a girl sitting on a large toadstool surrounded by an assortment of strange characters, and Lucy used this to keep track, scratching lines into the metal every second full moon. The last time she'd looked, the water had been barely lapping at the girl's toes, but by the middle of the Long Wet it would be up to her shoulder level. Lucy couldn't remember the girl's name now, although when she was a child her mother used to bring her here to climb on the statue. She recalled jumping from toadstool to toadstool, feeling the smooth, sun-hot metal, playing king of the castle with other kids. The bravest of them leapt from the hare to the man in the top hat or perched on the girl's head, gripping the long locks of her flowing hair. That wasn't Lucy, though. She never made it higher than the girl's lap—broad and solid and safe.

Now she moved quickly. There was no cover but scrubby grasses and spindly bushes. The ground underfoot had changed from loose, sandy earth to cracked, oozing mud. The lake was to her left. It had dwindled over the hot season to a series of small, murky pools surrounded by rings of soft, slippery sludge. A larger expanse of water lay far beyond her reach, as smooth as glass. Her fishing lines were marked by twists of bark. Lucy pulled them up, and, finding the hooks empty, tossed them back into the shallow water. All around her was the plopping sound of frogs, as they woke to her presence and alerted one another. The splashes they made sounded like a string of tiny firecrackers going off. She needed her spear to catch frogs. They were too quick, too alert.

The dogs had stopped barking. The night was silent again except for the small animal noises. Lucy crouched and submerged her water bottles to fill them. The flow of water gurgled gently. Her eyes darted around, her head lifted. She pushed her hood back so that she could see better. The quiet was unnerving after the cacophony of howls and barks. The hairs on the back of her neck rose. She was being watched. Slowly, she got to her feet, capped the jugs, and hung them from her neck, easing the rope into position so it lay across her shoulders. Then she loosened the knife in its sheath. She strained her ears, listening hard. Suddenly there were small, ominous noises coming from all around. A rat snake rustled past, its heavy black body as thick around as her wrist. There was the squeal of something just caught.

Lucy pulled her hood back over her face, trying to blend into the inadequate shadows. She froze. Directly across from her, at the edge of a pool of fresh rainwater, belly flat to the ground, was a cougar. So close she could see the pink tongue lap. They locked eyes. Lucy barely breathed. She tried to remember if the manual said she should play dead or make a racket. The cougar didn't move. Lucy's fingers fumbled at the hilt of the knife, trying to prepare herself for an attack if it came; quietly telling herself to slash a volley of cuts; reminding herself that the blade was broken, that stabbing would have no effect. But behind that voice, the knowledge that she'd be helpless against two hundred pounds of lithe muscle and bone, a natural killer, and the hope that death would be quick and the pain numbed by fear and shock. Maybe she shouldn't be making eye contact? Perhaps that was a threat? She closed her eyes and murmured a quick prayer. Her thigh muscles quivered. She ducked down, trying to move smoothly. Her feet slid awkwardly in the mud. She slipped and fell backward, the weight of the water bottles pulling her off balance. Quickly she was back up on her feet, knife in her hand. Her jeans were so coated in mud, they looked like a statue's legs. The cougar was gone, soundlessly, no movement of grasses even to mark its passing. And now Lucy realized that the dogs were yelping again, an excited chorus of barks, much closer, and she heard the crash and thud of many paws trampling the earth.

There was an ominous rumble overhead. Immediately, as if the sky had ripped open, the rain began, a torrent drenching her to the skin and plastering her hood to her skull. The ground was instantly hammered into sogginess. Lucy looked to her right. She saw hillocks of flattened grass too low to conceal a ground squirrel, and the tossing sea beyond. To her left was a series of muddy pools fast expanding and the shifting sludge that would slow her down, sucking at her boots, and beyond it the rain-shattered lake. She could make out the silhouette of the statue. The rainwater had already pushed the level up above the top of the toadstool, much higher already, she thought, than at this time last year. Directly in front of her, past a patch of soggy scrubland and up a slight rise, was a thick stand of trees, shadowed and dark. Behind her, she saw the first dog loping in her direction. Its muzzle grazed the ground, plumed tail up, fur raised in a spiky ridge over its back. Through the sheets of rain it looked like an illustration from a children's fairy tale cut out of black construction paper. Wolflike.

Without hesitation she sprang forward toward the grove, dodging around the hummocks of slick, sharp grasses, running, like a panicked rabbit, in a crooked line, until she was pushing through dense and prickly bushes, ignoring the barbs that caught and tore her skin and snagged her clothes. She secreted herself behind the nearest tree—a pine, wind-battered and salt-poisoned, with rough, shaggy bark, and no branches low enough or strong enough to hoist herself up on. The rain drove into her eyes. She wiped a streaming hand across her face. Her water bottles tugged at her neck. She lifted the rope over her head and hurriedly stowed the bottles under a nearby shrub. Her grip on her knife was slippery, and she rubbed her hand uselessly on her wet pants to dry the moisture from it. She tightened her grasp and leaned her forehead against the tree, trying to catch her breath. She had a cramp in her side and she kneaded it with one bunched fist. Pressing her body against the coarse bark, she squinted her eyes against the drizzle to make out the shapes of the dogs.

The throng broke apart, dozens of dogs fanning out and then coming back together as they caught a trace of her along the lakeshore. The moonlight made shadows everywhere. They had definitely found her trail. The rain might slow them down a little, the puddles she had sloshed through would mask her scent, but they were serious about tracking her and unlikely to give up. She could hear the heavy panting and excited bursts of barking as they called to one another, like the high-pitched yelps of puppies scuffling over a bone. They were so close.

Lucy forced herself to leave the comforting solidity of the tree and move backward, as quietly as she could, sliding her feet through the mush of wet leaves. She took shallow breaths, darting quick glances over her shoulder, making for the place where the trees grew thickest. Black shapes wove back and forth, just beyond the pines in front of her, as the dogs tried to pick up her scent on the wet ground. She crept toward a cluster of pine, elm, willow, and leggy maples. The tall trees stood trembling; water cascaded down from their branches. She backed against the smooth trunk of an elm, the biggest tree in the glade. Too high overhead, wide branches spread out against the dark, fractured sky. The moon was directly above her. She hunkered down, listening to the sounds of the dogs coming ever closer. She held her knife in both hands, the blade pointing straight out in front of her. She'd kill at least one or two before they savaged her. The cramp was back again, jabbing into her side with a ferocity that made her wince; her lungs felt starved of oxygen; her heartbeat echoed in her ears. Then the crack of a branch snapping, loud as a gunshot, made her look up.

CHAPTER TWO

THE DOGS

"What are you waiting for? Come on, grab it!" hissed a low voice. A hand dangled a few feet above Lucy's head. She blinked against the rain streaming into her eyes. Long fingers waggled. The rest of the person was shrouded in shadow. She stumbled backward, brandishing the knife. Behind her, at the perimeter of the small wood, the barks coalesced into a uniform baying and delighted howls, and she heard the sound of many bodies plowing through the undergrowth. They had found her.

The person made an annoyed explosive sound halfway between a curse and a grunt. "Well?"

She could tell it was a male voice. The hand gestured impatiently. "I can't hold on much longer. Are you coming or what? Do you want to be dog food?" She took one last look over her shoulder and jumped for the hand. Her fingers grabbed and slipped. The branch bucked under their weight. For a brief moment before she dropped to the ground, she saw his eyes—light-colored, not the bloody red eyes of the S'ans.

He grunted again. "And put that pig-sticker away before you cut off my nose. You're going to have to help yourself get up here, you know. I'm barely hanging on." Lucy hesitated; she didn't think the branch would hold them both. He leaned farther forward. His arms were bare and his skin was tanned, unblemished save for the silvery puckered scar of the vaccination on his biceps. She thrust the knife into her sweatshirt pocket, unsheathed. Dangerous, but she wanted it close at hand. Heavy bodies thudded through the underbrush. She turned and saw two dogs angling in, mouths open, black lips peeled back from their long, spittle-flecked fangs. They covered the ground with terrifying speed. She could see the lean muscles bunching as they prepared to leap.

She turned back to the tree and the hand that was still held out toward her and jumped for it. His grasp caught, slipped again, and then his fingers tightened around her wrist. She scrabbled at the trunk with the blunt toes of her heavy boots, reaching out for a branch or something to hold on to. The gash across her palm stung. She felt the wound split open again under the bandage. For one horrible moment she hung suspended just a few feet from the ground, and she imagined a dog's sharp teeth grinding into her ankle. There was a volley of awful noise: crashing, panting, and a chorus of snarls.

He heaved, she kicked desperately, her left foot hit something with a solid *thwack* and a yelp, and all of a sudden her momentum carried her up to the high branch he straddled, so quickly that she almost went over it and back down to the ground, but he kept hold, jerking her back. Lucy threw out her free arm and clasped it around the branch, then swung her leg across. Looked down. Ten or twelve dogs were clustered around the bottom of the tree. One blew a froth of bloody bubbles from its shattered nose. More dogs were coming, the pack, rearing up on their hind legs, jostling for position, black claws digging into the bark.

The earth tilted, pulled at her, and she squeezed her eyes shut, feeling her tenuous hold loosen and her equilibrium leave her with a stomach-twisting suddenness. Lucy fell against the stranger, a boy. Her head spun, and for a moment she thought she might vomit. Her stomach cramped. She bit down on her tongue until the nausea passed.

"I lost my balance," she muttered, even though he hadn't said anything. Her voice was gruff, and she was conscious of his hand still clasping hers, the warm solidity of his chest. Lucy scuttled back against the trunk, pulling her hand away and clutching the bark tightly. She had never liked heights, not even the swings or slides in the playground growing up. There was no room on the branch to move very far away. She carefully avoided looking down again. She could hear the dogs milling around, snapping and growling at one another. She tried to pretend she was not fifteen feet up. The boy stared at her with an amused expression that she longed to slap from his face. She cleared her throat. Her hand went to the knife inside her pocket.

"What?" she blurted out. She was painfully aware of the grime on her face and hands, the dry sweat that stiffened her hair, the stale, dirty stink coming off her mud-soaked jeans. He smelled clean. Soap—a memory so sharp, it hurt. His clothes were worn and patched, but not as filthy as hers. They were brightly colored, too—not the best choices for blending into the dull, beige landscape and shadows—as if he didn't care who could spot him from a mile away, and he'd cut the sleeves from his red sweatshirt as though he didn't feel the damp chill. She shot a look at him from under her eyelashes. He was about her age, with green eyes, dirty blond hair, and a generous mouth that was smirking at her. The grin slipped a little as her tone of voice registered.

"I'm waiting for you to thank me," he said. Her cheeks flamed.

It had been months since Lucy had been around another human being. She went out of her way to avoid them, to hide. She felt acutely uncomfortable; sort of like the feeling she used to get on the first day of school after the freedom of the summer holidays. She looked away from the intensity of his gaze. The dogs were sniffing around the tree. A couple of them had plopped down and begun licking themselves. They looked almost friendly, except that whenever she or the boy shifted just a little bit on the branch, they leapt to their feet and started growling and snarling again. Farther out in the brush she could see more shadowy sentinels waiting for her to make a break for it. How long would they wait for a meal? How soon before they'd give up and try for a mouse in a burrow or a rat on the garbage heaps? How long before she could climb down and go home? The boy was still looking at her, almost as if he could tell what she was thinking. The smirk was back. She dropped her eyes, busied herself with tightening the bandanna around her left hand. It was wet with new blood. She'd left a bright smear on the bark on her way up.

Clasping his hands to his chest and adopting a high-pitched voice, he said, "Oh, thank you, Aidan, for saving me from that pack of vicious dogs! That was *so* great of you to hang out of the tree like that and risk your life or possibly a serious accident for a complete stranger!" She scowled, wondering if she could jump off the far side of the tree, avoid the dogs, and get the heck out of there. She looked down at the new hole torn in the knee of her jeans.

"Thanks," she said, after a long moment. "I'm Lucy." Her voice sounded raspy, and she was aware of how dry her throat was. "Do you have any water?"

He shook his head. "Didn't plan on being here that long. Just came out to relax. See what I could see . . ." He stared at her and she wondered if her hair was bushing out.

"Are you scouting?" Lucy asked. She knew, of course, that there were others out there, loners like herself, but most people kept to their safe places and didn't wander. She saw campfires sometimes, heard voices from a long way off, but Aidan was the first person she'd seen in a while. As far as she was concerned, the streets belonged to the S'ans—survivors of the plague who were horribly scarred and sick in the brain.

He shook his head. The sarcastic curl was back in the corner of his mouth, and she decided it was just something he couldn't help, but it didn't exactly make her warm to him.

She looked at him properly. As far as she could tell, he carried no collecting bags, no blade, not even a big stick.

"What do you mean?" she said. "You're not scouting?" Lucy straightened up; her fingers felt for her knife again. "Are you a spy?" she blurted out. "Are you spying on me?" Her greatest fear was that someone would force her back to the shelter.

Aidan's eyes flicked to her face and then away again. He stared at his hands. She waited for him to say something. He cleared his throat. "Not spying," he said. "But I've seen you before."

She remembered the disquieting feeling that she was being watched and waved the knife in front of his face. "You've been following me."

He looked up. "No!" he said, as if horrified. She set her teeth.

"Your camp is visible from here if you know where to look. That's all. I noticed . . ." Now it was *his* cheeks that reddened. He stopped in mid-sentence, then shrugged his shoulders up and down and said in a louder voice, which set the dogs below whining and snapping, "It's lucky for you that I was here; otherwise you'd be dog meat. You ran to this tree. I didn't make you come here."

That was true enough. She eyed him, fingering her blade. "Sort of creepy, though," she muttered. "So what were you doing here, then?" she asked, lifting her chin and staring hard at him. "Are you just . . . hanging out?" The words felt odd on her lips.

"Yeah," he said easily. "I guess you could call it that. I just like to climb trees, and the view from here is pretty much three hundred and sixty degrees." He gestured wildly with one outstretched arm. Just watching the sweep of his hand made Lucy feel dizzy again, and she clutched at her tree branch, trying to do it inconspicuously. She was appalled. There hadn't been a moment in the last twelve months, except for when she was sleeping, when she wasn't doing something. If she wasn't gathering food, she was plugging gaps, collecting water, or baiting hooks. And in the evenings she'd plait coarse grasses into rough lengths for ropes or mats, cure skins, smoke meat, pound acorns, or mend tears and patch holes in her clothing and shoes. She definitely didn't have time to *hang out*.

Lucy stared at the boy thinking he was insane, but the *really* crazy thing was that he was staring back at her with the exact same expression mirrored in his eyes.

"Hello?" she blurted out now, slapping the branch so hard, it stung her palm. "Why risk everything for no reason except that you wanted to look at the view!" She pointed to the dogs. "This isn't a park anymore."

Aidan froze for a moment and then leaned back against the tree limb, his arms crossed behind his head. She had no idea how he was balancing himself, but he looked as comfortable as if he were lying on a couch.

"I think you *think* you know more than you do, wild girl," he said.

"What does that mean?" Lucy said, bristling.

"How long have you been out here?"

"Long enough to know how dangerous it is. The S'ans! The Sweepers! The scavengers!"

"I'm careful," he said after a pause. "And the scavengers aren't all bad."

"You're nuts." *And stupid,* she added silently. "The scavengers will rob you blind, the Sweepers will lock you up, and the S'ans will give you the pox. Or, if you're lucky, just plain kill you," she added, digging her knife into the tree trunk.

He was looking amused again, and her hand itched to slap him. A little snort of laughter escaped from his mouth.

She carefully swiveled her torso so that she was facing away from him. Less than a mile away, past the trees and the scrubland, was her camp. It might as well have been on the other side of the world. Aidan whistled a tuneless song under his breath and she did her best to ignore him. The dampness soaked into her skin, chilling her bones. She stunk of swampy mud. Her fingers cramped on the hilt of her knife, but she kept it out and ready.

The rain finally fizzled to a stop. Mist rolled in from the sea and wreathed the ground below. There was the tinkling splash all around them of drops falling from leaves onto the earth. Lucy's hand crept up to pat her head. Moisture made her hair frizz out. She probably looked a mess.

She scowled, shifting on the branch. Her butt was falling asleep and she longed to move, but there was no escape. The dogs panted and grumbled and prowled below. One, a terrier, Lucy thought, the sort of dog she'd once have thought was cute, just sat and whined pathetically at the bottom of the tree as if it was starving. A tussle broke out between two of them, a black pit bull with fur so short and slick it looked spray-painted on and a burly rottweiler. Smaller dogs darted in, nipping at flanks, and the chorus of barks was deafening. It was a short, vicious fight that ended with lacerated ears and bleeding muzzles. Tufts of fur floated in the air. The two dogs collapsed, chests heaving, licking their wounds. The audience of dogs lay down as well, as if exhausted by the excitement. Some of them seemed to fall asleep. Lucy carved out a chunk of bark and tossed it down onto one of the sprawled bodies.

The animal was up in an instant, growling ferociously and clawing at the tree. More dogs rushed in from every direction, baying in excitement. Their eyes reflected the moonlight, and thick strands of saliva sprayed from their jaws. Lucy wondered if they were rabid.

"Smooth," said Aidan. He'd been so quiet, she'd half-suspected he had fallen asleep.

She glared at him.

"Come on, seeing as we're stuck here for a while," he said, leaping to his feet. He was standing on the branch, perfectly balanced, one hand stretched out toward her. Below, the dogs were going crazy again, catapulting themselves up into the air, scrabbling at the tree trunk.

"Uh, no . . ." The thought of moving made her head swim.

"I want to show you something. Up there," Aidan said, shifting easily on the branch, his arms relaxed by his sides. He was wearing brightly painted high-top sneakers. His feet seemed to grip the bark. Lucy's heavy boots felt like weights at the ends of her legs. Her wounded hand twinged when she clenched it experimentally.

"Scared?" he asked.

She imagined pushing him down or kicking his legs out from under him.

"I'm not," she said, clenching her jaw. She got carefully to her feet, holding on to a branch above her head with one hand and tightening her grip on the knife with the other. Lucy ignored Aidan's outstretched arm, and eventually he shoved his hand in his jeans pocket as if to mock her, and started climbing. He moved with an ease that made her face flush red with annoyance. She rubbed her thumb over the bone handle. Her stomach twisted and she felt a rush of bile in her mouth. She bit her lip hard and forced herself to look ahead to where he was standing with his head crowned by new bright green leaves. *Not down, don't look down,* Lucy told herself fiercely. He was a jerk, and there was no way she'd let him see how terrified she was. She remembered how she'd followed her little brother, Rob, across a fallen tree in the park once, although her knees had turned to water, just because he'd taunted her. When she'd caught up to him, she had wrestled him down to the ground and stuffed handfuls of rotting leaves down his shirt.

Aidan walked casually to the end of the branch and then pulled himself up to the one above it. It was about chest-high on Lucy. She watched to see how he swung his leg over and then stood up. There were plenty of small branches overhead to hang on to, and she was pretty pleased with her performance. Just the slightest wobble on the way up, a misstep, forced her to drop to her knees and cling to the branch before continuing. But she'd sprung up again quickly before he'd noticed, not realizing until she was moving again that her fear of heights was being suppressed by feelings of irritation and a burning desire to prove to him that she was tougher than he would ever be. The tree was solid and broadly branched, and the bark smooth enough not to snag her feet but rough enough to give her some purchase. Aidan climbed and she clambered after him until they were near the top. The branches thinned out. Lucy gripped a handlelike pair of limbs and felt a little more secure. The air was much colder up here, and she pulled her sweatshirt hood forward, annoyed, too, that he didn't seem to feel the cold at all.

"So what's so special—" she began, and then she caught her breath. They were above the fog bank. Below it to the west lay the scrubby wasteland, the mudflats, the salt marsh, and just beyond, the vast waters of the Hudson Sea. To the south, under the low-slung moon, on a narrow wedge of rock and soil were the toppled skyscrapers—row upon row of fallen dominoes—and the ridges of pulverized concrete and steel girders like jagged, broken teeth. Such a strange skyline now, full of odd angles and deep chasms with no symmetry; it no longer seemed like something built by humans. The new wooden structures that bristled from every area of high ground looked like they would blow over in a stiff breeze. And to the east, Lake Harlem took the shape of a bulging Christmas stocking, the misshapen toe cupping the southernmost part of the promontory they perched above.

Lucy's rib cage felt suddenly too small for her lungs. The devastation was overpowering seen at this distance. An entire city leveled. Some structures brought down by the gale force winds and the earthquakes, others by friendly bombing. And buried deep within the mortar and brick and sheets of steel were millions of people who had sickened and died in a matter of hours, many dropping where they stood in the first and second waves of the plague.

"They're like giant gravestones."

"Easy to forget living out here, I bet," Aidan said.

"Yeah," she said slowly. "I had begun to forget." She shifted her weight without thinking and grabbed a branch to steady herself, ignoring the pain as her left hand flexed. In her camp, on her spit of land bordered by mud and water, it had felt as if she lived in a wilderness, when in fact the remnants of her old life were only a few miles away.

He pointed east over the mudflats. "Check it out."

Lucy could just make out the blurred shape of a landmass in the middle of the lake, a narrow island not more than a few miles long. Just visible against the blue-black sky was a darker silhouette. A tower, strangely shaped—an octagon or hexagon. At the very top blinked a red light.

"What's that?"

"That's Roosevelt Island."

The name stirred a memory in her, but she couldn't place it.

"That's where your Sweepers come from. The Compound."

There was another large, low, rectangular building attached to it. Just the outline was discernible, and it was unlit, but she could tell that it was solid, massive.

"The hospital," Aidan said.

And suddenly Lucy remembered.

She gripped her knife, feeling a chill creep up her spine. She remembered the dozens of newscasts, the mass hysteria that each one brought. The island was where the smallpox hospital was. In the early days of the plague, notices and warnings had originated from there, but as the epidemic had spread, the status reports had ceased. Anyone with common sense could just look around and see that most of the people they knew and saw every day were sick, no matter what the television might be telling them about vaccine supplies and control. The live footage of calm, white-coated doctors and pretty, smiling nurses had ceased, replaced by pretaped public service announcements, and the hospital had become just another derelict building. The little she knew about the S'ans and the dangers of the world she lived in now had come from those early news reports—a mixture of public service announcement and disinformation. "Stay in your homes. Avoid crowded places. Inform your doctor of any symptoms." And flashing across the screen 24/7, the plague hotline number to report your infected friends and neighbors. The hazard squads, they were told, patrolled constantly, seeking out pockets of infection, affected birds and animals, and those too sick to get themselves to the hospital. The white vans touring the neighborhoods and the white-suited men became a frequent sight, but they always gave Lucy the creeps. Once the disease took hold, most people had stopped believing that they were getting anything approaching the truth and ignored the reports and the government orders to remain in quarantine. People had left the cities in droves and the sickness had left with them, spreading like a wildfire.

There was something unsettling about the building, Lucy thought, taking a deep breath. In a landscape without any other artificial lighting, the red beacon at the top of the tower seemed like the baleful eye of some giant beast. There must be people inside, but whether they were doctors or government people or squatters, she couldn't tell.

Aidan grabbed her arm. "But look," he said, turning her to

face north. His face was lit up with excitement. He stood on the highest branch capable of holding his weight. The wind rustled the leaves. Far beyond the Hudson Sea—out where, Lucy knew from childhood Sunday drives with her family, there had once been farmland and apple stands, cows and pumpkin patches and the sweet cider donuts Maggie had loved and eaten by the dozen, and where the land was now given over to wilderness—a flickering light had appeared, followed by another farther away, and then another, strung out like shimmering golden beads on a necklace. A crooked line of fires. Aidan's fingers dug into her arm. She would have pushed him away, but she was afraid of falling.

"Oww," she said.

He barely took any notice of her.

"There are people out there who don't have to hide. Who are just . . . living. That's where I'm heading someday."

"So why don't you go, then? What are you waiting for?" She tried unsuccessfully to keep the sneer out of her voice. He was probably one of those people who didn't move without someone telling him it was okay.

He looked at her, taking in her expression. He let go of her arm. "Oh, so you're happy, right? You're having fun hiding from everyone, playing survivor out here with the dogs, eating frogs and acorns, being cold and wet or hot and itchy? Bathing once every few months?" His voice was scathing. His nose wrinkled, and once again she became aware of the smell wafting from her grimy clothes and her hair, which must resemble a bird's nest.

Her face reddened.

"I'm not leaving here."

"The Sweepers will find you sooner or later."

"I thought they were just looking for diseased people. Or the S'ans?"

Aidan shook his head. "No. Now they're looking for whoever they can find. And who's to say the plague won't come back again? Another wave that'll take out more survivors? Maybe it's breeding in the sewers. In the rats. Or in the birds again."

She pressed her lips together. "Sounds like a good reason to stay away from people."

"Nothing will get rebuilt without people," he said.

"*People*"—she put a snotty emphasis on the word—"are the reason we're in this mess in the first place. Too many people, and most of them are a waste of oxygen."

She glared at the tree limb, dug her fingers into the cracks in the bark. He snorted. She could just tell without looking that his mouth was twisted in a sneer again. She felt heat flood the back of her neck. *What a jerk!*

"The waters are rising," he said. "Every season, they creep a little higher. You can tell by Alice."

She looked at him uncomprehendingly.

"The Alice statue. Isn't that how you keep track of the lake levels?"

"How did you know about that?" She tightened her hold on her knife. "You have been watching me!"

He rolled his eyes. "You don't own the park, you know. It's not yours."

Eyeing him suspiciously, she thought about what he had said.

Alice! That was the name of the girl sitting on the mushroom. Now that she heard it again she had no idea how she could have forgotten. She'd seen the animated movie, and her mother had read the book to her, stopping when it gave Lucy nightmares about having her head chopped off. There were so many things she had forgotten or blocked out, as if she couldn't help squashing down all the memories with the ones that hurt still. She stared at the tower. And then at the water, knowing that what Aidan said was true. The rains would come again with staggering ferocity like something out of the Bible; the oceans would swell, devouring the new brittle edges of coastline; rivers would spill over; and the lakes would grow until they swallowed the land. They were due for something big and devastating, she could feel it. Locusts, maybe.

"Where do you live?" Lucy asked, shrugging the crawling feeling from between her shoulder blades.

He turned to look at her, one hand rumpling his shaggy hair until it stuck out in all directions. The smirk was gone. He pointed into the darkness. "See?"

She shook her head.

He grabbed her shoulder, turned her a few degrees to the east. Past the hollow where her camp was, a tall silhouette loomed. She recognized the Egyptian-style marble column which stood there, as out of place as a camel, and to the northeast of it a plateau and a series of gorges where a massive earthquake had caused the concrete slabs of a big road to slide and sink and bunch upward like a swathe of gray ribbon.

Aidan pointed with his finger, and she followed the invisible path with her eyes. "See the plateau? If you keep going across the escarpment about three or four miles as the crow flies, you'll come to the canals. It's pretty hard going." She could just make out the slender silhouettes of rope bridges slung like webs above the cement-veined crevasses, and clusters of stilt houses sticking up along the slopes like bunches of strange flowers.

"There," he said, stabbing the air with his finger, "the Hell Gate." He sounded proud and embarrassed at the same time. "The camp was actually part of Wards Island before the floods."

"What's with the name?" she asked, thinking it sounded overly dramatic. "I thought the Hell Gate was a bridge or something?"

"We adopted it because it seemed appropriate."

"Sounds homey," she said sarcastically.

A dog howled suddenly from outside the thicket. Under their tree the pack lurched to its feet, barking raucously. The howl came again, a long, sustained cry like a signal of some kind, and the pack, jostling one another and snapping at the air, scrambled about in excitement, tearing up the mossy ground with their thick claws. Lucy tracked them as they milled and broke apart, never moving more than a few yards away from the tree. Something had gotten them riled up again. She sensed his eyes on her.

"You can't just hide in your hollow like a mouse."

She stared at him. "I'm not hiding," she snapped. "I'm surviving. And I've been doing just fine on my own."

His gaze flicked away. She felt him tense beside her.

"Those are not feral dogs," he said. "They're hunting dogs."

"So what are they hunting?"

"Well, I'm pretty sure it's not me. They didn't appear until you did. They're trackers. They're looking for something."

She felt her jaw drop open. "What do you mean?" Her voice was a croak. "What are they looking for?"

"I don't know exactly." He frowned. "But something makes them go crazy. I've watched them before," he said. "They're sent out from the Compound. I've seen them around, out on the Great Hill, on the Cliff, in the Hell Gate, down in the Village. They go out, they find people who are hiding, and then the Sweepers come."

She blinked. Her brain felt fuzzy. Her knife was in her hand again. It felt clumsy in her hand, as if she couldn't will her fingers to hold it properly.

"So they're just keeping us here until . . ."

"Until the Sweepers arrive."

"How did the dogs know?" she asked.

He shrugged. "I guess they smelled you."

She shot a swift glance at him, but he wasn't smirking. His eyebrows were drawn across his forehead and one hand raked through his hair.

She judged the jump to the ground. Maybe she could push off from a branch before dropping, get some distance from the dogs before running. She thought there were maybe a couple of dozen of them. And more beyond her sight, out there in the gloom with the dog that had howled the announcement of their location. She squinted into the gathering darkness, straining to see a sign that the Sweepers were coming. Could she kill a dog? If she had to. But would that stop the others? Or would the blood drive them into a killing frenzy?

"Give me that bandanna," he said, pointing to her wounded hand.

"Why?"

"Come on!" He made an impatient gesture when she remained frozen. She held out her arm and he untied the knot from the bandage. Dark, fresh blood clotted the blue and white paisley design, and there were older, rusty stains where it had dried. He shoved it in the back pocket of his jeans and pulled two large, smooth rocks and a slingshot from the pouch of his sweatshirt. "Stay here until they're gone, then run as fast as you can," he said.

"What are you going to do?"

He grinned, his teeth very white.

The dogs were huddled beneath the tree in a solid mass of resting bodies. Aidan fitted a rock into the rubber pocket of his sling and then drew it back between two fingers. The stone whistled through the air, hitting the trunk of a tree at the edge of the grove with a sharp *thunk*. Furry heads came up, and the dogs bolted toward the sound. He quickly aimed and shot the second rock at a tree farther on, and then, with one easy motion, swung out from the branch catching the limb below him. Quickly he made his way down before Lucy could even gasp out a word. He jumped the last ten feet, landing softly on his feet. The bandanna was out and in his hand, and he ran in the opposite direction from the pack, ducking every few feet to trail the material along the ground. Once he'd cleared the woods, he stopped and turned. He stood for a moment at the top of a small grassy hill, and then a wild, almost joyful cry burst from his lips. It rang through the trees and was answered by the dogs. Outlined against the sky, he raised the bandanna like a flag and waved it. He whooped and hollered. Lucy watched him disappear toward the lake. A chorus of barks rang out, and then the pack rushed back in a boiling frenzy. The small black-and-white terrier she had noticed before fought to get to the front. Its nose was down to the ground, a steady whine rising from its throat, its stump of a tail wagging furiously. It sent up an excited yapping, which was echoed almost immediately by another chorus of mad barks, and the small dog sped away. The other dogs hurtled after it, shoulder to shoulder in a melee of bristling fur, passing underneath her tree and onward in the direction the boy had taken.

CHAPTER THREE

THE TIME BEFORE

Lucy half climbed, half fell out of the tree. Her knees were shaking and her muscles felt stiff and cold. Her hand was sore and so caked with congealed blood that she could barely close her fingers. She clambered backward until she reached the crotch of the tree, grabbed hold of a branch, and slipped, wrenching her shoulder. Her feet skidded against the wet bark. Her heart in her mouth, Lucy inched her way down, staring fixedly at her boots and letting the ground fuzz out at the edges of her vision. Any hope she had of natural coordination abandoned her, and the memory of Aidan's confidence frayed her nerves even more. She dropped the last twelve feet gracelessly, slithering down against the trunk and scraping the side of her left arm and the length of her ribs against the bark. She came down hard on one foot, jarring her ankle.

By the time she had hobbled all the way to the clearing that surrounded her camp, she was panting and hunched over. Her ankle had swollen like a golf ball; her hair was glued to her face by a combination of sweat and moist air. Every shadow cast by the moon, every whisper in the grasses, sent a surge of panic through her body. So much adrenaline was coursing through her that she felt physically sick with it.

But there had been no sign of the Sweepers, no sign of the dogs beyond the occasional echoing howl carried over the mudflats from the lake. Lucy stopped in the middle of a barren patch of ground where she could see in all directions and listened hard, forcing her breathing to slow so she could pay attention. Would she hear if Aidan was being torn to pieces? Could she tell if the dogs had caught up to him? A lone insect stilled its buzz-saw melody as she slowly turned in a circle. There was no other sound.

The night wrapped around her, and with a soft sigh the rain began to fall again, passing from sprinkle to gushing torrent in a few seconds. She moved forward at a jog, then an all-out run, frantic suddenly to reach the shelter of her camp. But then she paused, fiercely reminding herself to be cautious and check the silhouetted hummocks. She added them up and felt her heartbeat calm. Twenty-three hunched shapes, and that one fallen tree stump that looked like the curved back of a breaching whale—everything as usual. Lucy started forward again. It was impossible to move quietly. The ground was covered in puddles, some treacherously deep. She splashed forward, hands out in case she fell on the slippery grass, muddy streams on either side of her feet. Around the circumference of her camp, barely twenty yards from her concealed front door, dozens of paw prints were gouged into the wet soil.

Casting one final look around, she bolted the last ten feet to her door, ignoring the pain in her ankle. She dragged the willow screen aside and ducked inside. Her shelter was smoke-filled and thick with the briny smell of stewing turtle. She pulled her sweatshirt sleeve over her hand, picked up the pot by the scalding handle, and moved it from the smoldering fire, setting it on the ground. She raked the meager embers with a stick and added the last of the wood to the pile, then sank down, holding her hands out to the pitiful warmth. She was soaking wet. Her waterlogged sweatshirt dragged at her body; her filthy jeans were pasted to her legs. Her toes squelched in the two inches of water inside her boots, and she could smell the stink of her sodden socks even without taking her boots off. Her hands shook, and then the tremors traveled swiftly up her arms and down her spine. She knew the smart thing would be to strip, dry herself off as best she could, and then put on a change of clothing, but she was too exhausted to do more than stare at the flames and shiver. Her fingers were slathered with mud and blood and covered in scratches. Her whole left side, where she had fallen from the tree, felt bruised and raw. She peeled her sweatshirt and tank top up. Furrows of skin were scraped from her ribs and along her forearm. Her shoulder was bruised; purple bloomed above the bone. Lucy looked at her upper arm: smooth, unblemished except for four freckles set in a line as if someone had pierced her with the tines of a fork. No scars. She pulled her shirts back down, gasping as the cold, wet material touched her body. She wrapped her arms around her chest and rocked back and forth, slitting her eyes against the tendrils of smoke that wreathed the floor.

The rain pounded the branches above her. Occasionally a drop would force its way through the densely woven wood and fall on her head. She had a plastic tarp she could sleep under, but it was splotched with mildew and it crackled and rustled and slid away from her sleeping bag. She always had nightmares when she used it, waking in a confused tangle and feeling as if she were being suffocated.

Seeing another person, talking to Aidan, had thrown Lucy off balance. She was perfectly fine living on her own, relying on no one else, but she'd almost forgotten that there were other people out there. It was easier if she could pretend that she was the only survivor. Then her mind was completely occupied with foraging and hunting and all the small problems she had to solve, and she'd crawl into her sleeping bag at the end of another long day with no troubling thoughts. But now she was remembering how things used to be, and it was almost like a part of her, the human part, which was social and—she hated to admit it—craved conversation and interaction, had awoken again.

Lucy hobbled over to her backpack, unbuckled it, and pulled it open. She pushed her hands down to the very bottom, letting her fingers dance over her flint and tinderbox, her journal, a dead flashlight, her transistor radio, one last precious book of matches, until she felt the smooth leather cover. She hardly knew why she had kept it when so much of her life before was strewn in piles on the floor of her New Jersey home. The last weeks there were a blur in which only endless phone conversations with her parents' doctors and the countless forms to be signed stood out in her memory. A jumble of decisions were made while she could scarcely remember her own name, until at last the bodies were packed into the ambulance and taken away, leaving a silence that felt heavy and buzzed in her ears. She'd scanned her mother's phone book, called women she remembered as being kind, but the phone rang and rang and no one ever picked up.

And after that the house was almost unbearable, and the neighborhood she'd grown up in felt empty and forlorn, like a ghost town. She had become increasingly nervous, jumping at sounds, scared of the lights that came on in the adjacent houses in the middle of the night, the strange, silent men in hazard suiting who seemed to be looking for something, the white vans they drove. Lucy had taken to sleeping on the cold linoleum floor in the mudroom, which had no windows but did have a door that double-bolted and let out into the yard with its thick screen of cedar hedges. She'd listened to reports on the solar-powered radio her dad had kept on a shelf by the cellar door with stubs of emergency candles and freeze-dried camping meals. The college stations she was familiar with were not transmitting, and one by one the big news stations stopped, until finally there'd been nothing but a pirate channel, fuzzy and frustrating to pick up strongly. But in the early days, she'd lie on an inflatable mattress with the radio pressed to her ear, happy to be hearing another human voice. The host, who called himself Typhoid Harry, had been the first and only person to explain the plague in words she could understand. From him she'd learned that most people had contracted the plague in the first wave of contagion. Out of every one million people, 999,999 had died. Most of the survivors were picked off by the second wave. However, there were a scant few who seemed protected by the routine childhood vaccine given out with those for chicken pox, measles, polio, and bird flu, and an even fewer number who somehow survived the disease, horribly scarred and insane—the S'ans.

On the day she'd left for good, she'd run from room to room, breathless, crying jagged sobs that hurt her chest, careful not to look at too much, but becoming transfixed by the sights of her mother's faded dressing gown still hanging on its hook on the bedroom door, her shawl draped on her favorite armchair, her father's coffee mug on the draining board in the kitchen. She'd spent most of the time in her dad's home office searching for she didn't know what, catching the lingering scent of his aftershave, and finding the hunting knife and sheath in the bottom drawer of the desk.

Lucy had taken the knife not so much for defense. At that point everything was odd, surreal, but she had no notion of any physical danger to herself. She'd slipped it into her bag with her mother's shawl, a box of assorted freeze-dried food, and a bottle of spring water, because it was so unlike her father to own a weapon. He was all about leather attachés and legal briefs and dark, perfectly pressed suits. It was a puzzle to be gnawed on.

And she had taken her tenth-grade yearbook, too, even though she'd hated school, never infiltrating the groups of popular kids. The yearbook was a superficial slice of high school life that completely ignored the pain and boredom of it. She couldn't help thinking that Aidan would have fit in perfectly at her school, although she had to admit there was an edge to him that was different from the preppy, stuck-up boys she used to have classes with.

She opened the yearbook. The blank pages in front and back were empty of those insipid *Have a great summer!* messages. Inside she'd scrawled over pictures of the hair-sprayed, shiny lip-glossed, made-up girls in her class with a big, thick, black pen, giving them punk hairdos and raccoon eyes and thought bubbles that said stuff like "Do you think I'm pretty?" Somehow their deaths had changed it all. The yearbook touched on the life before. It had become something to remind her that things had been normal once.

Lucy flipped the pages with difficulty. They'd swollen from the damp and stuck together, and the red cover was warped. Past the graduating seniors' portraits, where everyone was posed like they were selling wristwatches; carefully avoiding the formal photo of Maggie, who was smiling so widely, happy and secure in the knowledge that she had her pick of Ivy League schools; past Rob and the rest of the ninth graders who looked like little kids and always would be. She got to her class picture. Ran her eyes over the list of names: Julie, Scott, Chad, Angie—people who'd barely noticed she was alive even though they'd known one another since kindergarten. In the class roster she'd been marked absent, but she'd been there. It was like a bad joke that even her teachers seemed unaware of her existence. She stood at the end of the row toward the back, shoulders hunched and hair pulled forward across her pale face, which appeared to float like the moon above the unrelenting black of her combat boots, jeans, T-shirt, and zippered hoodie.

Chad was standing next to her, but he'd squeezed over so that there were at least a couple of feet between them. God, she had hated him! He'd always acted as if she were diseased or something.

Lucy chewed her thumbnail, remembering how strange life had been that spring. The flyers with the lists of symptoms had appeared, plastered all over school, and it seemed as if everyone visited the nurse's office complaining of headaches and muscle cramping and fever. A few girls had fainted in class. Lucy had felt perfectly fine. She turned the pages of the yearbook slowly, flicking past photos of football teams and teachers and school staff. She paused at the picture of the nurse, Mrs. Reynolds, looking so neat and trim and motherly in her white outfit.

But she hadn't been so calm the last time Lucy had seen her, when she was called into the health office for yet another blood test. Mrs. Reynolds had seemed distracted. Even her smooth blond hair, normally pinned in a neat bun, was messily tucked behind her ears, and she'd had dark circles under her eyes. There'd been none of the usual chatter, the casual questions about Lucy's health or how the school year was going. She'd been nervous, preoccupied. And she'd flubbed the test somehow. Instead of blood squirting into the needle, it had dribbled all over Lucy's arm and the black-and-white tiled linoleum floor, and quite a lot of it had spattered onto the woman's white brogues. And although Lucy knew from sex ed class the previous year that the nurse could field the most embarrassing questions lobbed at her by Chad and his idiot posse, she had mumbled when Lucy asked her how many kids were sick and if it was contagious.

"What is it?" Lucy had said. "Strep? Or is it mono?" For some reason there was a coolness factor associated with mono. It meant you'd been kissing someone. Julie Reininger's rep had been cemented by having mono and being out of school for a whole month last winter.

"Maybe that bird flu they were talking about on the news?" Lucy had continued, and she'd been almost mesmerized by the weird spasm that quivered across Mrs. Reynolds's fingers and the way her eyes skittered away. And then she'd bitten her lip, as the nurse jabbed the needle into her arm again. Shortly afterward, Mrs. Reynolds had left the room, clasping the full tube of blood and closing the door firmly behind her. Lucy had heard the sound of the lock clicking shut. She had waited, until her sweaty thighs had stuck to the paper covering the gurney and she realized that she had to go to the bathroom. Finally, after looking at the closed door and the frosted glass window, she got up and walked around the small room, sliding drawers open and checking out the plastic-wrapped syringes, the tongue depressors flavored with cinnamon, the model of the female reproductive system all shiny purple and pink plastic—she'd wondered if the colors were anatomically accurate—and blowing balloons with a couple of powdery surgical gloves. She tried not to think about how full her bladder was. One of the bottom drawers held a thick stack of folders. Lucy was about to close it when she noticed Chad Grey's name and casually flipped the cover open. Chad had been absent for the last few days, and Lucy couldn't say she missed him. He always had some lame comment to make when she walked past his locker in the hallway, and he liked coming up with stupid words to rhyme with her name. Being called "Goosey" or "Moosey" might not have been exactly insulting, but it was almost impossible to walk to your desk with any kind of poise when a crew of boys was hissing it under their breaths. Maybe he had an STD or something. . . .

A wallet-sized student photo was clipped to the top of the page. A black bar was slashed across his eyes in marker, and the letter *D* was carefully marked next to his name. Lucy would have liked to believe that it stood for *dumb* but even then she was afraid it meant something much more terminal. She read: "Student complains of abdominal pain, fever, headache, backache, nausea. No lesions. Subconjunctival bleeding, subcutaneous bleeding. Hemorrhagic variant suspected. Sent to Dr. Lessing/R. Island for confirmation."

And there was a folder for Hilly Taylor and one for Samantha Barnes and that massive jerk AJ Picard, and, come to think of it, she hadn't seen any of them around for a while. She had trained herself to ignore them for so long, but now it seemed crazy that she could go from class to class and sit there doodling in the margins of her notebooks without noticing the empty desks. And each photo had been altered in the same way, black bars slashed across their eyes, the letter *D* written in thick, black lines, and the same listing of symptoms.

Suddenly she had to pee so badly, she squeezed her legs together like a toddler. She kept rifling through the papers and there, almost at the bottom of the pile, was one marked "Lucy Holloway." It was thicker than the rest. Seeing it made the latest needle hole in her arm twinge. They'd turned her into a pincushion these last few weeks. And there'd been no explanation. Just more tests following the first physical exam, when Mrs. Reynolds had run her fingers over the smooth skin of Lucy's upper arms, looking for the puckered scar of a vaccination that wasn't there.

"My parents didn't believe in them," Lucy had whispered when the nurse had finally thought to ask her and she'd begun to feel afraid that there was something really wrong with her. It was one of the only ways her straight parents deviated from the norm. She remembered when Maggie had told her, in a hushed voice, about their older brother, who'd died when he was barely two years old from an allergic reaction to a shot. "That's when Mom and Dad moved out of New York to Sparta, here in New Jersey," Maggie had said breathlessly, her eyes round with delicious horror. "Because it's less crowded and people are healthier, so it doesn't matter." Then she'd added, "Alex's face swelled up like a pumpkin, and his hands looked like shiny pink balloons, and then his tongue turned black." And even though there was no way Maggie could have known all that, the image had given Lucy nightmares for years.

Now she opened the folder slowly, half-afraid she'd see the black bar and the *D*, but then thinking that if she did then that would indicate it meant something other than *deceased*. And that would be good, right? Her startled face looked back at her from the photo. It was a copy of the picture on the student ID she was supposed to wear clipped to her backpack but never did. Her thick, curly bangs obscured her left eye completely, and her mouth was pressed into a thin line that almost made her lips disappear, but there was no black bar, no letter *D*.

She'd picked up her folder and stumbled backward to the gurney, spilling pages covered in weird symbols, rows of numbers and decimal points, percentages and charts. Too much information for someone who had suffered many scraped knees and cuts and broken bones but had never contracted anything worse than a head cold. One thing you could say about Lucy Holloway was that she had near perfect attendance.

She wasn't able to make heads or tails of the science stuff, and her bladder had finally demanded that she do something about it. She peed in a blue plastic cup and then dropped it in the biohazard receptacle, trying not to tip it over. The can was filled with used syringes and marked with a yellow and black skull.

And then Mrs. Reynolds had come back; the clicking of the lock opening gave Lucy just enough time to stuff her folder back into the drawer and vault onto the examining table. The nurse had jotted down a few notes and then made the calls that brought a legion of white-coats in, their faces blank behind their masks, and the battery of testing had begun again, until finally her father had shown up. He'd seemed twelve feet tall standing in the doorway, swinging his briefcase like an axe, his face purple with rage. She had never seen him with his cuffs undone, his tie unknotted, his carefully combed hair bristling. Something stony in his face had stopped her from asking any questions when he'd dragged her out of the room. Afterward, there'd been no time. Lucy never went back to school. Missed final exams, never picked up her report card, and soon there had been no reason to think about school. She'd received her yearbook in the mail a month or so later, sent directly from the printer with a computer-generated mailing label affixed.

A few pages further and there Lucy was again, a shot of her hunched over her journal, her hair a tangled curtain drawn across her face, scribbling away furiously. All around her were people caught in the midst of laughing and talking, their hands a blur of motion, moving around her as if she weren't there. And she kind of hadn't been. In her mind she'd been traveling and thinking about the day she could escape, and she had written it all down in her journal. Even to herself, though, she had to admit she looked like a strange, dull girl. Lucy closed the book, thinking not for the first time that she should burn it or throw it away, and ended up stowing it safely in a fold of the orange tarp against the wall. She sat back down next to the fire and clasped her arms around her shins, resting her chin on one bony kneecap. Her body thrummed with exhaustion.

If Aidan had gone to her school, she wondered if he'd have talked to her or if he'd have gravitated toward the in crowd. She could picture him: confident, easy, and relaxed. She could see Julie and Hilly hanging on his muscular arms, imagine him in a letterman jacket or a numbered basketball jersey. What was his deal, anyway? He reminded her of the boys at school. He had that swagger, that confidence, which she could only suppose came from having things always go your way. And from looking like he did, like something out of a preppy sportswear catalog. But he was different, too, in a way she couldn't put her finger on.

Two things bothered Lucy: One was that Aidan seemed to know quite a lot about her and where she lived. She wondered if he was spying on her after all. She'd felt as if she was being watched for a long time now. And if so, that begged the question *why*? And the other, far more important, was, what if he was right about the dogs? She could think of no reason why someone would be tracking her, but it made her feel unsafe for the first time since she'd found the hollow and the willow grove. She'd built her camp. It was as warm and dry as she could manage. It was comforting in a weird way, maybe because it was completely hers and proof that she could survive on her own, away from other people.

At first the thought of being alone had been terrifying. It was what had driven her to leave her family house and venture back into the city, searching for someone to tell her what to do next. She'd wandered blindly, attempting to mesh her memories of various streets with the rubble-strewn desolation around her, and eventually followed a cluster of scared-looking teenagers who seemed to be heading somewhere.

The shelters that had been organized after the first and second waves of the plague had passed were depressing and crowded with survivors looking for answers or authority figures that weren't there. There were maybe five of them set up in gutted churches and schools and sports arenas around what remained of the city, and they all looked the same: long rows of camp beds, flickering tube lights, and huddled bodies under thin blankets. People bundled under the covers like they were children afraid of the dark. She couldn't help but be reminded of the last time she'd seen her parents in the hospital, lying on gurneys side by side in the hallway with sheets pulled up over their faces.

It had been impossible to sleep. Every three hours there was the grinding roar of old generator-powered fans starting up and pushing around the warm air and the thick smell of unwashed clothing, unwashed skin, and instant noodles. And always, from one bed or another, a constant keening, like a wounded animal had crawled inside to die, and strangled sobs sometimes exploding into rage. The woman in the bed next to her, her gray face sagging with exhaustion, had never stopped crying and moaning, "The Sweepers took my boy away, the Sweepers took my boy away," until it started to sound like the lyrics to a sad song. Lucy had slept in her clothes with her boots on and her backpack clasped to her chest, too scared even to visit the bathrooms at night, when grimy, wild-eyed people gathered for secret reasons of their own.

One day, as she was coming back from a solitary walk around a swampy, mosquito-infested neighborhood that used to have the best used record stores, she'd seen a squad of people in white hazard suits come out of the shelter with the sad woman and a few others—mostly children—bundle them into a white van with darkened windows, and speed away. The men's faces were covered with blue surgical masks and their hands were gloved. The lady had left her purse behind, pushed halfway under her pillow, as if she was planning on coming back in a few minutes; as if she hadn't meant to leave. By the next morning it was gone, and the pillow, too. Pillows were in short supply. After that, Lucy had gotten out of there as soon as she could. She'd been better away from people and among the trees, where she felt like she could breathe.

A sudden flurry of raindrops forced their way through the roof and dripped onto her head and neck. She blinked. She'd set bundles of sage burning in the corners and the purple smoke was thick on the ground, the spicy fug strong enough to mask the briny scent of cooked turtle. Her clothes were still damp, but beginning to stiffen. She had been sitting for an hour at least, staring at nothing. She peeled off her wet things, scrubbed her skin with a scratchy towel, and put on dry clothes. The thick woolly socks on her feet felt like heaven, even though her big toes poked through. She wrapped herself in her mother's shawl, and then slipped on her leather jacket, pulling the collar up around her ears. She pushed her waterlogged boots close to the fire. Then she peered into the depths of the cooking pot. It looked like a thick soup, greenish-brown, and it smelled salty and wild. Chunks and strings of indefinable matter floated on the top. Lucy's stomach turned an unhappy somersault, but from nausea or hunger, she wasn't sure. It had been at least sixteen hours since she'd choked down a heap of lukewarm acorn mush, and she dipped a bowl in now, being careful not to stir up the murk too much. It was stronger tasting than she expected. As salty as boiled seaweed, and although she was careful to sip with a pursed mouth, straining it through her teeth, there was plenty of sand and little bits of turtle shell floating around with the gluey wild onions and the chewy dried mushrooms. It was slightly less repulsive than the salamander stew she'd made before finding out it was better to skin them first, and she reminded herself that the survival book had praised turtle meat as being high-protein and low-fat. However, she would not be recommending it to anyone.

She forced the food down, and then sat determinedly not thinking about what she had just eaten for a few minutes until she could be sure that it was going to stay down. Instead she found her thoughts returning to Aidan. Lucy decided that she was pretty sure she disliked him intensely, his attitude, his annoying self-assured way. The fire wheezed and snapped and sent out tiny wavering flames that occasionally puffed gouts of smoke as if they concealed a small dragon. The flicker of rain falling beyond the walls reminded her of snow on a television screen. Lucy fell asleep, sitting up, her jacket pulled tight around her, the smell of worn leather comforting.

In her dream there were dogs swimming in the lake, their pelts dark and streaming water like seals, and they were herding the small boat she was in, pushing it toward shore. There was something hidden in the pitch-black that terrified her. Was Aidan somewhere? She could hear him, but the sound of his voice echoed all around her, and she couldn't tell where it was coming from, and it was too dark to see him. Suddenly she was certain that the dogs were pushing her away from the safety of land, into the open waters.

She came awake in a rush, not sure what had roused her. Her eyes felt as if they were filled with grit. The camp was flooded with a soft gray light. It was too quiet, and after a moment Lucy realized that the storm had blown itself out and that it was the encompassing stillness that had wakened her. She could hear the trickle of water sheeting down the walls of her shelter, but other than that there was a deep silence, muffled, as if she still had her head under her arm, or she were still asleep. It was eerie. She got up, forced on her boots without tying them, and moved the screen aside. She was definitely awake. Her boots were clammy, the leather stiff. It was not quite dawn. Droplets of moisture glistened on the grass stems. The rain must have just stopped. The trees about her shook as though a giant had flicked their tops carelessly as he walked past, and Lucy realized that the roof of her shelter was swaying as if blown by a strong breeze. But there was not a breath of wind now. It was still and so, so hushed, it seemed the entire world was frozen between moments.

Lucy stumbled out toward the shore. Wet reeds slapped against her hands. Her jeans were already soaked to the knee.

The air was warm. All the myriad sounds of animals waking up were missing. No frogs. No birdsong. No rustle of mouse or vole in the long grass. The sun was rising now, just cresting the purple edge of the horizon behind her. She felt the heat on the back of her neck and shrugged out of her leather jacket and the shawl, carrying both under one arm. She checked to make sure her knife was sheathed at her waist. Everything seemed crystal clear, the curious quality of light so sharp it hurt her eyes. Her booted feet squelched and slid in the sand, the loose laces clumpy with mud. A sound like the *flip-flop* of a car's windshield wipers in a rainstorm reached her ears, but magnified a hundredfold. Ahead of her, the surface of the sea appeared to be seething, like molten silver at a boiling point. She stopped and slit her eyes, shading them against the brilliance of the light. She'd seen the ocean just before a sudden storm, with a blazing sun overhead, when the waves seemed picked out in metal wires and the sky was almost black, but this was different. This was like a spilling of gleaming coins.

She realized that she was looking at fish flopping on the beach, thousands of silver bodies leaping like dancers. The tide was out so far, she could see nothing but the fish and the brown sugary sand, the water drained away as if someone had pulled a giant bath plug. Far beyond, reflecting flickers and flashes of sun, she could see the ocean. It was retreating, the waters drawing back like a tide in reverse.

She turned and began to run. Panic spilled into her mouth like bile. The waterlogged sand tugged at her feet, slowing her down and threatening to trip her. She pushed on, forcing her knees higher. No time to bend and tie her laces. Only two thoughts yammered in Lucy's brain and she grabbed hold of them: *Get my stuff. Get to the highest ground I can find.*

CHAPTER FOUR

SEA

After the first disasters, they'd had emergency drills at school: what to do in case of earthquake, cyclone, and flash flood. They'd watched countless hours of video footage, of Maui engulfed by lava and the devastating eruptions of Mount St. Helens and Mount Vesuvius, massive explosions that buried all of Portland, Oregon, in ash and molten rock, and tilted the city of Naples into a boiling sea. Even the youngest kids knew to find a doorway or a desk, a cellar or the highest ground.

So before the thought had hit her brain, Lucy had turned and started running. She had twenty minutes if she was lucky, ten if she was not, and considering how things usually played out in her life, she'd better not count on having enough time.

She had to abandon her home. The thought of it was a physical pain in her chest. Lucy was past the sands now, resisting the urge to turn around and look behind her, fearing the sight of that wave building as it rolled back in. She'd seen films of tsunamis towering a thousand feet, waters so high and fierce you expected to see Godzilla charging through them with tiny destroyers and navy boats bobbing around his leathery ankles. And she'd seen the footage of what was left behind: miles of wreckage, houses splintered, buildings mowed down and crushed, and the drowned bodies of humans and animals flung on the shore like driftwood.

Time seemed to slow down and then speed up again. Lucy felt like she was watching herself in a movie. Short, flickering scenes, as if the film were old and missing frames, the whole thing spliced together badly. She found herself in the salt marsh with no idea how long it had taken her to get there. It seemed mere moments. The ground was firm under her feet; she ran faster, and then the bristly grasses gave way to low shrubs and spindly bushes, and she skirted some and leapt over others, letting the panic take the lead. Ahead of her was the clump of supple trees that marked her camp. And the ground was wetter, slippery as oil, where it had flooded from the rains. She dodged hummocks of greasy grass, her breath coming in heaving gasps. Sweat trickled down her back. Just before the entrance she slid in a foot of water, but was up on her feet again before she felt the wet soak through her jeans. Lucy pulled the screen aside, hurled it from her, ducked down, and was in, casting her eyes around.

What should she take? No time to think. She unbuckled her backpack, pulled at the laces until it gaped open, stuffed the shawl inside, and jammed her arms into the sleeves of her leather jacket. Her brain was taking snapshots of each corner of her camp. Sleeping bag; the survival manual from the table; her clothes from yesterday, a damp, dirty pile on the ground. She shoved everything in, pushing it down as much as she could, feeling to make sure her journal was there, and then the bag was buckled and slung over her shoulder. She paused to kick dirt over the smoldering fire, then berated herself for wasting time. Tons of water were about to crash down on her, but it was a habit learned during the Long Dry when a wayward spark could destroy everything. One last look around. She didn't have much. The pots and pans were an unnecessary weight. What food stores she had left were not worth taking. She grabbed a half-full water bottle, not sure if she'd find a stream or a spring safe to drink from. She hung her spoon and fork around her neck. The hammer of her heart seemed to be counting off the seconds. Was there anything else? She turned to leave, then suddenly remembered and ran to the place where her sleeping bag had been spread on a flattened pile of dried grasses, shoved her hand against the wall, and pulled out her yearbook. She clasped it to her chest, took one last look around, and ducked outside.

She bent and tied her laces, fumbling for a moment and finally settling for two tight knots which would be impossible to undo later. She stowed her yearbook in the bag and shrugged it back over her shoulders. The beach was still empty, the fish a thin layer of throbbing silver at this distance, with the deep blues of water and sky above. Choosing which way to go was a nonissue. West was the sea. East and south ended in water as well. North would take her up a slope and eventually to the Great Hill, and from there she could make a decision. A small voice in her head piped up and reminded her that the Hell Gate, Aidan's camp, also lay in that direction, but she pushed it down. From the Great Hill she could journey on for a few days and cross the Geo Wash Bridge if she wanted or loop back around. Maybe come home in a day or two and try to salvage something, rebuild. She told herself she could completely avoid the Hell Gate if she wanted to.

Lucy hurried along the narrow track—a muddy animal trail worn into the grass by sharp deer hooves when they came down from the heights to drink from the lake. Beyond the scrublands the ground rose sharply. She went straight up, taking it at a run, her backpack bouncing with every step, reaching forward with her hands, low to the ground, ready to catch herself if she fell. The terrain became loose, crumbling earth and pebbles, spiked with rocky outcrops and straggling trees. Stones rolled under her feet, threatening to bring her down. She pulled herself up, grabbing at slender branches and roots to keep her balance. A few hundred yards up, she paused for breath. Her sprained ankle was a hot ball of pain. Her throat was raw. Her ribs hurt. Her fingers were scratched and bleeding. The wound on her palm had opened again. She'd left a trail of blood on the stones. The thought crossed her mind that the dogs would have no trouble tracking her this time. Lucy felt a jolt of fear and suppressed it. Drowning in a monstrous wave would fix that problem. Just ahead was a thicket of wind-twisted fir and pine clinging tenaciously to the slope, and beyond, she knew, was a bare cap of gray rock at the summit of the hill. And surely that would be high enough. She ran on, limping now, her leg muscles trembling with exhaustion. There were pine needles underfoot; it smelled mossy, pleasant. Dappled light filtered down. She paused, her breath hitching in her throat, and drank the water in her bottle in a few, panicked gulps. She felt safe under the canopy of trees, but her fear pushed her onward. She had just reached the far edge of the wood when she heard a roar like a subway train hurtling through a tunnel. It seemed frighteningly close.

Lucy broke through the line of trees, clawed her way up to a rocky ledge, and looked down from the height. She had a panoramic view of the drained beach, so peaceful at this distance. The thin slice of land where she'd lived for more than a year fell away beneath her only a mile or two from where she stood. She could see the green dome of her camp, the line of grass hummock sentinels, the black trunks of salt-burned trees by the shore, the wide swathe of sand. And then the wave came. Suddenly there was water everywhere, rushing in as fast as a jet plane. The waves jostled to fill every available space. The bowl where her home nestled was an upended snow globe shaken with a ferocity that robbed the breath from her lungs. Trees were uprooted and flung into the air; bushes and slabs of earth were ripped loose, rolled and tossed into the seething mass of water. The stone needle was completely submerged. The wave grew higher as it came, a cataclysmic wall of water dwarfing everything before it, taller than her father's office building. It smashed against the hill like a massive fist, and she felt the tremor vibrate through her body. It broke less than a quarter mile from where she stood. A quarter mile was only 1,320 feet, she remembered from some math class long ago, and yet it seemed closer. If she hadn't forced herself to take more than 1,320 steps, it would have caught up to her. She looked into the wave, a dizzying swirl of stormy blue and emerald green, darkening to purple at the depths and exploding with foam at the crest. It was near enough that Lucy felt the soaring spray hit her face and her nose filled with the smell of salt. Her eye was caught by a splash of bright orange within the brown swampy swirl of pulverized tree and bush and earth, and she recognized the tarp from her camp. When the wave rolled back out with a sucking sound that she felt as a pressure around her throat, it left nothing behind but a thick sludge. The ground steamed in the morning sun. It was quiet and nothing moved.

Lucy realized that she had bitten her lip. Blood trickled down her chin. She rubbed it away, staring at the bright red smear on her fingers before wiping them on her jeans. She looked down at the devastation, trying to will her brain to comprehend it. The splintered trees, the slick layer of mud and pools of water. Nothing remained of her shelter. Even the tarp had been dragged back to sea. There were shapes left sprawled in the mud. Rabbits, groundhogs, other small animals, drowned in their burrows. Bile flooded her mouth and she vomited. Turtle soup. And that brought on more heaving until her stomach was empty.

After some minutes she got up, moved away from the steaming pile of puke, and sat down with her back to the wreckage. She peeled her sock back from her ankle. It was soft and puffy to the touch, but she could rotate her foot and flex her toes. She stripped the sock off and tied it around her ankle and then put her boot back on. The sole and heel of her foot were covered in calluses about a centimeter thick—she could walk without a sock for a while. Next, the wound on her palm, split open again and weeping a little blood. She wrapped it with the only bandanna she now owned, pulling the ends tight and securing them with a knot. Lucy's fingers were shredded from the rocks and the tips throbbed, but at least it was a distraction from the pain in her ankle. She leaned back against her backpack, listening to the thud of her heart. The slope ahead was a gentler rise topped with cracked and weathered gray stone. Tiny pink-flowered plants anchored themselves in the crannies. In the sky, so brilliant a blue that it seemed unreal, a hawk climbed in ever-tightening circles. *It must be wonderful to be so free,* she thought, *to be able to travel away from everything.*

It was the yucky taste in her mouth more than anything else that propelled her to her feet eventually. She walked up to the crest of the hill, favoring her ankle and working the stiffness out of her legs, and scanned the area in front of her, wondering if she could find a spring or a small stream where she could refill her bottle, maybe soak her ankle. The hill dropped off into a gorge, but it was not so deep that she couldn't scramble down into it and up the other side. It was what lay beyond it that made her pause and begin chewing on her thumbnail: a long expanse of buckled highway, driven up into a series of concrete ridges by the powerful earthquake that had collapsed the Empire State Building three years ago and pulverized most of Midtown. Strewn with rubble, the road dropped twelve feet in places and climbed twenty feet in others. The concrete was crumbling and pierced with weeds. Dandelions bobbed their yellow heads from every crack. She'd always liked dandelions. They seemed like free spirits, growing wherever they wanted, and springing back no matter how often her mother dug them up. Lucy started walking toward the first crevasse.

CHAPTER FIVE

THE HELL GATE

Lucy wiped her mouth. After three hours of steady hiking, climbing, and risking severe bodily injury crawling in and out of crevasses, she'd found a puddle of rainwater that tasted of tarmac but wasn't too gritty. The water made her stomach cramp and she realized how hungry she was. The sun climbed in the sky. It looked huge and more orange than yellow. She guessed the time must be close to noon. She wanted to be off the ridge before night fell. She felt exposed and vulnerable with no foliage above her, and although the sky was cloudless, Lucy knew that a vicious storm could move in with unnatural speed. The day had become humid, still, as if the tsunami had driven out most of the oxygen when it took the trees. Her bangs hung in limp ringlets over her eyes, and she could tell by touch that her hair had frizzed up. She wished for an elastic band or a piece of string to tie it back with, but she had nothing. She touched the hilt of her knife, rubbing her thumb over the smooth bone. She could hack off the mass of hair, cutting it close to the nape of her neck, but then she'd have the same problem in another month or two, and in the meantime she would look like a freak, or a boy. She wasn't sure which was worse, but she did know that she didn't want Aidan to see her looking like a head-injury victim.

Aidan was an uncomfortable thought. Lucy pushed it away. She wasn't going to see Aidan. She was going to stock up, rest, and figure out where she would live now. Aidan was where people were, and where food was, that was all. She cupped her hands, scooped up more lukewarm water, and dribbled it over her head and neck, then smoothed her hair down as best she could. The road was flat for a few hundred yards. Beyond that it dropped off again, but she couldn't tell how far. She walked, watching out for loose rubble. In places the mangled tarmac was marked with a broken white line, but it was no longer straight. It deviated from the middle and twisted suddenly and disappeared. She estimated that she was around Second Avenue and 92nd Street, although acres of road and earth had been shifted in the big quake, the landscape completely reconfigured. Sometimes she thought it looked as if a toddler had built a city out of blocks and then knocked them all down in a rage.

Lucy had reached a gorge that was as big as a canyon. It went down about forty feet and then climbed back up nearly the same distance in a series of trenches like giant steps. There was no way around it—it crossed the entire width of the ridge. When she finally pulled herself up the last craggy slope, bruising her knees in the process, she found herself on top of a plateau. Straight ahead of her was a deep, wide ravine, and stretched across it, ridiculously fragile, a suspension bridge. It swung in a gentle rhythm, although there was no breeze. This must be the Grand Canal. For a minute or two Lucy looked across the chasm. She chewed on her lip. Sweat trickled down her back and her heart thumped painfully against her breast bone. It was so high. The bridge was anchored on her side by several loops of rough-looking braided rope attached to an outcrop of rock. Lucy tugged on it and then stepped onto the bridge, which dipped with her weight. Each step created vibrations that traveled the length of the bridge and then bounced back, throwing her off balance. She crept forward, holding on to the rope supports with both hands, her arms outstretched to their full length. She tried to keep her eyes on the far side, but she couldn't control her gaze. It was drawn to the ground far below. The channel bed was almost completely dry. The two downpours they'd had at the beginning of the Long Wet were not enough to flood it yet. Sharp rocks and rubble were strewn on the bottom, along with mounds of garbage. She saw a baby stroller, a dented refrigerator with its door hanging loose, wads of rain-soaked paper, tattered clothes and blankets, the twisted wreck of an old metal bed—the kind they used to have in hospitals, with wheels and coiled springs.

The rung she shuffled onto snapped with a sharp crack, half of the wood breaking off jaggedly and spinning out into the air. Her already weakened ankle twisted. Her foot went through the hole; the weight of her body threw her forward onto her knees, and the bridge swung crazily from side to side, tilting so that she was no longer on a level surface. Now one edge was vertical. She was being tipped off. She grabbed at the ropes, burning red stripes across her hands, and halted the fall. For several minutes she didn't move. She lay there sideways with her head hanging over the edge, waiting for the bridge to stop swaying and right itself again. Lucy squeezed her eyes shut, trying to erase the image of the rocks sticking up like spearheads at the bottom of the canal. Slowly she shifted her weight toward the middle. The bridge leveled out. Once her heart had stopped pounding, she pulled her foot from the hole. Like a bear trap, splinters of wood had pierced her jeans and the sock she'd tied as a bandage over the bone. Her ankle was ringed with scrapes like tooth marks. She moved from her knees to her feet and began to inch her way forward again. Her teeth chattered so hard, her skull hurt and her jaw ached. By the time she got halfway across there was a sheen of sweat across her face, which she dared not wipe off, and her legs were trembling. She forced herself to keep moving. When she stepped off the bridge onto firm ground, her legs gave way beneath her.

After a few long moments with her head down around her knees, Lucy got up again. Her hair was plastered to the back of her neck with sweat and her damp arms clung to the lining of her leather jacket. Her throat was parched and her stomach growled with hunger. In the forefront of her brain was the fervent hope that wherever Aidan was, it would be straight ahead and not across any more suspension bridges. She looked around at the dilapidated buildings, the mountains of pulverized concrete and twisted girders. This may have been a neighborhood before, but now it was just the shell of one. A path, barely discernible, snaked through the rubble, disappearing a dozen yards ahead between the remnants of two brownstones, their roofs missing, their foundations sagging so that they almost touched at the top. The Hell Gate. The question was, were you entering hell going in or coming out? As far as she was concerned, the jury was still out on that one.

The terrain was unpredictable, and in most places sharply inclined on crumbling slopes made up of equal parts soil and man-made materials. Cinder blocks, sandbags, and planks of wood shored up the various levels like a humongous ladder. She followed the track—so narrow a goat would have had a problem with it. She went slowly, testing the ground, which was loose and studded with rocks. She kept her eyes open for people. Scavengers. Bands of roaming thieves who scoured the streets for anything that could be reused or resold. Rumor was they stole the fillings out of the mouths of corpses.

Suddenly Lucy was conscious of a hum not far ahead, down the next hill. She unclasped her knife, making sure it slid freely in the sheath, and pulled her leather jacket tighter around her body. It was too hot for leather, but it gave her confidence. She hoped it made her look tough. She walked slowly toward the noise, unable to tell if it was machinery, music, or the buzz of human voices. A guide rope was fastened to stakes where the edge of the hill dropped precipitously, with white flags of cloth tied onto wires to make the way clear. Wooden pallets were laid over deep puddles. She stopped. A curve in the trail along the edge of a crag revealed a view of the settlement below: tents clustered like mushrooms, lean-tos made of rough pieces of plywood. She was barely fifty feet above the source of the jumble of noise. She ducked down, feeling nervous all of a sudden. Lying on her belly in the loose dirt, Lucy peered over the edge. A few pebbles rattled down the slope. Just ahead, the path dropped down and opened onto a crowded square.

A wide road, which had somehow escaped devastation, rose high over the canal and ran southward; small walking alleys radiated in all directions, leading to more plywood shacks and, farther up, to the other suspension bridges she had seen from a distance. The central area had been part of the big street. You could tell because it was relatively flat and by the broken white line running down the middle, but the surface of the tarmac was cracked and uneven, giving it the appearance of large black paving stones. Reappropriated awnings and large lengths of canvas were slung on poles around the edges as protection from the sun's heat and the rains, but the middle circular area was clear.

More people than she'd seen since she left the emergency shelter massed in small groups. They seemed to be mostly children and teenagers, with a sprinkling of gray heads, which didn't surprise Lucy. It was the middle-aged population that had suffered from the plague the most. People like her parents.

She heard the hubbub of human voices. They sounded excited, happy. And unexpectedly she heard music. A guitar, she thought, and a few singers. People jostled and bantered; some pushed wheelbarrows piled high with broken appliances, and others lounged cross-legged on long benches. Smoke gusted from a massive fire pit. A large black pot steamed above it. Lucy scanned the crowd for Aidan, unable to stop herself from feeling a jolt of excitement at the thought of seeing him again and ruthlessly reminding herself that she didn't like him.

And there he was, taller than she remembered. His shaggy blond head, his red sweatshirt. He leaned against a crumbling wall that was covered in faded posters and graffiti. As she watched he threw his head back, laughing at something his companion, a girl standing very close to him, said. The girl reached up and smoothed her hand across his face. Even from this distance she was striking. Her thick black hair so sleek it looked oiled and a jumble of silver bracelets on her tanned arms that caught the light.

Lucy wasn't sure what to do. She'd crossed miles of treacherous ground. She'd lost everything but what she carried on her back. And now she just felt like crawling away. She couldn't imagine walking downhill into that crowd of people. Knowing her, she'd probably trip and fall. The buzz of dialogue almost hurt her ears. She wasn't even sure if she remembered how to start a conversation. "Hi," she said experimentally, and her voice cracked.

On the other hand, they had water, and whatever was cooking above the fire smelled good. Dusk was approaching, and the thought of sleeping out here was daunting. She could cut through the settlement to link up with the Geo Wash Bridge farther north if she meant to keep on going. Or backtrack the way she had come, across the rope bridge again, and then go miles around, and that was an unbearable thought.

She stood up, brushed the dirt from her clothes. Her hands crept up to her hair. The humidity had matted it into the corkscrew curls she despised. She spat on her fingers and dragged them through the unruly mass, but it was no good. She scowled. This was stupid. She didn't need anybody. There was no one down there whose opinion meant anything to her. She squared her shoulders, shrugged the backpack into position, checked her knife, and took one last look around.

Suddenly she stopped in her tracks. She saw a billow of dust coming from the south along the road. Not a cyclone. This hugged the tarmac, and it moved fast and low. The cloud dispersed, and now she could see a line of vans speeding toward the square. Four white vehicles like delivery trucks, but unmarked. The same type of van she'd seen crawling through her neighborhood sixty days after the plague arrived, searching out the sick and dead, dragging people from their homes. "Sweepers" was what the TV anchors had called them. Cleaning up the mess. Her eyes darted to the thronging crowd. She remembered what Aidan had said, that the Sweepers were hunting survivors now. She was gripped by a fear so strong, it cramped her belly. She was still too far away; the vehicles were moving too fast. How could she alert them?

She waved her arms in the air. No one noticed, not even

when she jumped up and down. She could yell, but her voice would be drowned by the tumult of voices below. A sound. Something unexpected. Something that would carry across the square. She pursed her lips. She was pretty good at wolf whistling, a skill she'd mastered to annoy Maggie. But her throat was too dry, and her tongue felt thick in her mouth. She couldn't whistle, but she had an idea. She filled her lungs and howled, a long wail that cut through the air like a knife.

CHAPTER SIX
SWEEPERS

The mournful cry seemed to echo. Down below people snapped to attention, froze for a long moment, and then the jumble of noise started up again. There was some laughter and excited chatter, as if it were a prank. Heads turned this way and that looking for the source of the howling. Then someone screamed. She heard shouts: "The Sweepers are coming!" and a dozen arms pointed at the speeding vans barely one hundred yards away now. So close that Lucy could hear the rev of the accelerators, smell the sharp odor of gasoline. They arrived in a column, the exhaust fumes and the dust boiling up along the road behind them.

And then, like an anthill kicked open, people were running everywhere, making for the alleyways, melting into the shadows. It seemed like everyone was yelling. Kids disappeared under tarps and into tents. It was chaotic, but in a way it seemed rehearsed. Aidan was lost in the tumult. She leaned forward, crouched against the ground, searching the crowd for his bright sweatshirt, and found him bent over an old woman who was frantically trying to tie the corners of her blanket together around a pile of fruits and vegetables. Shriveled apples rolled in the dirt. A child stumbled and fell, screaming when he scraped his palms on the rough surface. Aidan scooped him up. A boy and girl, eight or nine years old with identical rats' nest hair, scabby knees, and dingy undershirts, squatted under an awning with their arms around each other. Two older kids threaded their hands through a column of bicycle tires. They could barely walk with their load. The dark-haired girl yelled at them and they dropped the stuff and scuttled off. Lucy pressed her body into the earth, lifting her head to see. She had a clear view. The square had emptied out. About fifteen or twenty people remained, and most of them seemed to be Lucy's age. A few of them picked up rocks and sticks from the ground. Some pulled short knives and slingshots from their pockets. They spread out in a thin line. Their faces were set and grim.

Brakes squealed. The clamor of the engines seemed incredibly loud. One of the vans sideswiped the edge of a caved-in building, dislodging pieces of brick. Another plowed through a heap of pots and pans, sending them flying into the air. The vehicles slowly pulled up in a wedge and came to a stop, although the engines continued to roar. They effectively blocked the road. The front and rear windows of the vans were tinted. Heavy steel bars were welded to the bumpers. Huge truck wheels lifted them up four feet from the ground. The engines cut off simultaneously. The back doors were flung open, and a dozen figures in white hazmat suits spilled out. They wore shiny headgear and heavy, laced boots and carried small black boxes. Their hands looked like they were made of marble, and Lucy realized they were wearing white surgical gloves. Someone else appeared around the side of a van, holding the ends of several thick leashes in his black leather-clad hands. Four vicious-looking dogs struggled to free themselves from their trainer. They were powerfully built, with barrel-chested black and tan bodies. Rottweilers and German shepherds, Lucy thought, watching their noses scent the air, ears pressed flat against their skulls.

Aidan stood with the dark-haired girl and an older man, who was muscular with a shaved head and the glimmer of gold in both ears. He looked five or six years younger than

Lucy's father had been. Mid-thirties, she guessed. His bulky arms were inked with swirling blue tattoos, his calves bulged, and his back was ramrod straight. There was something military about him, as if he'd been trained for conflict. Lucy glanced from the teenagers standing in their thin line to the Sweepers who had spread out in a solid row. The Sweepers stood shoulder to shoulder, their helmets reflecting the sunlight. They looked as impenetrable as a steel wall. The teenagers didn't stand a chance.

Lucy fought the urge to run. Adrenaline scurried up and down her spine. Things seemed to be happening in slow motion, but she knew it had barely been a minute or two since the vans arrived. The Sweepers moved forward. Aidan and the others faced them, flimsy weapons ready. The bald man raised his hand. Chunks of stone flew through the air. Lucy heard the clatter as they connected with the Sweepers' headgear. Aidan yelled something indecipherable, but the anger was clear, and a second volley of rocks flew. One of the Sweepers broke ranks and took a wild swing at him—the blow missed his nose but connected with the side of his head. Aidan staggered and threw a punch back. The Sweeper dodged it and darted back to his line. Aidan pressed his hand to his cheek. Lucy winced. She could see the scarlet welt.

The black-haired girl erupted into a barrage of curses. Another volley of stones flew through the air, followed by a hail of garbage: old tin cans and bottles. It had no effect from what Lucy could see. Slowly Aidan and the others were forced backward against a wall. Lucy stood up. No one was paying any attention to anything that was happening outside the square. Anxiety coursed through her; she felt ill and riled up all at the same time. She had a clear view from where she stood. The Sweepers looked like white chess pieces in their close ranks. Two of them were sidling to the right, trying to flank the kids. Lucy pursed her lips and howled again. Aidan shouted something and another volley of garbage spattered against the dark visors. The Sweepers reformed into their solid line. Lucy couldn't understand why the kids didn't just rush them. They seemed to approach no closer than ten feet. She narrowed her eyes, trying to see more clearly. The slim black boxes that the Sweepers carried looked like old-fashioned transistor radios. She didn't notice any weapons.

Suddenly the bald man rushed forward with a roar. Eight of the Sweepers closed around him. The remaining four faced Aidan and the rest of the teenagers. They stood locked in some kind of staring contest. Lucy couldn't understand it. Only the bald man did anything, and he was a blur of motion. He jabbed a punch, ducking low and driving up with an uppercut that struck a Sweeper under the chin and sent his head snapping back on his neck. Another Sweeper rushed him from behind. He pivoted, kicking out with one leg. His booted foot connected with an arm. Lucy heard a *crack* like the snapping of a twig. His momentum carried him forward.

He spun again and slammed his boot into the chest of the nearest Sweeper who fell to his knees. The bald man skipped backward, keeping a safe distance. The teenagers cheered.

Aidan picked up a discarded length of metal pipe. "Leo," he shouted, darting into a clear space. Leo ducked a blow and raised his arm high. Aidan threw the steel bar. Leo caught it and swept it around in a circle. The men fell back. Leo swung the bar as if it were an ax, catching a Sweeper behind the knees and bringing him down. Moving so quickly that his hands were a blur, he brought up the pipe like a spear and jabbed a second man in the back and another in the belly. His breath was coming in gusts now, and his broad chest was heaving. His movements slowed, but they were no less deadly or accurate. The five or six Sweepers who were still on their feet circled him warily. He held the bar easily in one hand, his head swiveling to clock their movements, but there were too many of them.

Aidan and the teenagers moved forward with their rocks and pieces of wood. The Sweepers moved back.

And then, all of a sudden, the dogs were among them, loosed from their leashes, advancing slowly, the fur raised along their spines, tails curled against their flanks. Even from where she crouched, Lucy could hear the rumbling growls, and, terrified, she buried her face in her arms.

Could they smell her from here?

The Sweepers broke ranks, two remaining in place while the dogs circled, growling continuously, keeping the teenagers at bay. A red-haired boy, not much older than Lucy's brother, darted forward, screaming and stabbing the air with a heavy stick. The dog trainer made a gesture with one hand, and immediately one of the German shepherds was on the kid; hurling him backward, its jaws clamped on his forearm. The boy screamed, an awful high-pitched noise. The trainer shouted something and the dog released the arm, but settled its weight across the kid's chest, pinning him on the ground. Its jaws were inches from the boy's pale face.

Leo dropped his weapon and stepped back. His eyes were on the boy and the dog. None of the teenagers moved. It was as if they were frozen.

The hazmat-suited men dispersed; only the dog trainer remained where he was. Making their way around the perimeter of the square, the rest of them conducted a search, shining powerful flashlights into the tents and plywood huts.

Lucy heard a patter of voices and an excited yell from inside one of the shelters.

"Hold your ground," Aidan shouted. At his side, the dark-haired girl tossed a stick from hand to hand. Her face was turned toward his, and Lucy could see the rage disfiguring her features as she argued with him.

"No, Del," he yelled, putting out a hand, which she smacked away.

Leo shook his head at her, barked a command and then held up one arm, keeping the teenagers back. A bottle flipped end over end through the air and smashed in front of one of the dogs. A volley of growls erupted, but the dogs stayed in position as though they were tethered by invisible lines.

None of the teenagers moved, as two grimy children were pulled from their hiding places and thrown over broad backs like they were bags of potatoes. A woman with drooping shoulders was shoved forward with such force, she staggered. An old man with a shapeless cardigan and a fringe of mousy hair followed, as though he were sleepwalking. A cluster of seniors with their arms around one another were forced through the open double doors and pushed down onto the floor of a van. The men Leo had hurt were helped to their feet and bustled away. The dogs, summoned by a whistle or gesture that Lucy didn't notice, returned to the trainer, who placed his black leather-clad hands on top of their rough heads before ordering them into a vehicle. The German shepherd was the last dog to be summoned. The dog moved slowly off the prone redhead and backed away. Del rushed to the boy, kneeled on the ground, and helped him up. Blood dripped from his arm, and it hung limply at his side.

A fat drop of rain splattered on Lucy's cheek as she watched in horror. In the next second, the sky had cracked open with an explosive blast and the rain poured down in a solid sheet. Lucy wiped the water from her eyes in vain. She was almost blinded. Engines started up, wheels screeched, and the column of vehicles drove off. And now people moved. They ran after them, yelling and throwing stones.

The rain fell in heavy sheets, reducing everything to slippery mush. The path was a treacherous mess of mud and rushing rivulets of water. Lucy didn't know what to do. Part of her wanted to disappear. She stood there, shifting from foot to foot, trying to decide. Aidan looked up, spotting her. Lucy cringed—too late to duck down. She should have remembered that she'd be silhouetted against the sky and that he'd be wondering who had made the signal. He frowned, but then his expression cleared. He raised his hand, and after a moment she waved, too. She felt the rocky soil slide under her boots as she made her way carefully down to the square. She pulled the collar of her leather jacket tight around her throat. Why hadn't she joined the fight? What would Aidan think? Chances were he already considered her some kind of coward, hiding in her camp, ignoring the reality of life outside her safe acres.

But when Lucy finally reached the bottom of the path and stood there, water streaming down her neck and filling her boots, at a loss for anything to say, he pulled her into a hug. She buried her nose in the shoulder of his sweatshirt, smelling a clean, fresh scent, like lemons mixed with his sweat. Her heart gave a little skip before she realized that all his concern was for those who had been taken. He probably just needed someone to hold. His arms tightened around her, but she made herself step away, ignoring the confused expression in his eyes.

"Hi," she said. Her voice only cracked a little. Inside her pocket, she dug her fingernails into her palm. She felt herself flush. She had to stop this. It was ridiculous. He clearly had feelings for that Del girl.

"Lucy. I should have guessed it was you." A hint of the crooked smile appeared on his face, but it vanished quickly. He scraped his hand through his wet hair and steered her under an awning. Others slowly appeared from their hiding places, assembling in small groups under the shelters. Lucy glimpsed more people who hovered in the shadows at the perimeter. *Too scared to come out even now,* she thought. The murmur of subdued voices rose. Brightly striped umbrellas went up around the fire pit, shielding it from the rain. They seemed too cheerful in contrast to the stunned atmosphere, a splash of color in a scene as monochromatic as an old postcard.

They stood quietly as the rain poured down, washing the dust from the road. The frown was back on Aidan's face, but he didn't talk. He rubbed the knuckles of one hand. Lucy saw that the skin was broken and bleeding, and the flesh over the bones looked swollen. His cheek was red and bruised. The viciousness of the attack had been shocking. Now that it was over, she felt a weariness that threatened to submerge her. If she'd been able to, she'd have crawled into her sleeping bag, drawn her jacket over her head, and slept for two weeks. The pain of losing the safety and comfort of her home squeezed her heart.

Aidan looked past her. His arm went to hers, cradling her elbow, and he turned her to face the bald man striding toward them. He was huge. Tall, and as broad as a brick wall.

"Lucy, this is Leo." Leo nodded but did not smile. His shirt was damp with sweat, and beads of moisture flecked his scalp and upper lip. He wiped a ham-like hand on his cargo pants and then held it out, pumping her own in a bone-crushing grip. His blue eyes studied her with an intensity that made her nervous.

"Leo just needs to check you out," Aidan said, giving her a little pat and then a push on the back.

"Wha-a-t?"

Simultaneously Leo's hand gripped her forearm and she was directed toward one of the larger army green tents. There was no question of breaking loose. His hold was bruising. She tried to grab her knife, but it was out of reach. She threw a panicked look at Aidan over her shoulder. He nodded at her reassuringly, but his eyebrows were bunched and his expression was worried.

CHAPTER SEVEN
EXAMINATION

Inside, the tent was dark and smelled of mildew. A bench heaped with clothing stood in the middle of the packed dirt floor along with a table, two chairs, and some milk crates stuffed with wads of material. A few sheets hung from rings on the ceiling, making a small enclosure. A large bucket of water rested nearby. A hurricane lamp smoked gently and gave off a pungent odor.

And by the wall—her heart started beating quickly—stood a wheeled hospital gurney, like the ones her parents had died on.

Leo had finally let go of her arm. She stood rubbing it, eyeing the doorway flap and his bulk in front of it. She wondered if she could squeeze through the tiny gap under the tent where it was pinned to the earth with stakes, tried to decide if he was as slow as his height and weight suggested. But then she remembered the grace with which he had fought and resigned herself miserably to being his prisoner.

"You can put your backpack down and take a seat," he said, motioning toward the chair. His voice was brisk, impersonal. It gave away nothing.

He busied himself at the small table. There were small glass bottles and a few odd-looking metal implements on a steel tray, which he pushed to one side.

Lucy remained standing, balanced on the balls of her feet so she could run if she had to. Her hand went to the knife. She wasn't sure what to think. She tried to read him. It didn't seem as if he was about to attack her, but her nerves were zinging anyway.

What was she in for? Torture? Execution? And the more nagging thought: Why had she ever trusted Aidan?

Leo now turned to the heap of clothes and rummaged through them with his broad back to her. It was such a target.

She half drew the knife and prepared to pounce. If she could get the knife to his neck, she could make him let her go.

His words distracted her.

"Henry's not here, but I've learned enough from him not to cause you too much discomfort. Let's see, might as well get this sorted. A medium should do, I think."

Henry? Medium what?

He swiveled suddenly, as coordinated as the cougar she'd seen at the lake, and tossed something at her. She almost dropped the knife in her attempt to catch the soft bundle.

His eyes widened as he caught sight of the blade. And then a grin spread across his ruddy face.

"It's not what you think."

She held up two pieces of clothing. Worn, black faded to gray—a pair of loose drawstring pants and a baggy thermal shirt.

"For you to change into. After."

He nodded at the tarps hanging behind her. "There's a makeshift shower in there. Water's cold, I'm afraid. No disrespect, but I'm thinking it's been a while." Her cheeks flamed. Then he pointed to a box spilling more clothes on the floor. "Underwear and so on in there." And now she could have sworn *he* blushed, but the light was pretty poor. "They're secondhand, but clean."

He took a step toward her, his fingers spread out in a non-threatening pose.

She held her ground. "What do you want?"

"Can you put the knife down, Lucy?" He had stopped moving toward her, and his voice was gentle. She felt tears pricking at her eyelids. He sounded like her dad. The same burr in his voice.

She got a grip on her emotions and did not lower the knife.

He picked up something small and metallic from the table and flicked a switch. A small dot of light came on. She recognized the scope doctors used. Like the one they'd used on Rob when he was four and stuck orange pips up his nose.

He showed it to her, moving slowly, as if she were a little kid. The circle of light bobbed around.

"I need to ask you to trust me. Just for a little while."

She thought about her choices. Surprise! She didn't really *have* any. Seemed like that was the way it was recently.

She scowled and nodded.

"I'll trust you, too," he said, his eyes on her weapon. "I just need to look in your mouth and ears. Check your glands for swelling, your fingernails for blackening."

With the worst cases of the plague, bleeding started under the skin, a darkness spreading like crude oil on water, and a high fever boiled the blood. In the first few months she'd been obsessive about checking every bruise, every lump, but she was a klutz, and she always had some cuts or contusions sprinkled across her legs and arms.

He shone the light in her eyes and grunted. "Your eyes are clear."

"Are you afraid I'll infect you?" she asked sarcastically.

"Frankly, right now I'm more worried about your blade." He shifted around so he could peer into her ears. She hoped they were moderately clean.

He checked her fingernails, pressing along the edges. He turned her palm over. The knife cut on it still oozed, and the edges were raw.

"Nasty," he said. "There's a salve here somewhere." He placed her hand palm up on her knee and rummaged through the clutter on the table, emerging with a flat tin and a rectangular piece of material. He opened the box, revealing a paste which resembled brown Vaseline. It had a pungent smell like oregano.

"Goldenseal, echinacea, and comfrey," he said, as though that meant anything to her. "Grammalie makes it."

He smeared some over the wound, wrapped it tightly in a cloth bandage, and used some thin strips of cloth to bind it in place. The edges of the wound stung briefly and then stopped. She clenched her fist experimentally. The pain was numbed.

"Here." He handed her a surgical glove. "To keep your hand dry."

She was oddly reluctant to take it. The Sweepers wore gloves like that. She was reminded of a question she'd wanted to ask. "Do they always send dogs?"

He considered. "Lately." He squared his shoulders and rubbed his chin thoughtfully. "Lately it seems like they're looking for something in particular."

She couldn't control the shiver that snaked up her spine.

"How can you live like this, not knowing if they're going to come back?"

"We try to prepare as best we can. Look out for one another." He glanced at her with narrowed eyes. "You were living alone? Out in the Wilds?"

She nodded.

"Easier, I bet. But lonely, maybe?"

She shrugged, feeling the sudden prickle of tears. She rubbed vigorously at her nose.

"People just naturally cluster together, you know. Everyone's got a version of the same story." He cocked an eyebrow at her. "Probably for the first time ever, we have an understanding, a compassion for one another, you know? Everyone has lost someone."

She said nothing, though a part of her wanted to. Alone, she could squash down all the emotions. He was making it hard.

"Say *ahhh*."

She wondered how bad her breath smelled.

He put the scope down and reached behind him. When he turned around again, he held a thermometer. "Open again."

She opened her mouth and he placed it beneath her tongue. The thermometer was uncomfortable in her mouth. She moved her tongue. He frowned slightly and repositioned it. "Hold still for two minutes." She exhaled through her nose.

"Family maybe means something else these days," he said. "It's not about blood ties anymore."

She grunted and shifted on the chair. She ducked her head so she didn't have to meet his eyes.

After a seemingly endless time he said "Open" again and removed the thermometer. He shook it a couple of times and squinted at it, trying to read the numbers.

"People are scared. They fear that the disease is just dormant, that it might mutate again, resurge. We have to face the possibilities," he continued, holding the thermometer toward the light. "Normal." He placed the thermometer back on the table and faced her. "Good."

Lucy ran her dry tongue across her lips. The thought that the plague could appear again was terrifying.

"I could have told you that. I'm not sick."

"It's hard to tell. By the time the bleeding and fever appear, it's usually too late. And contagion usually occurs before the symptoms show themselves. We're barely hanging on here. We can't let you into the camp if there's even the smallest chance that you could bring infection."

"Aidan's the first person I've seen in six months. None of this is necessary." She stared at him, her chin thrust out. He looked amused. "I don't know if I'm staying past tonight," she said.

"Even so. We'll have to dispose of the clothes you're wearing, too. We ran out of bleach a month ago, and none of the herbal concoctions do the job."

She remembered her mother burning their family blankets and pillows on the pyres.

"You can't take my leather jacket. Or my boots! I'll leave." She pulled her jacket around her. She'd had the boots so long that, ripped and shredded as they were, they felt like old friends.

He shot them a glance, then looked at her stony face. "You can keep them. It's the plant fibers that hold the disease. Let's finish up." He moved slowly, holding his hands out where she could see them.

Then he pressed his thumbs in under her jawline and behind her ears. His hands were quick and firm. She closed her eyes and tried not to think about how her father had smoothed her hair away from her face or tweaked her nose when she was little and didn't want to take her fish oil gel tabs. "Anything hurt?"

She shook her head impatiently. He exhaled and wiped his sweating forehead. She wondered if he was more nervous than he admitted.

"Henry will ask you some questions when he gets back. He's out on hunt detail right now."

"Hunting animals?" Lucy asked.

He shot her an amused glance. "What else would it be?"

She shrugged. "Who's Henry?"

"He's our resident medical expert." He sat back on the stool, spreading his large hands on his knees and leaning so that only one chair leg still touched the floor.

Lucy suffered another twinge. Her dad used to sit like that at his desk. Even though her mom always complained that it scuffed the floor.

"Any more clothing in your bag?" he asked.

She nodded, unlaced the opening, and pulled out the sodden mass of her clothes. Her nose wrinkled. They smelled of mold and ancient sweat and the iron tang of blood from her wounded hand. She dropped them on the ground. They were torn and disgusting and probably unwearable anyway. She continued to dig, dropping her dead flashlight, tinderbox, journal, yearbook, survival manual, and her musty, polyester sleeping bag in a heap. Her fingertips touched soft wool at the bottom of the bag and her heart leapt. Her mother's shawl! Surely he wouldn't take it from her? He had said plant fibers, like cotton. This was wool. Wool was okay, right?

She withdrew her hand and raised her eyes. "That's it," she said firmly, indicating the pile of things. His glance passed over them slowly, and then he nodded and she shoved everything but the clothing back in and tied the laces tightly.

"That's it?"

"Yeah. Yes," she said hugging the bag to her. Could he tell that she was lying?

A furrow appeared across his forehead. "How long were you out on your own?"

She exhaled.

"About a year." His eyebrows went up, but all he said was, "There are more clothes over there if you need anything. No towels, but you can use them to dry off with, too." He got up heavily and pointed toward the shower stall. "You've got about three gallons of water there. If you use it all before you rinse off, you'll have to hike a ways to get more." He handed her a slab of rough soap. It smelled overpoweringly of peppermint and lemons and felt greasy against her palm.

"So? Okay?" he said, preparing to go. "I'll be outside if you need anything."

Wait. Now that he was leaving, she felt the familiar lump of dread settle in her stomach. Funny how she felt safer when she was out in the open and could see her surroundings. Anyone could approach the tent and she wouldn't know until it was too late.

"You can leave your old clothes there on the ground. I'll be right outside." He met her eyes, nodded, then ducked out the tent flap. She heard his deep voice as he greeted someone. It was comforting to think of him so close by.

The water was not as cold as she had feared. She made a washcloth out of her tank top and paid particular attention to her armpits and the back of her neck. The soap was gritty and so pungent, it made her want to sneeze. She gave up trying to work it into a lather after a couple of minutes, doused her head, and tried to work through the worst of the tangles. She washed her mouth out and ran her finger over her teeth to clean them. When she was done, her skin tingled and she could bear to smell herself.

It was a relief to kick her old clothes to the side. She'd been wearing the same two pairs of jeans for almost a year, the same T-shirts and tank tops and hoodie, washing them in the lake when she could. She'd tried to make her own detergent from soapwort and the fat layer from the belly of a dead squirrel, but it had been a disaster. The stink of cooking lard had driven her from her camp for a few hours, and she'd ruined one of her only saucepans. She sniffed her sweatshirt before tossing it onto the discard pile in disgust. It was funny how she hadn't really smelled her stink before. She'd gotten so used to it.

She dragged her fingers through her curls one last time, both wishing for and glad there wasn't a mirror.

The new clothes smelled strongly of bleach and were rough and slightly itchy against her newly scrubbed skin, but they fit okay. She rolled the pant legs up a little, laced her boots, and then dug through the pile looking for a sweatshirt. She needed something with a hood, preferably dark-colored, so she could vanish if she had to. *Aha!* She pulled out a sweatshirt. It was faded with washing and too big, but she slipped it on, instantly comforted by the fleece lining. Over that went her leather jacket. Now she could rough it outside for a few nights if she had to. She also grabbed another change of clothes, underwear, socks, and a couple of tank tops and stuffed them into her bag.

She shouldered the backpack and ducked outside. The rain had stopped, and the ground steamed slightly in the blazing sun.

Lucy shaded her eyes. The hospital tent stood in its own little area apart from the other lean-tos and awnings she could see scattered on the outskirts of the big square. People clustered together, exchanging worried glances and talking in low voices. None of the young kids were unaccompanied. Each had an older guardian, grim-faced and wary. Some of the teenagers were gathering piles of rocks; some stood along the path Lucy had traveled down, acting as sentries.

Feeling shy and awkward, she spotted Aidan a dozen yards away. He was standing close to *that Del girl*. Funny how she'd just started calling her that in her mind. Petty and sort of mean, actually, but there was something in the way the other girl held herself, as if she knew that she was beautiful and expected attention for it, that was really annoying.

Aidan leaned into her. Their heads were almost touching. His hand was on her sleeve. She yanked her arm away. A torrent of angry words spilled from her lips. He frowned and made a series of exaggerated gestures with his hands, and suddenly she laughed and pulled him close, her left arm slung around his shoulder. His arm slipped around her waist. It was an intimate gesture, and it halted Lucy in her tracks.

Lucy fumbled with the too-long sleeves of her sweatshirt. She must look like an elephant. And it was way too hot to be wearing all her clothes. Del was in a tank top and a pair of faded cargo shorts.

Slowly, Lucy walked in their direction, her eyes fixed on the pebbly ground. She tried to look as if she had a destination, a purpose. She kicked a rock. A minute ago she'd felt clean, refreshed; now she was sweating. She touched her hair, pushing the riot of damp curls back without success.

"Lucy!" Aidan said, and waved.

Del moved even closer to him. She didn't smile. Lucy had never been so conscious of tripping as she was now, covering the ground that separated them. She prayed she wouldn't stumble in front of Del's piercing blue eyes. And if she did, she hoped she'd be knocked unconscious or something.

"Hi," she said, reaching them. She was striving for unconcerned and cool, but it came out sounding like a question. Del smirked.

"Del Flowers, this is Lucy . . . ?"

"Holloway," Lucy said. "Lucy Holloway." *Man, even the girl's name is exotic.*

They shook hands. Del's eyes slid away from hers, and as soon as she'd given Lucy's hand the expected up-down shake, she dropped it like it was a snake. Her fingers crept around Aidan's forearm.

Lucy put her backpack down and shrugged her arms out of her leather jacket. The sun was beating down. The glare beating off the broken tarmac was giving her a headache. She remembered how long it had been since she'd eaten. And most of that she'd puked up. She felt suddenly dizzy.

Del was tiptoeing her fingers along Aidan's biceps now. He stepped away and bent down to tighten his shoelace. "How'd it go with Leo?" he asked.

Lucy was instantly angry. She remembered the fear she'd felt. "You could have warned me."

"Would you have stuck around?"

"I almost knifed him."

Del snickered. "Leo is a black belt. I think he'd probably manage to defend himself against you."

"Not if he wasn't expecting an attack," Lucy fired back.

Del rolled her eyes. "Oh *come* on! He took on six guys today." She tugged at Aidan's arm. "Tell her!"

Aidan shook his head and mumbled something incomprehensible. Del glared at him, and then turned a poisonous gaze on Lucy.

"Whatever," she said, and stormed off.

After a long moment, Aidan said, "It's been a bad day. She's upset."

You think? Lucy barely stopped herself from voicing the thought.

Without speaking, they walked to the center of the square. Although it was still midafternoon and bright, the shadows were creeping forward. The sun was suddenly obscured behind boiling black clouds. The air felt heavy.

Rain again, thought Lucy, and then the fat drops fell. In just a few seconds, they became a torrent. Pools of already saturated mud surged under her boots. She felt the weight of the water in the weave of her clothes. Aidan's shaggy hair was plastered against his scalp. It seemed as if the weather never did anything by half measures anymore.

He pulled her under a pale blue awning, but he released her arm far too soon. At a loss for anything to say, Lucy stared at her feet. Aidan looked toward the wide road by which the Sweepers had come. His face was set. She followed his gaze.

"Where does the road go?" Lucy asked.

"It dips down and follows the shoreline for a few miles and ends up at the island."

"So they've got a straight route from here to there?"

"Yeah, it's one of the only routes still accessible. They keep it clear for the vans. Otherwise they'd be on foot."

An older woman, her head covered by a black scarf, dragged

a cover over the big pot on the fire and then joined Lucy and Aidan, who instantly made room for her. She walked slowly, as if her joints were stiff. Lucy's Grandma Ferris had moved like that. Her solid body was swathed in black shawls. Her nose was curved like a beak and she wore heavy gold hoops in her ears, which had elongated the lobes. Lucy recognized her as the woman with the fruits and vegetables. Her black eyes flashed. "They took the priest, Walter, and sad Olive?" she asked Aidan. Her voice was accented, the consonants thickly pronounced. "My little *zabkos*, too?"

Aidan nodded. "And some others I didn't know." She made a guttural noise in her throat and then sighed. "At least Emi and Jack are still together. They had barely settled in." She sighed again.

She turned toward Lucy. "And who is this?"

Lucy tried to meet her gaze but failed. Water dripped from her hair into her eyes. Her nose was running like a faucet. She thought about wiping it on her sleeve but didn't. Not in front of this fierce woman.

She pulled her sweatshirt hood up, but it was too late. She was already soaked.

"This is Lucy. She gave the signal," Aidan said. "And this is Grammalie Rose," he told Lucy.

The woman stared at her for a long moment. Her dark eyes were framed by thick, black brows. They gave her face a strength that made Lucy nervous. She felt like a mouse pinned by a hawk.

"The howl?"

Lucy cleared her throat. "Yes," she said in a raspy whisper, and then, louder, "Yeah." She shot a quick glance at the stern old woman, wondering if that had sounded sort of smart-alecky.

"You are a wolf, perhaps?" She made a dry coughing sound which Lucy realized with surprise was a laugh.

"I just thought the sound would carry. And people would notice."

The old woman stared at her openly. Her eyes were very black. There was no definition between iris and pupil. It made it hard to look away.

"So," she said eventually, nodding her head. "Good. We need people like her."

"What?" said Lucy, glancing at Aidan. The corner of his mouth twisted and then flattened into a thin line again. "I'm not much use in a fight."

Aidan touched the welt on his cheek. "Yeah, well, neither am I." He looked down the road and frowned. "Especially when we're up against Tasers and a plan, and we've got nothing but some teenagers and senior citizens with sticks and stones."

"Tasers?" Lucy echoed. Those were the black boxes she'd seen the Sweepers holding. Stupidly she'd thought they were radios. No wonder the kids had held back.

"They don't always use them. Not against the young ones at least. It's as if they don't want to injure them or something," Aidan said.

Grammalie Rose said, "They will have their attention on Leo now."

Aidan nodded.

"So you don't really know what they're doing with the people they take?" Lucy asked.

"No idea, but I doubt it's a spa treatment," he said.

"Nothing good," Grammalie said heavily.

They both fell silent.

After a few seconds, Aidan loosened his shoulders. "Grammalie Rose, do you think . . . ?" He paused. She swiveled those piercing eyes toward him.

"Do I think they will come back?" Grammalie Rose exhaled. "Do I think we should try to find them?"

Aidan nodded. His hands were clenched in fists, but Lucy thought he was unaware of it.

"I think that would be both dangerous and foolhardy." Aidan made an impatient gesture. The old woman raised her hand and pointed her forefinger at his chest. "And I think we will have a meeting soon and hear from everyone."

"Soon? Tonight?"

She shook her head. "Feelings are running high. Not everyone is here."

Aidan grunted.

Her black eyebrows bunched. "Okay?" she asked.

"Okay," said Aidan.

She glanced at Lucy. A quirk appeared in the corner of her mouth.

"I will see you soon, *zabko*. There are still a few hours of light left."

"Ummm. Okay." Immediately Lucy berated herself. Why hadn't she said she had no intention of hanging around? That she was just passing through?

Grammalie Rose walked away, and Lucy watched her make slow progress, pausing to speak to one person, lay a hand on a bowed shoulder, give a swift hug to a small child who ran up to her, chattering away.

Lucy turned to Aidan, who was flexing his bruised hand. "What's . . . *jabco?*"

"I think it means 'little frog.' She calls everybody under sixty that."

"Oh. So should I be worried? She scares me."

"She sort of scares me, too, but don't be nervous." Aidan stared out into the rain. "I'm glad you came."

Lucy glared at the ground. She pressed the backs of her hands against her hot cheeks.

"No choice," she mumbled, and then wished she'd kept her mouth closed.

He shot her a quick smile which turned to a frown. "Why?"

She told him briefly about the tsunami, skipping over the

details in case she burst into tears at the thought of her lost camp. The frown got deeper.

"Well," he said after a long pause. She looked back at him. She'd been focusing with all her might on a cloud shaped like a teapot. "Now you can join us. We all pitch in together. No one is alone."

She wasn't at all sure about this. She felt nervous surrounded by people, and there was the danger of the Sweepers. She'd decide later. She could always sneak off in the middle of the night.

Finally she cleared her throat. "Why do you think they take them?"

"I honestly don't know."

"Well, where—"

"To the hospital on the island. That's where the white vans come from. That's where the answers have always come from." He frowned. "And the lies."

"That makes sense," Lucy said slowly. She dreaded asking the next question, so she asked a different one. "How many times has this happened?"

"Twice before. They used to grab the older folk, the ones who didn't move as quickly. But now they're taking anyone who is healthy. Mostly the kids. Today there were a bunch of people from . . ." He paused, searching for the correct word. "From elsewhere. Come for the trading. They didn't know the drill."

"The people," she said through a tight throat. She desperately needed a drink of water. Funny that she could be so wet and so thirsty at the same time. "Do they ever come back?"

He stared at her, and then his face sort of went blank.

When he finally spoke, she could barely hear him.

"No."

CHAPTER EIGHT
GRAMMALIE ROSE

The old woman glowered at her. Lucy dropped her eyes. A thin trickle of sweat crept down her neck. The rain had stopped again as suddenly as it had started, and now the sun was blazing once more. She'd taken off the sweatshirt and dumped it and her leather jacket in a pile with her backpack. Even in just the thermal shirt she was hot, and also grimy with mud and what she had a sneaking suspicion was manure. Whatever Lucy had been expecting, it wasn't this. She leaned against her shovel and looked out over the straight rows of vegetables, the vines rambling over wrought iron gates planted in the earth like trellises, the greenhouses made from old storm windows. In the distance she glimpsed others working. They moved slowly and their faces, from what she could see, were sort of strange. There were bumps and ridges where there shouldn't have been, and their skin was smooth but strangely colored. They wore hoods and long robes. Monks, maybe? But she was too exhausted to ponder it for long.

This mean old woman had made her dig potatoes, carrots, and beets; pick beans and zucchini; stake straggling tomato plants; and remove slugs and beetles from the leaves of Swiss chard and spinach until her fingers were covered with a gluey black residue of insect slime and guts. She hadn't complained, though, mostly because she couldn't. Grammalie Rose, who must have been in her seventies, had worked right alongside her, silently, one of her black shawls pulled over her hair and tied under her chin. Lucy had stared at her tough, reddened hands with their short, blunt nails as she squished bugs between her fingers and brushed dirt off of waxen potatoes before piling them into plastic buckets and tubs. She pulled rows of peas with a minimum expenditure of energy. None of the wrestling with tough stalks that Lucy was doing. Another one of those situations where her awkwardness wasn't doing her any favors. She could almost hear her brother, Rob, pipe up, "Lucy loses to a plant!"

Lucy kept waiting for the woman to ask her questions or just make small talk, but she didn't. It was like she conserved energy. She marched along the rows, picking or digging, her back hunched, keeping up a solid pace while Lucy had trailed a few yards behind, *her* back screaming and *her* knees aching, barely able to drag the full container behind her. Finally, Lucy had casually asked where Aidan was.

"Out scouting, probably. Hunting or foraging. He likes to roam, that one," the old woman said before pointing out a cluster of bright green caterpillars on a head of lettuce.

And now that they were finally sitting down at the edge of the lot, Grammalie Rose was sticking with the silent treatment *and* giving her the evil eye. It was making her feel uncomfortable. The thought that Aidan had probably known what was in store for her and had uttered no warning *again!* made her stutter with rage, but she shoved it down to her belly where it simmered and spat. She ground her teeth and shot the old lady her best under-the-bangs-slit-eye stare. Grammalie Rose just looked amused and lit another one of the foul-smelling brown cigarettes she liked. The threads of black smoke it gave off stunk like burning hair.

"Have you never shelled beans, *zabko?*"

As she said this, Grammalie Rose was stripping the leathery pods from the dried beans and tossing them into a pail where they rattled like marbles. She made it look really easy. Snap the end, pull off the string, split the shell with her thumbnail before spilling the purple and white beans into the palm of her hand, and throwing the shriveled ones onto a compost heap. Lucy had tried to copy her and ended up cutting her fingers to shreds and losing most of her beans in the dirt. They rolled everywhere, and who would have known that the dry pods sliced flesh like the edges of thick envelopes? Lucy hunched her shoulders, ignored the pain in her fingers, and yanked on a stubborn pod string.

"Did you eat nothing but meat and acorn mush?"

"Cattail bulbs. Chicory," Lucy said. "Wild onions."

"No wonder you are so skinny. And without energy."

"I outran a tsunami today, and then I hiked over a couple of mountains," Lucy said, feeling her ears go red. She hurled a handful of beans into the bucket with force. Her legs were falling asleep and it was impossible to find an inch of soil without rocks to sit on. "Shouldn't we be preparing or something, in case the Sweepers come back?" she asked the old woman.

"They will be back."

Lucy stared at her. "So?"

"So, people must eat. Life goes on."

"You're saying that we shouldn't do anything?"

Grammalie Rose just nodded and kept shelling. Her plastic bucket was full already, and she hooked Lucy's with the toe of her clog and drew it closer. Her hands dipped and rose and dipped again.

Lucy bit her tongue. She felt like she might explode.

"But . . . that's . . . just . . . grrrrr!" she shouted finally, leaping to her feet and pacing back and forth.

After a few seconds, Grammalie Rose thumped the ground beside her. The frown was back on her face. Despite her annoyance, Lucy marveled at the bushy blackness of Grammalie Rose's eyebrows and the wrinkles fanning across her crumpled-tissue-paper face. How old was she?

"Sit down," she said.

There was no arguing with her tone, and Lucy could hardly pull her knife on the old woman. She exhaled through her nose and sank down ungracefully, crossing her legs and shifting until she found a comfortable spot. Grammalie Rose thrust a bucket of bean pods at her.

"We *are* doing something, *zabko*," she said.

"I'm not a frog!" Lucy said, turning a hot stare on her.

Grammalie Rose snorted out one of her dry laughs again. "*Wilcze*, then," she said, seeming amused.

"What does that mean?" Lucy snapped, suspecting that she was being teased. She felt like she was being treated like a three-year-old and struggled to control her temper.

"Wolf cub," she said, gesturing to the full bucket. "Full of snarls and bites." She chuckled and held Lucy's gaze until she sat and began work again.

Lucy slid her nail into the tough bean skin and split it, finding a rhythm that was missing before. Gradually she relaxed. *I could still leave,* she told herself, *anytime I want.*

She pushed her hand into the bucket and let the smooth beans sift through her fingers. She played with a pod, crunching it, and cast her mind about for something to say.

"How many people live in this settlement?"

"About thirty-five now. There were close to seventy-five when I first came, but some chose to move on. North. Some prefer to live on the outskirts and come in on market days. And others were taken."

Less than forty, Lucy thought. *And most of them kids.*

She cleared her throat and reached for a bottle of stale-tasting water. She'd drunk about a gallon already, and it seemed that she'd never get enough.

"Did you build all of this?" She waved her arm. Around the periphery of the lot were tumbled dinner plate–size slabs of concrete, rubble, and mounds of garbage big enough to climb. A chain-link fence sagging and busted through snaked around the edge.

"Not me personally."

Lucy stared at her. The black eyes gleamed through their veil of smoke. Was she joking with her?

"It was an old landfill. A dump, literally, and next to it, a cement parking lot which did not fare too well in an earthquake. Pickaxes and a lot of sweat did the rest." She pointed.

"See the low walls over there?" Lucy nodded. Gray walls sectioned off various rectangular areas.

"Corn and herbs. We're trying wheat and barley for the first time, now that flour can't be had for a song or a prayer. We built those out of blocks of concrete we dug up out of the parking lot. It is backbreaking work, but a creative use of salvage."

Her hands stopped working for a moment and she gazed over the furrows of sandy earth.

"It is not good soil, but it is good enough for what we grow here. The manure helps."

"So there are animals?" The thought of eating meat that was not newt or squirrel made her mouth water.

"Not anymore. We lost our last five goats just last week. Poachers." She scowled blackly. "The cows and the chickens died in the second wave." She sighed. "What I wouldn't give for a good honest egg."

"And the vegetables?" asked Lucy. "I mean, these are like what you used to get in a store. Not foraged daylily bulbs and wild greens."

"This was a neighborhood once. The kind that existed before all the troubles. People owned their homes and they grew extra food for their families. We adopted their gardens and their sheds. We used whatever we could find. That's what scavengers do." She picked up a trowel and turned it over in her hand. The clunky handle had obviously once belonged to some other implement and was kept in place with coils of wire.

Scavengers. Grammalie Rose said it with pride, but Lucy had always thought that scavengers were no better than thieves. She remembered what she had said to Aidan up in the tree and she blushed. Fortunately, the sharp-eyed old woman didn't notice. She had risen to her feet, uttering small complaining noises as her knees creaked, and picked up the two full buckets of beans. She jerked her head at Lucy and then at the other tubs overflowing with produce. Lucy slid her arms through the handles, two on each side. She was balanced, but she felt the tug across the back of her shoulders and the promise of pain to come. Not for the first time in the last year, she thought longingly of a hot bath.

They walked back toward the square. A few people were sweeping the grimy puddles of rainwater away. Others were making piles of cans, rocks, and chunks of brick and sharpening sticks. More were unrolling large carpets woven from bright strips of plastic or squatting on the ground making repairs or dismantling pieces of machinery. Lucy could only guess where the heaps of gears and chains and oddly-shaped metal bits had come from and what use they could be now.

After Grammalie Rose's explosion of conversation, she'd reverted to silence again. When they reached a long awning, she grunted and stopped. A narrow table of pine planks stretched at least twenty-five feet beneath the canvas tent. It was supported in five or six places with sawhorses. Knives of varying sizes gleamed on the rough surface. There were pots and pans, wooden cutting boards, colanders, and more of the plastic tubs. A fire crackled and smoked at the far end.

Lucy dropped her containers on the ground with a relieved groan and eased her backpack off. She worked her arms around, trying to loosen her shoulders. Maybe now she could go sprawl out somewhere, enjoy the last of the sun's warmth, and take a nap.

Grammalie Rose raised an eyebrow as if she knew what was passing through Lucy's mind. They locked eyes for a long moment. Lucy was on the verge of walking away when Grammalie Rose said in a mild tone, "You don't work, you don't eat."

Lucy nodded shortly. Her stomach felt like an empty balloon. She'd had no food for more than twenty-four hours. The old woman thumped her on the back. "Not so sullen, *wilcze*. The preparers get to eat first," she said, "and everyone must take a turn. This is not some cruel sort of punishment dreamt up especially for you." She made a croaking noise that sounded suspiciously like a chuckle and pushed her toward the table. There were people down at the far end scrubbing potatoes. They were surrounded by mounds of dirty yellow spuds, and yet they chattered and laughed together.

"Henry!" Grammalie Rose called, and pointed to one of the tubs Lucy had hauled.

Henry was small and dark, maybe in his early twenties, with brown hair that stuck up in a duck's tail over his forehead and twinkling brown eyes.

"Henry, this is Lucy."

Henry grinned at Lucy and stuck out his hand. She shook it, conscious of her filth-encrusted fingers. "Leo told me about you," he said. "He said you seemed okay."

"I am."

"Hmm." He ran his eyes over her in a not entirely clinical way.

"You don't look like a doctor," Lucy said, trying to cover her embarrassment.

"Oh, I'm not a doctor, but I do my best."

She felt vaguely unsettled.

He checked out the rest of their containers. "Looks like bean soup tomorrow. We'll have to soak them first."

Grammalie Rose grunted. "I've been making bean soup since your father was your age. Let tomorrow take care of itself." Henry made a face and skipped backward to avoid a slap. "First things first," the old woman said in a louder voice. "Take the onions and the carrots, *malpa*."

Henry staggered off, bowed under the weight of two tubs, and Grammalie Rose showed Lucy where a large bowl of tepid water was. Next to it was another slimy block of soap, this one off-white and shapeless. "Wash well, *wilcze*," the old woman said, sinking down on a bench. Even though her eyes had closed as if she were resting, Lucy still felt them on her back.

She rolled her sleeves up above her elbows and scrubbed her hands with the soap. It smelled of industrial strength solvent and lard. Her fingers tingled now as if they'd been sprayed with an acid solution, and the bandaged wound across her palm stung. She also took the opportunity to wash her arms and the back of her neck, too, so although she smelled of paint stripper, she felt a little cleaner.

There were six skinned dead things on the table that needed their innards removed, and she was pretty sure that was next on the list of chores. Whoever had skinned them had left their little white tails attached. "Letting us know they are not cats," Grammalie Rose said, touching a cotton ball tuft.

"Do you hunt cats often?" Lucy asked. Meat was meat, but cats were carnivores and never tasted good. Most carnivores didn't. She'd caught a weasel in a snare once and boiled it up, and the meat had been stringy, gamey, and really tough.

"Not often, but when the hunters bring them, they remove the fur *and* the tails so we can pretend it is something else."

Looking away from the sad little carcasses, Lucy's attention was captured by a hooded, cloaked figure that approached the table and carefully picked up the tub Lucy had used to wash her hands. The water was almost black with grime and bits of insect wings floated in it. His hands were gloved.

"Good," said Grammalie Rose. "Sammy, please bring us some fresh water if you can."

The man nodded. His hood slipped back a little and Lucy gasped. His features were covered completely by a mask. It was smooth and beautifully ornate, painted a luminescent white with gold filigree and flourishes around the cutout ovals where the eyes should be. His own eyes burned red behind the mask. A bow-shaped mouth was molded half-open and colored with more of the gold paint. The skin of his neck where the mask ended and his cloak gaped was blackened and cracked, as if it had been charred in a terrible fire.

Lucy stepped backward. Her heart was hammering in her chest, and she was unaware that her arm had knocked over a bowl and sent garlic and beets spilling onto the ground. He was a S'an. He was infected. A walking time bomb.

Without realizing it, she must have spoken out loud. Grammalie Rose pinched her elbow. Lucy half turned, and her fists came up defensively. The old woman batted them down. Lucy tried to form words but was unable to. Her brain was speeding. Those other strange people in the fields must be S'ans, too. She didn't understand how this could be. Everything she had ever been told said that they were carriers of the disease, as much as the urban birds were. They were to be avoided, and yet they were here. Working and mingling as if they were regular people.

The pinch became increasingly painful. She dragged her gaze from the S'an and stared at Grammalie Rose.

"I will slap you if I have to," the old woman said in a ferocious voice. "Are you going to faint?"

Lucy shook her head. Her legs felt weak, but her head was clear.

"Listen to me. You hate because you are scared, and you fear because you don't understand."

A shiver of horror ran up Lucy's spine.

"The S'ans are to be pitied, not feared," Grammalie Rose said. "They have survived the disease, but they are damaged. Their skin, their bodies, are ravaged. Do you hate him because he is not so pretty as you?"

"No, I . . . I . . ." Incredibly, through the fright, she felt a flush of shame. The S'an was three feet away and Grammalie Rose was carrying out this inquisition in front of him. "No," she said again, feeling like she was being hauled up in front of the class and reprimanded for cheating on a test. She knew that everyone under the awning was staring at her.

"Do you know where the name came from?" Grammalie Rose asked, relaxing her grip a little. Lucy felt the tips of her fingers buzz as the blood flooded back in. She thought back to the news reports.

"They are escapees from the sanatoriums, right? Driven insane by the second wave of the plague? After the disease mutated, people started losing their minds and their legs fell off and they craved fresh brains and stuff. . . ." Her voice trailed off. It sounded sort of stupid when she said it out loud.

Grammalie Rose snorted. "Zombies, huh? I used to love those old movies." She let go of Lucy's arm, nodded to the S'an who was still standing there, holding the sloshing tub in both arms. He shambled off, spilling water in a trail behind him, but before he went he winked at Lucy.

She stared after him, her mouth open. She closed it with a snap.

"That is an urban myth arising out of fear; because they were infected, but against all odds survived with their skin burned and cracked and their eyes bloody. They are not crazy people."

"But don't they carry the contagion still?" Lucy asked. Her hand had gone to her knife; she rubbed her thumb over the hilt, tried to control the shaking.

"No."

This was contrary to everything Lucy had heard.

She rallied her thoughts. "I thought the symptoms meant the sickness is still there. His eyes are red. He's still bleeding under his skin. He was wearing gloves."

"No. His immune system remains weak, but they are no more sick than we are. The gloves and robes shield his damaged skin from the sun. He wears the mask to protect *our sensibilities.*" Grammalie Rose put stress on the words. Her black eyes were flashing with anger. Lucy stepped backward, tripping over a beet. She bent down to pick it up, noticed the other vegetables and the fallen bowl, and started piling them together.

It seemed impossible, but surely if the S'ans had been living with the settlers for all this time then they must be all right. Leo had said that people were scared so they had to be careful. Somehow Sammy and the others had checked out. She got to her feet. She needed time to get her head around this.

Grammalie Rose bent with a grunt and picked up a garlic bulb that had rolled near her foot. She handed it to Lucy, who put it in the bowl with the rest.

"You look to be good with a knife, *wilcze.* Think you can deal with the rabbits? Small pieces for a stew." Grammalie Rose spoke calmly, as if nothing had happened.

"Uhh." Lucy was startled.

"Good. I'll be over helping to peel that mountain of potatoes. Otherwise we'll never eat today." She nodded grimly at her and made her slow way to the far end of the table where Henry and the others stood. After a few seconds more of staring at Lucy, they got back to work and the hum of conversation started up again.

Lucy rubbed her nose with the back of a hand covered in blood. She'd already gutted and filleted three of the rabbits. The chef's knife she was using was very sharp, the edge honed beautifully. The S'an—Sammy—had not come back again, but the expectation of seeing him was making her jumpy. Part of her wondered where Aidan was. He was the only person she sort of knew in the camp, and he'd disappeared. She cut the pieces of glistening red meat into chunks and pulled another rabbit toward her. Using a cleaver, she chopped off the cotton ball tail. The knife whacked through the bone and into the board. She rocked it back and forth to loosen it.

"Whoa!" Henry jumped backward, his eyes wide in mock alarm. "Do you think you can put the knife down for a second?"

After a moment, Lucy recognized the teasing note in his voice. She smiled back reluctantly. The wood in front of her was covered in deep cuts. She hadn't noticed how much pressure she'd been exerting.

Henry slouched against the table. Freckles sprayed across his nose and cheeks. His eyes were dark brown and round like a child's. The spike of hair made him look like a cartoon character. He held a plate. On it was a loaf of bread and a small bowl filled with green-tinged oil.

Lucy's belly rumbled audibly, but she was so hungry, she didn't care.

He pushed the food toward her. "I thought you might be hungry. It came out of the oven about fifteen minutes ago."

Hastily wiping her filthy hands on her pants, Lucy tore off a chunk of bread and shoved it into her mouth. It was still warm. Henry watched her with an amused expression. "You can dip it in the oil, if you like. We have to make our bread with water, no milk you know, and it makes it sort of dense . . . and hard to swallow."

She stopped chewing for a minute. "Tastes pretty good to me." She took his advice, though, and swirled the next chunk in the oil. It was fruity and rich, and absolutely delicious. From the far end of the awning, the mouthwatering smell of onions, garlic, and carrots simmering in oil wafted into the air. She hadn't realized how much she'd missed fried food until now. The thought of fried potatoes made her giddy.

Henry pointed to the other side of the square where the remains of a building stood. Someone had attached frayed lengths of canvas from the two remaining corner uprights to make a rough roof. "Used to be an Italian deli," he said. "Nothing survived in the shop, but they had a cellar filled with wine and bottles of oil. The wine's gone now, unfortunately," he concluded. He met her eyes with a wry look. "But we've got enough oil to fry a mountain of potatoes." He rummaged in his back pocket and brought out a stub of pencil and a tattered notebook. "Can I ask you a couple of questions?"

"Sure, I guess," said Lucy, brushing bread crumbs off the front of her shirt.

"We keep an informal sort of census now. So many people coming and going," Henry said. "Name?"

"Lucy Holloway."

"Age?"

"Sixteen. I'll be seventeen in a . . . few months." She realized that she wasn't sure exactly how soon her next birthday was.

He nodded. "Nice to have another mature person here. It's mostly little kids and the DAs."

Henry answered her querying look, lowering his voice: "Doddering Ancients, but don't let Grammalie Rose hear it."

"What did she call you? *Malpa?*"

"Polish for *monkey*. She thinks she's so funny!"

He jotted Lucy's responses down, and then swept his gaze over her. His eyes widened in appreciation. "I'd say you're healthy. Very healthy." Henry scribbled something else.

She blushed. There was no mistaking the fact that he was checking her out. He must be, what, at least twenty-one? Her hand crept up to her messy hair. Boys were so weird. Working in the fields all afternoon had covered her skin with a fresh layer of stink. Plus manure. And blood. And still, he was flirting.

Henry put his notepad away and leaned on the table.

"So. Grammalie Rose was a bit rough on you?"

"Yeah, because of the . . ." She corrected herself. "Because of Sammy."

"Hey, it was a shock for me, too, when I first came here, but soon enough you realize that they are just regular people."

"I guess," Lucy said. "So how many are there?"

"Three in this settlement. But there are more out there." He waved his hand in a vague way.

"And they help with the chores?" She fought to keep her voice neutral.

Henry shot her a look. "Yeah, everything but the cooking. Bits of them, you know, fingers and the like, kept falling into the stew, so we put a stop to that."

Lucy gasped, and then caught the wide grin spreading across his face. She went red. Henry put up his hands in a conciliatory gesture.

"Sorry—couldn't help myself. Corny as it sounds," he continued, "we're like a family. Literally, in some cases."

She looked at him.

"Emi and Jack are siblings." His face fell, and Lucy remembered that these were the names of the little kids who'd been grabbed earlier. "And Sammy is Aidan's brother."

"Really?" Lucy said. "I mean, how could that be? That one of them is fine and the other is . . ." She broke off. No one else in her family survived.

Henry raised an eyebrow and she got the feeling he'd read her mind. "There's no clear answer. Most people died if they got sick. Sammy's lucky to be alive," he said.

She nodded, and tried to swallow the lump in her throat.

"If you think about it, Sammy and Aidan beat the odds. Two brothers in the same family."

"But Aidan didn't even get sick. He has no scars . . . does he?"

Henry's mouth twisted. "Luck again, I guess. Of those who contracted the mutated hemorrhagic smallpox in the second wave, maybe one in a million survived, even with the vaccine. Most died within seventy-two hours. Those are some bad numbers. The regular pox left about one in one hundred thousand alive, so if you look at it like that, you and I, and everyone else here are blessed. Right? A few scars here and there, maybe, but nothing like what the S'ans have to bear. Pretty soon you won't even notice a difference." He shot her a grin, and she couldn't help but grin back at him.

"How do you know so much about it?"

"I was a premed student before."

"So how many unvaccinated people survived?"

He looked startled. "None. Big fat goose egg." He made a zero with his thumb and forefinger.

"No, seriously," she began before noticing his face. The smirk was gone. He shook his head.

"Basically that's why the majority of the deaths were adults aged thirty to sixty. The kids and teenagers were okay 'cause they were up to date on their shots including the reinstated ones."

Lucy nodded. She remembered her classmates back in grade school complaining that they'd had to get a whole slew of new injections after the first bird flu cases had been diagnosed.

". . . and the older people like Grammalie had been given live smallpox inoculations during the War, but the rest of them . . . Nope. One hundred percent mortality."

Her mouth shaped itself into an O. Her hand crept up to her left shoulder and pulled the rolled sleeve of her shirt down so that it covered her upper arm.

None. Zero. That made her an even bigger freak than the S'ans. She remembered the thick folder in the nurse's office. The countless blood tests. What exactly was wrong with her?

"Are you all right?" he asked.

"Yeah, yeah, I just ate too fast."

"Okay, well give a holler when you're done," Henry said, pointing to the cutting board, and sauntered away.

CHAPTER NINE
CAMP SCAVENGER

After Henry had gone back to his potatoes, Lucy forced her fingers to continue cutting up bunnies. Her brain was yammering away at full speed. If what Henry had said was true, she should not be alive. Unless she *had* been vaccinated when she was a kid and Maggie had been wrong or lying. Her sister wasn't the type to play tricks on her siblings — that was more like something Rob would have done — but maybe she just hadn't had the facts straight.

Could she have forgotten? The first time she'd run through the glass doors had completely faded from memory, so maybe something in her just preferred to ignore unpleasant events.

Lucy pressed her fingers against the skin of her upper arm, trying to feel for the raised scar of a smallpox vaccine. She felt nothing. She needed to go somewhere where she could look. Find a mirror. Examine every inch of her skin. But she couldn't do it with all these people around. She wondered about bathrooms: Did they have them? Were there latrines out in the fields or something? Surely someone here owned a mirror. Perhaps Henry? He looked like he spent time getting his hair just right.

Another part of her brain reminded her that if she did have a vaccine scar, she would surely have noticed it before now.

Her stomach twisted. She *had* eaten too much too fast. Lucy took a sip of water and tried to think. Maybe she should leave? Go back out in the Wilds? But the Sweepers . . . Now that she'd seen them in action, she was scared. No one seemed able to stand against them, and by herself she'd be totally helpless. And the dogs — they were hunting people with the dogs.

She wished there were someone she could talk to. She might be sick and not showing symptoms. She could be a carrier like Typhoid Mary, who'd shown no symptoms but had infected people just by cooking their meals. She looked down at the chunks of rabbit glistening on the chopping block, the pile of cotton ball tails. Her stomach heaved again. Cooking would kill the disease, right? *If* she had it. Lucy imagined her body swarming with virus. She grabbed the edge of the table and pressed her fingers into it until her gut settled. Maybe she could tell Aidan. Or maybe she shouldn't say a word.

As if the thought had summoned him, Aidan appeared behind her and hopped up onto the table. "Hey," he said casually. "I was looking for you."

Lucy fought to control her panic. She made a noncommittal noise and stared at the table. She drew a bowl of water toward her and sluiced the blood from her hands, scrubbing at them with her nails. Slowly, her heart stopped racing. She peeked at Aidan under her eyelashes.

His sweatshirt was damp with sweat; there were mud stains on the knees of his jeans and a few dry leaves caught in his hair. She stared at his fingers, thinking how strong they seemed. That made her heart race again and distracted her from morbid thoughts. He tore off a piece of bread, swooshed it in the oil, and popped it into his mouth. He eyed the portions of chopped-up meat. "Cat?" he asked sadly. Lucy flicked a rabbit tail at him. "Oh good," he said and flicked it back at her.

"So where have you been?" she asked, looking at Aidan's dirty fingernails.

"Out," he said.

Lucy felt a surge of irritation. Which was good. It banished the last of the fear and made it possible for her to meet his eyes without blushing. "With Del?" she asked before she could curb her tongue. Aidan looked at her and then jumped down, ignoring the question. Maybe he picked up on the sneer in her voice? She vowed to keep her mouth shut about the other girl.

He picked up the cutting board and transferred the meat into a plastic serving bowl. "Come on," he said, grabbing her arm. He led her to where the others were standing around a large pot on the fire. It was blackened iron and big enough to bathe a child in. About forty pounds of carrots and onions simmered at the bottom. The smell that rose was heady. Henry stirred the mixture occasionally with a long wooden spoon. A young girl, maybe eleven years old, with long blond pigtails was cutting up the last of the potatoes, helped by two small kids and a gray-haired old man with a walrus mustache. Grammalie Rose was no longer there.

"Ready for this?" Aidan asked Henry, hefting the bowl of meat.

"Sure, pile it on," Henry said. "Potatoes next, Sue," he told the pigtailed girl. He lifted a bucket of water and held it poised for a few seconds before upending it into the sizzling pot.

The good smells were making Lucy woozy. She sat down on a bench and closed her eyes, letting the fragrant steam wash over her.

Aidan sat down beside her. "About fifteen minutes," he said with an amused tone in his voice. "Can you bear it?"

"Possibly not."

"Well, at least we eat first," he said.

"*We?*" Henry said, waggling his eyebrows at Aidan. "And how exactly have you helped with this fine meal?"

"I believe I hauled that water," Aidan said. "And I washed up last night."

Henry spread his fingers. "All right, all right." He turned to Lucy. "Can you help Aidan with the bowls and spoons?" He pointed toward the stacks of mismatched kitchenware. "We need thirty, forty of everything."

Lucy grabbed a handful of spoons and shoved them in her back pocket. She stacked bowls along the length of her arm and anchored them with her chin. It was a brave move. One clumsy step and she'd drop everything; but amazingly she made it to the table safely. She set the places. Aidan put down plates, water jugs, and three more loaves of the crusty bread, and scattered a few bread knives along the length of the rough pine table. He started cutting slices and, grabbing a knife and another loaf of bread, she did the same. With half an ear she listened to the surrounding chatter.

People materialized from the corners of the kitchen tent, wiping their wet hands on their pant legs, removing stained aprons, and stretching sore neck muscles. They each grabbed a bowl and lined up for a few ladles of thick stew. Dishes clattered. A dozen conversations were going at once. Lucy felt the familiar shyness creep into her bones. It was like the high school cafeteria. She'd always eaten alone, outside in the quad or in the library. Aidan pulled her to her feet and shoved a bowl into her hands. "If you don't get in there, you'll never eat," he said, elbowing a space for her.

Henry grinned as he served her. He leaned forward and winked. "I gave you a little extra."

She smiled shyly and sat down at the far end of the table, away from the little clusters of people. For the next few minutes, she concentrated on eating. It wasn't until she looked up that she realized Aidan was sitting right across from her. He was smirking like a maniac.

"Never saw anyone actually inhale food before," he remarked.

"Oh God, I . . ." She put her hand up to her mouth and wiped it clean. A few spots of stew were speckled across the front of her shirt. There may even have been some caught in her hair. She wished she could just sink through the floor.

He pointed to the corner of his lip and tapped.

"What?"

"You missed a spot."

He half stood up and reached across the table. Was he going to touch her? And then suddenly he jerked away.

"Make room," Del barked, squeezing in next to him. The kid she'd forced farther along the bench glared at her but said nothing. He just picked up his bowl and turned to his neighbor, Sue. They bent their heads together, whispering furiously and darting covert glances at Del.

"Hi," Lucy said, determined not to get into a situation with her again. She even managed a small smile before returning her attention to her bowl.

Del stared, then nodded.

Score one maturity point for Lucy! She carefully scooped up a minute amount of stew and carried it to her mouth. The food had reached her stomach, and she felt a soothing warmth spread to her limbs. *I could fall asleep right here on the table,* she thought. She listened sleepily to Del.

"Did you scout today?" she asked Aidan. "I couldn't find you."

He shook his head. "I went a mile or two up the road. I thought about setting permanent sentries, but there's too much area to cover."

"What about pit traps? We could dig some around the periphery and then just keep watch by the road," Del said.

"Too dangerous for the little kids. You know they run around everywhere."

"Well, how about blocking it off? Then they couldn't drive the vans up to the camp." Del banged her spoon against the table for emphasis.

Aidan rubbed his forehead. He looked as if he hadn't slept for a week. "Leo figured out that it would take a ton or more of rubble to block it off. We can try, but it'll take weeks. And it's harvest time. We can't really spare people from the fields right now."

"There must be something!" Del stared at the table. "What'll they do to them?" she asked suddenly in a gentle voice, sounding completely unlike herself. "To Emi and Jack?"

"They'll be okay."

She gripped his arm hard. Aidan winced. "Promise me."

He shook his head, looking uncomfortable.

Del subsided into a stormy silence. The conversation along the table had dwindled, the sound of cutlery against bowls quieted; people finished and left. Others hauled water for washing up. Lucy was thankful not to be summoned for more chores. She rested her head on her arm.

Things were bad. She was scared, but she was also not hungry for the first time in months. She felt strong and revitalized. If she had to, she could run for miles, cross New

Venice, and find somewhere safe on the outskirts. Or travel farther. North, perhaps, like Aidan had said.

She didn't realize she'd fallen asleep until someone shook her gently by the shoulders. She opened drowsy eyes and looked into Aidan's face. Directly behind him stood Del, her arms crossed tightly, her mouth flattened in a line.

"Del said you could share her sleeping tent," Aidan said, helping her to her feet.

"Scout's been sleeping somewhere else anyway," Del said with a bitter laugh. She didn't look as if she'd offered freely, but at this point Lucy didn't care. She swayed and shook her head, trying to drive the cobwebs from her brain.

Aidan picked up her backpack and handed it to her. She clasped it to her chest. He led the way inside a small tent tucked between the gutted remains of two buildings. Trickles of the day's fading light fell through gaps between the canvas panels. Lucy caught a glimpse of three tarps on the ground arranged around an unlit hurricane lamp, two covered with blankets and clothing, before Aidan pushed her gently toward the third. She bumbled forward, tripping over her feet, and let the backpack slide to the ground as she sank down to her knees. Too tired to even dig out her sleeping bag, she pulled her sweatshirt and jacket firmly around her, tucked her knees in, and curled up on her side. She was asleep again almost immediately.

CHAPTER TEN

ATTACK!

Lucy was awakened by an excruciating pain in her wounded hand. She opened her mouth to scream but someone's fingers pinched it shut before she could emit a sound.

"Quiet!" Del hissed viciously. Lucy gripped Del's forearm and squeezed as hard as she could. "Don't yell," the girl said, slowly removing her hand from Lucy's mouth.

"Get off me," she replied between clenched teeth. The lamp in the middle of the tent threw a small circle of light. It was enough to make out Del, fully clothed, balanced on the balls of her feet as if she was expecting an attack.

Del shifted her weight and the boot lifted. Lucy decided it had been an accident; the opposite was too much to consider. She clutched her squashed fingers to her chest. She wiggled them. They seemed bruised, but not broken.

She wondered if it was close to dawn, but then through the gap in the roof she glimpsed the moon, half-hidden behind clouds. Standing above Lucy's bed, Del was a still form against dark shadows. She could see the other girl's rib cage move in and out with her breathing. She seemed to be waiting for something.

"What's going on?" Lucy asked. She'd only slept a few hours and her body was stiff and achy.

"I heard someone outside the tent," Del murmured. Her head darted around. She cocked it to one side like a dog. Lucy listened, too, straining to hear.

Distantly she heard a rumble. Thunder? Or could it be car engines? She sat up. She'd gone to bed with all her clothes and her boots on. Under the triple layer of jacket-sweatshirt-thermal, her skin was clammy with sweat. Her head felt groggy, her eyelids rimmed in sand.

Del was as immobile as a statue.

A crescendo of rumbling rose, followed by a shout and, closer still, the thud of running feet. And now she could hear voices raised in panic coming from all around and the sound of tires on sandy soil.

Cars!

"It's them. The Sweepers. They came back," Del said.

Lucy was instantly awake. Her heart pounded as if it would spring out of her chest; every muscle twitched. She scrambled to her feet. Through the canvas, she could see the dim shapes of figures moving outside. They had lights. Maybe flashlights or torches. She couldn't tell if they were scavengers or the enemy.

"Stay low," Del breathed. "They might have brought the dogs." She was frozen in a half crouch. Lucy mimicked her posture.

"If they brought the dogs, we should get out of here!" Lucy said, trying to breathe normally.

"Don't move," Del said with an imperious hand gesture that made Lucy bite her lip in annoyance.

The other girl moved slowly, her eyes on the hurricane lamp in the middle of the floor.

Lucy suddenly realized that their silhouettes must be visible from the outside.

Before she could say anything there was a thump as Del kicked the lamp over. The flame went out. Lucy blinked, trying to accustom her eyes to the sudden gloom.

"Let's go," Del muttered.

Lucy fumbled for her knife. It wasn't at her waist. For the first time, she had forgotten to fasten it on her belt before she went to bed. She cursed herself and dug into the sweatshirt pocket. Not there, either.

It must have fallen out.

She bent to the tarp she'd been sleeping on, searched the surface with trembling fingers. The thick layer of clothing made her clumsier than usual.

"Come on," said Del. "And be quiet, would you?" Lucy thought but couldn't be sure that she'd muttered something about a "buffalo."

"My knife."

"Leave it."

"No!"

Del snorted with impatience. "Hurry," she said. Lucy felt around the edges of the tarp and was finally rewarded with the hard outline of the hilt under her fingers. She picked up the knife, instantly feeling more confident.

A motor revved nearby. It sounded as if it was right in front. The tent flap was tied shut, but it was flimsy. They couldn't go out that way.

"We've got to get out of here," Del whispered, making for the back of the tent. She pulled on the bottom where it was pinned to the earth by metal hooks.

"Help me get this loose. Quietly."

Lucy joined her and, stowing her knife in her pocket, grabbed a handful of canvas and heaved. The ground was hard, compacted mud; the stakes had been pounded in, and they couldn't pull it loose. Del muttered a few choice curse words under her breath.

"Wait," Lucy said and pulled her knife back out. She stabbed at the heavy material. The sound of tearing canvas seemed incredibly loud. Del stifled an angry exclamation, which Lucy ignored. Once she had a big enough hole, she held it open and Del clambered through it, swearing as her boots caught in the folds of material.

Lucy started to follow her, and then she remembered her backpack. First rule: Always carry what you need with you. She hesitated. She could imagine what Del would say, but the habit was too ingrained. For over a year she had survived on her own because she was always prepared for the worst, and because her backpack held everything necessary for her survival.

She couldn't leave it.

Del was just about through, but it would just take a second.

She turned back to the tarp, scooped up her backpack, and shrugged it over her shoulders. Then she ran back to where Del's foot had just disappeared through the gap.

"What are you doing?" Del hissed, sticking her head through the hole.

"I'm coming!"

Someone burst into the tent. A heavy body struck Lucy in a tackle. She fell to the ground, biting her tongue hard on the way down. The taste of blood was in her mouth. She was pinned by strong arms attempting to grab her own and the weight of someone's body across her legs. She flailed, striking out wildly, and twisted around so she was lying on her back. Lucy kept struggling and kicked out with both feet. A sharp *crack*. She had hit something hard enough to make her ankles throb. An explosive grunt, the sound of fumbling, and then a helmet thudded to the ground near her head. The visor was smashed. Before she could struggle to her feet, the man threw himself forward. Lucy brought her knees up, trying to force him off of her. She lashed out with her fist, feeling the vibration in her elbow as she connected with his face. His breath was hot against her cheek. She felt a slick wetness on her forehead. Her blood or his?

A thick arm pushed against her neck. She tried to land another punch, but it was hard to breathe. Black dots danced in front of her eyes, and her pulse pounded in her temples.

Lucy attempted to scream, but the sound was choked off in her throat. With one last burst of energy she raised her head and bit down as hard as she could. It wasn't much—the man's arm was covered in thick material, denim or heavy cotton, but it was enough. He shifted and she arched her back, simultaneously rolling to one side, and managed to push him off. She scrambled to her feet, panting, and aimed a kick at him, not caring where it landed. She heard the satisfying *thump* of impact.

The man groaned and threw out a hand, closing his fingers around her ankle, and suddenly she was pulled off her feet. She landed hard on her back, the blow cushioned by the bag across her shoulders, although she felt a sharp pain radiate up her spine. She must have landed on her dead flashlight. The breath left her body in one involuntary gasp. And then he was dragging her toward him. She dug her fingers into the dirt, but it was useless.

Lucy twisted her body, trying to break free, and then from the side and slightly behind him, a shadowy figure appeared. Del raised the hurricane lamp high, then brought it down. Some instinct must have warned him because he moved slightly, and rather than hit him on the head, the lamp smashed into his shoulder. Still, it was enough to break his hold on Lucy's leg. Shards of glass flew everywhere. Lucy felt a chunk sting her face. Del hauled her to her feet and dragged her out the front of the tent.

They ran toward the shouts and screams, then stopped, blinded. The square was lit up. The vans were positioned in a half circle, their engines idling. On top of each one was a powerful searchlight.

Lucy shielded her eyes. She could see little pockets of people to either side, mostly younger kids clutching one another and crying; the old man with the walrus mustache she'd noticed at dinner. No one who looked like they could defend themself. Many of the shelters had been destroyed, the wooden supports smashed, canvas tarps trodden into the dust. There were perhaps a dozen Sweepers scattered around.

She could hear yelling coming from other parts of the camp. They must be everywhere. The scavengers were divided. She wondered where Aidan was. Henry, Leo, Grammalie Rose? Had they been captured already?

Del swore again under her breath.

Lucy cast a glance behind them. A Sweeper stood there, blocking the way back into the maze of alleyways. Why hadn't they run in that direction?

"Get ready to fight," Del said.

Lucy pulled her knife out and held it ready.

Del moved so she was standing with her back to Lucy's. She bent and scooped up a length of twisted metal. They circled, taking small steps and trying to look in every direction at once, to find a hole they could break through. A searchlight was moved so that it pointed directly at them. Lucy tried to see past it, but the intense light threw everything else into deep shadow. She caught a glimpse of white-suited figures rushing toward them, flanking them.

Del shouted and was suddenly yanked away from her. Lucy moved her knife, blade edge out, in a sweeping motion. She was grabbed from behind, her knife hand pinned. A muscular arm settled around her neck, restricting but not cutting off her breathing. "Easy," a voice breathed in her ear. She felt a pinching sensation in her wrist, and her fingers opened. She dimly heard the thud as the knife fell to the ground. She was lifted off her feet. There was a flurry of movement to her left. And then Del was free. She swung the metal bar, aiming at her captor's groin. The blow connected and the man dropped to his knees. She swung again with a ferocity that was terrifying, catching him across the back, and he fell forward, groaning. Lucy's Sweeper was distracted, and she took the opportunity to stamp on his instep with all her might. With a roar of rage he pushed her away with so much force that she stumbled, falling to her knees.

"Duck!" Del yelled, swinging the metal rod like a madwoman. Lucy made herself as small as possible.

Her knife gleamed in the dust a few yards away. It might as well have been on Mars. She began to crawl toward it. She could hear Del cursing, panting, and, amazingly, mocking the Sweepers. But there were too many of them.

"Del!" Leo bellowed, appearing from an alleyway at a run and beating his way to the girl's side. He was armed with a two-by-four studded with nails. The Sweepers fell back for an instant, and then, as if obeying an order, advanced in a solid line on the two of them.

Two more Sweepers joined them, effectively containing the scavengers within a small area. Leo circled.

And then, surprisingly, one of the Sweepers moved forward alone. It didn't make sense. The scavengers were totally outnumbered. Lucy had reached her knife. She picked it up. No one was paying any attention to her. She crouched in the shadows, looking for an opportunity to help.

Leo pushed Del behind him and faced off with the Sweeper. A grin spread across his face. "Come on then," he yelled, advancing. He slapped the wood against his palm.

The Sweeper moved in closer and suddenly lunged forward, his arm outstretched. Concealed within his hand was a small black box. Lucy screamed a warning, but her cry was drowned out.

Leo raised his club.

And then there was a flash of electric blue light and a sound like meat being seared on a hot grill.

Leo collapsed to the ground like a felled tree. His body jerked spasmodically, and then he was still.

"Leo!" Del shouted, running toward his prone form. She'd taken only a few steps when another Sweeper stepped into her path. The blue light flashed again, and she crumpled.

Lucy shrank back into the shadows, drawing her hood forward around her face.

The Sweepers were gathered around Leo and Del, who were as still as corpses.

Were they dead? Leo groaned as one of the Sweepers nudged him roughly with a boot. Lucy felt a surge of relief.

Another man picked up Leo's nail-studded two-by-four, studied it, then hurled it to the ground in disgust. It bounced, landing not far from where Lucy lay hidden.

She thought she could see smears of blood on the board. What could she do? If she tried to help, they would capture her, too. She was safe for now. She felt a sense of relief mingled with the shame of escaping capture. If she had not paused for her backpack, then Del might still be free.

Slowly, Lucy forced herself to crawl backward toward the collapsed shelter behind her. Once she was concealed under the tarpaulin, she curled into a ball and tried to control the tremors that racked her body. She listened to the heavy sounds and grunts of the Sweepers, picturing them as they loaded Del's and Leo's unconscious forms into the nearest van. She heard the low rumble of voices and the piteous sound of a child sobbing. The doors slammed shut, the engines roared, and heavy tires crunched through the debris.

The rumble of the vans slowly died away, and afterward there was silence, which felt oppressive and filled with threat.

It was hours before she moved from her hiding place.

Lucy sat on a small hill above the camp and watched the sun rise. She was cold and cramped, but she could see everything from this vantage point. As soon as she had dared, she'd scuttled out from under the tarp and run, heading for higher ground.

Her thoughts went around and around in her head. She'd been arguing with herself for hours, unable to sleep.

She'd figured out this much. One: She was scared. Two: She badly wanted to leave. Three: That was the one thing she could not do.

The reality was, she was involved. Not only because she'd been right there when Del and Leo were taken, but because probably—*definitely*—Del wouldn't have been caught if not for her.

She untied her backpack and scanned the contents. A journal, a few pieces of clothing, her sleeping bag, a yearbook, a broken radio, a flashlight without batteries, a sharpening stone, and a tinderbox with a book of soggy matches in it.

Nothing she owned was worth someone else's life.

She looked down on the settlement. All the shelters around the square had been ripped apart. Flimsy supports lay twisted and snapped in two, plywood lean-tos were scattered in splintered heaps. The soft, packed earth where the trading market had been held just a day ago was torn up, and the deep tire tracks of the vans snaked through the devastation.

She looked south in the direction the road curved. The road that ended at Roosevelt Island. From here she couldn't see the red light flash at the top of the tower, but she knew it was there.

She got to her feet with a sigh.

A small group had assembled in the square. She recognized Aidan, Henry, Grammalie Rose, and a few others.

Lucy paused. Turned and looked in the opposite direction. She could make her way inland, find another perfect place to build a home, go back to life as she knew it. Alone.

A shout wafted up from below.

She gazed down. Henry had lifted his hand in a wave. He flourished it back and forth as if he were signaling an airplane.

Slowly, she waved in return and started down the path.

CHAPTER ELEVEN

AIDAN

The scavengers stood in a close group near the kitchen. Lucy shuffled her feet, not sure if she should interrupt, and was grateful when Henry hollered at her to join them. His left eye was blackened and puffy, the whites shot through with red. His hair was plastered to his head with sweat and filth and he bounced from foot to foot with nervous energy. He moved over to make room for her in the huddle.

"Lucy," Aidan said. His eyes went to the cut on her cheek and she touched it, shaking her head. It stung, but it was little more than a scratch. She'd collected a few more bruises, but she'd been lucky. Most of the blood on her belonged to other people. "I'm fine," she said.

Aidan's knuckles were scabbed and raw. A deep gash ran across his forehead, and there was dried blood in his hair. Lucy looked away from the expression of anguish on his face.

She stood apart and he made no attempt to move closer to her.

There were two teenagers, a boy and a girl, Lucy hadn't seen before. They both appeared to be about nineteen.

"*Wilcze*," Grammalie said, and nodded as if she was pleased she was still around. "This is Connor and Scout."

Connor was tall and rangy with red hair and a very direct gaze. Scout was tiny and had a pixie cut and worried brown eyes. They exchanged awkward greetings.

"We were out hunting," Connor told the group. "Didn't get back until this morning."

"How many this time?" Scout asked, wringing her fingers together. Connor grabbed her hand and enfolded it in his own.

"Five," Henry said. "Two more kids, Lottie and Patrick, and Hank—you know, walrus mustache, who helps out in the kitchen? And . . ." He took a deep breath. "Del and Leo."

Scout groaned.

"We're trying to decide if we should keep everyone together or disperse," Aidan told her.

"We cannot decide anything until we have a camp meeting," Grammalie Rose said.

"Fine. We're *discussing* it, then," Aidan rejoined. Lucy was surprised at the anger in his voice.

Grammalie Rose shrugged. "We all need to calm down first."

Aidan nodded curtly. He stalked a few paces away and stood with his back to them. Lucy understood how he felt. She wanted to be doing something. Right now she felt like she was just waiting for the next awful thing to happen.

"There are shelters farther out, near the bridges, that are harder for vehicles to reach. There are hiding places. Bombed-out buildings. We can lie low for a while," Henry urged. "I spent last night in one of the canals."

That explained the mud encrusting his clothing.

"The Long Wet is just beginning. There is the danger of flash floods," Connor pointed out.

"Well, high ground then," Scout suggested. "The plateau, maybe?"

"No protection," Henry said. "Gales, lightning storms, fire." He checked off the points on the fingers of one hand.

Connor glared at him. It was turning into a shouting match.

"How will people be fed if we are spread to the winds? The little ones? It is mostly little ones now," Grammalie said. "Here we have shelter. Supplies. Water."

"They're just picking us off," Henry said. "We're like sitting ducks!"

Lucy silently cheered him.

Grammalie Rose put up a hand, forestalling any further argument. "We may indeed end up moving, but nothing can happen until everyone is here to decide what is best. Sammy and Beth are still out foraging. They have a voice in this as well."

Her brows drew across her forehead, giving her sharp eyes a hooded appearance. Lucy thought she looked older suddenly. She noticed how bowed the woman's back was, and how swollen the knuckles on her work-reddened hands. Suddenly she wanted to offer Grammalie Rose a chair, but there were none.

"In the meantime," she continued, "there is food to gather, washing to be done, injuries to tend." She looked pointedly at Aidan's forehead and Henry's eye.

Henry muttered something unintelligible.

"We need water," Grammalie Rose said. "That is paramount."

Aidan whirled around.

"We'll get that," he said, scooping up a few large plastic jugs and thrusting them at Lucy. She took them, too surprised to say anything. He grabbed four more and steered her out of the square. She pulled her arm away and stood still. She hated how he just grabbed her and started moving. Like she was a kid who couldn't cross the road by herself. He stopped, surprised.

"Listen, I've been working my butt off ever since I got here," she said. "Maybe I don't want to haul water!"

"I wanted to talk to you alone. I've been thinking about stuff," Aidan said.

"Okay, so talk."

"If Grammalie Rose sees us just sitting around, she'll put us both on latrine duty, and you don't want that, believe me."

Lucy had already caught the earthy odor coming from the row of narrow tents on the west end of the camp.

"Okay," she said slowly. It would actually feel good to be moving. "Listen, all this talking stuff is kind of irritating, though. Why can't someone just make a decision and then we act on it?"

"You mean like someone in charge?" He shook his head. "That's not how it is here. Sure, Grammalie Rose is kind of the boss, because she's the oldest and she's had experience living in a commune. And Leo—" Aidan's voice hitched. "He was a natural leader, but everyone is equally important here. That's the point."

"But doesn't it drive you crazy? I mean, how does anything ever happen quickly?"

"It doesn't."

At least he sounded as frustrated as she felt. Lucy began to feel a little thrill of excitement.

They started walking again. Aidan took a narrow path between two rows of old brick houses. The second floors were still mostly intact, but the foundations were crumbling and the roofs leaned together like two people about to kiss. Wooden scaffolding pressed up against the masonry on both sides, keeping it all standing, but Lucy couldn't help but be glad when they came out on a demolished area filled with rubble. Some kids were playing kick-the-can in the dust. They hollered when they saw Aidan and he waved back. A green garden hose coiled on the ground like a big snake. It was attached to a pipe that stuck up out of the debris. Aidan turned on the spigot. Water, rust-colored and full of debris, started to flow in a series of jerks and spurts.

"Why don't we get fresh water from a spring?" Lucy asked.

"I've found a couple of sources out in the woods, but it's a long trek. This is more convenient, at least until the cistern dries up."

The water cleared. He fitted the lip of a jug over the hose end and stood back up.

"So, what's the big plan?" asked Lucy, feeling a shiver race along her spine. Standing around waiting for bad things to happen was worse than actually doing something. "Were you trying to find a way to get onto the island?"

"Are you crazy?" he said, looking thunderstruck. "I'm not James Bond. Where would I even start?" Aidan scratched his head with his free hand, completely missing a leaf that was trapped there. "No, I was just working out ways we could post lookouts, cut off entrances to the camp, prepare for the next raid. And . . ." He seemed uncomfortable. "I was thinking that this isn't really your battle. You can leave. No harm done."

She was instantly furious. It didn't matter that she had been considering the same thing. That was her choice to make, not his.

"Don't be stupid," Lucy said. "I was there when they grabbed Leo and Del." She choked on the words, she was so mad.

She met his gaze. "I hid." He dropped his eyes and stared at the gushing water. "They could easily have taken me, too," Lucy said.

He looked flabbergasted.

She was pretty surprised herself. Saying it out loud made it all clearer in her head. She could try to make things right, and she could always leave afterward.

"I get the whole 'camp is the safest place' thing," she said. "And it is for the little kids, but there are the rest of us."

Aidan nodded.

"I was thinking rescue mission," she continued, trying to sound convincing.

"Some day, sure; but we know nothing about how things are set up, the layout of the place. We don't even know what kind of weapons they have. Or how many of them there are. Believe me, I want to get Del and Leo and the others back worse than anybody, but if we go charging in there, we'll get caught."

Lucy stared at him. This talk didn't seem like him. It wasn't what someone who climbed to the tops of trees should be saying.

He must have read the surprise in her eyes. "What?"

"You said no one has ever come back. We don't know what's happening to them. So what are you waiting for? An invitation?" She bit her lip. This was one of her worst faults, speaking without thinking, but she couldn't help it. The words just kept bubbling out of her.

He looked as if she had slapped him in the face. She tried a gentler approach.

"You're so calm about it. The Sweepers took your friends, and it's like you've given up without even trying."

"I've been thinking about this all night!" Aidan yelled. "There's no easy solution. You think me and maybe two others can just barge in there like ninjas?!"

They glared at each other. The water overflowed the container, but he made no move to replace it with another. He paced back and forth, savagely kicking chunks of brick out of his way.

"You don't know. It's not the first time," he said in a calmer voice. "Leo was the fighter, the planner, and even *he* couldn't think of a way to get the others back. With him gone . . ." Aidan shrugged his shoulders. "We're just not that organized."

"What about all of this?" she said, pointing to the shelters, the cultivated fields in the near distance.

He scowled. "It took us about six months to get all the shelters up, the water situation figured out, and the vegetable gardens planted. It was mostly Grammalie Rose's doing. And it takes the best part of every day to keep it going."

She understood that. It had taken all her energy to keep herself fed, warm, and dry.

"Yeah, but we can't just do nothing," she said.

"You're a lot like Del," he said. "Hot-tempered. What's the nice word? Impetuous." His mouth twisted into a wry grin.

Lucy wasn't too pleased to be compared to Del. She'd caught the admiring note in his voice. She pressed her lips firmly together. He was looking off into the distance—probably thinking of *her*. Lucy lifted the hose and stuck the end into another jug. The water was flowing more freely now and was less brown. She resisted the temptation to spray him.

"You said Leo was the fighter. We might not be able to throw a right hook or a roundhouse kick, but we could arm ourselves and go after them," she said. Aidan jumped a little, as if he'd forgotten she was there.

"You saw the kids in the square?"

She nodded. "The ones collecting projectiles?"

"They were so upset about Lottie and Patrick and the rest of them that they begged for something to do. I couldn't think of anything else. We've got rocks and cans, but they've got stun guns and chloroform gas and masks. The best thing for us to do is to keep watch and to hide."

"Watching and hiding didn't do much good last night."

"We weren't expecting it."

Lucy felt a surge of frustration. "We'll never be able to expect it. They've got the element of surprise on their side. They'll just pick us off."

He looked so miserable; she felt awful, but she couldn't stop talking. "We don't even know what they're doing to them." She was remembering the sad lady and the children from the shelter. The vans coming and taking them away. This had been going on for months.

Aidan shook his head. "We have to think about everyone in the camp. How would it be if most of the adults were gone on some disastrous rescue mission? There are kids here who can't make it on their own."

"Grammalie Rose," she said feebly.

"She's eighty, did you realize?" Aidan shook his head.

Lucy kicked out at a rock as big as a bowling ball. Her toes stung but she ignored the pain. Aidan bent down and placed another bottle under the tap.

She stared at his thick blond hair with the leaf caught there. "I thought she was your friend." It was maybe a low blow, but she couldn't stop the words exploding from her mouth. Part of her wanted to hear what he would say. Part of her didn't.

He looked up. His green eyes flashed with anger.

"She is!"

"Well, you don't act like it! If she were my friend, I'd be out there looking for her." She recalled his comment to her back in the tree, about being a mouse in her safe hollow. "I wouldn't be skulking around here."

"You don't know me!" he yelled, leaping to his feet. "You drop in and you think you even know what's going on? Well, you don't. You don't know me, you don't know us, you don't know how we live!" He was so angry now, he was practically spitting.

Lucy felt the rage well up in her belly. Who did he think he was? "I can see that you're all hiding instead of fighting," she threw out. Her hands were shaking.

"You have nothing at stake. These aren't your friends. This isn't your family."

"I'm here right now."

"For how long?"

She froze. Aidan was right. She hadn't exactly decided whether to stay or go yet. She opened her mouth and then closed it again.

He was only a few inches in front of her now. The long muscles in his arms flexed. A vein pulsed in the column of his neck. She could smell him. Sweat and lemons. He looked like he was going to hit her. She tensed, and then he stepped away. He filled the last two containers in silence, kneeling down and keeping his back to her.

Lucy felt all the annoyance and anger drain away, and it was as if they took her energy with it. All of a sudden she was bone tired.

Aidan was moving. He carried two jugs in each hand, leaving three for her. He was already halfway across the lot, calling to the can-kicking kids to come with him, before she'd even picked hers up. The weight made her wrists ache. She staggered after him, throwing mental daggers into his broad back.

CHAPTER TWELVE

THE RETURN

Two days of hauling and digging helped keep the fear at bay, but the frustration was eating her alive. Lucy had agreed to every duty Grammalie gave her as long as the job took her away from people and the camp. And as far away as possible from Aidan.

She carried in the last load of cabbages and dumped the tub on the floor by the long table. She stretched, easing the cramped muscles along her spine. She'd been stooped over for so long, her back protested. She stifled a yelp.

Henry looked up from peeling onions. His blackened eye had turned shades of purple and yellow, and tears leaked from between the swollen eyelids. He wiped his nose on the sleeve of his shirt. He smiled at her.

"Thanks. Haven't seen much of you lately."

Lucy jumped up on the edge of the table and swung her legs, noting that her injured ankle had swelled again. "Been out in the fields mostly." She picked gravel out of her knee.

He nodded as if he understood. "Normally I'd do anything before peeling onions, but it feels good to keep my hands busy."

They were both quiet for a few seconds. Slowly, shockingly, things had started to feel like normal again. The busy pace of days spent worrying about food, water, tending fires, and rebuilding shelters didn't leave much room for anything else. Still, Lucy felt guilty every time she thought of Leo and Del.

"Need any help?" she asked.

"You can go check the soup. We're eating at the big tables since the rain's holding off. Grammalie Rose thought we needed a group night."

She nodded and wandered outside. The lanterns were lit, casting wavering shadows and filling the air with stinky smoke. The sun sank down behind the Great Hill in a flush of crimson clouds.

In the square, the awnings were rolled back and tied with lengths of rope. Long tables and benches had been moved out into the open and arranged around the fire pit. It was piled high with roughly chopped wood salvaged from the Sweeper-leveled houses all around, and more fuel lay stacked nearby. The flames roared. The big black cooking pot hung above it in a welded cradle. Even from where she stood, Lucy could smell the mouthwatering combination of root vegetables and browning meat. From the opposite corner of the square she caught sight of Aidan hauling more water. She paused, waiting to see if he would notice her. He responded to a few greetings. His eyes seemed to wander in her direction, but she couldn't be sure. Lucy watched as he crossed over to the pot and set his jugs down. He emptied one in, then another. Steam rose in great billows, his forehead shone with sweat. She moved toward him, a conciliatory smile pasted on her face, but then, before she'd made it to his side, Aidan was gone, crossing quickly and disappearing into one of the side alleys that ran like a maze around the dilapidated houses. She stared after him. He was avoiding her. If she were able to catch up to him, she was pretty sure she'd have punched him in the nose or at least kicked him really hard in the shin. She should have known he was a brooder. They never knew how to fight. Instead of yelling, they kept it all inside. She'd been all ready to continue their discussion from the other day, but he obviously couldn't handle anyone disagreeing with him, and that's why he was acting like a baby. She felt mad all over again.

Lucy checked the soup. Rabbit. Or was it cat? She couldn't tell. It seemed too thick to her. Aidan hadn't even added enough liquid, she thought, annoyed. She bent to pick up a water container. Her arms, sore from carrying pounds and pounds of vegetables, complained.

Henry hurried over to give her a hand. He reminded her of a puppy. If he'd had a tail, it would have been wagging. She found a smile for him. He grinned back. Between them they poured the rest of the water into the pot. Henry stirred it all together, pushed the lid over the top leaving a gap for steam to escape through, and raked up the embers with the toe of his boot. Almost immediately the water began to simmer.

The heat was strong enough to crisp her eyelashes. Lucy stepped back, looking up at the sky. For the first time in a while, the night was clear and cloudless. She sniffed for the scent of rain but smelled nothing except for the aroma of meat, vegetables, and broth. Henry winked at her.

"Soup's on!" Henry said. "Give it five minutes."

From somewhere nearby came the sound of a pot being pounded with a wooden spoon, and at once people appeared in the alleyways. They hovered in groups of three or four, as if they were family units: one or two small kids and then the older people, the DAs.

Shadows danced across the square. Henry steered her toward the food prep tent, where teetering rows of stacked bowls, platters of the dense, chewy bread, and an assortment of mismatched spoons were laid out. There were saucers of the green olive oil and roughly chopped tomatoes scattered with shredded green leaves. Lucy smelled the pungent scent of basil and her mouth started watering. Yet another thing she'd missed without knowing it—herbs.

Henry grabbed a bowl and a spoon and handed it to her. He ladled tomatoes into her bowl, then filled his own. He shoved a loaf of bread into the front pocket of his sweatshirt, along with a bottle of water. "Can you snag some of that oil?" he asked. She juggled her bowl and picked up a saucer, trying hard not to spill it. They made their way back out past the line of people and sat at a table directly across from the fire. Lucy eased herself down with a sigh. The bench was hard and splintery, but it was the first time all day that she was off her feet. She could feel her toes tingling inside her boots. Her sore ankle throbbed. She closed her eyes and took a deep breath. The fire was like a wall of heat against her face. Slowly the taut muscles in her neck loosened and she opened her eyes. The lanterns were mostly behind her and cast bobbing shadows that made the ground appear to tilt and the dark silhouettes of the shacks on the hill seem to vibrate. It softened edges and concealed the mounds of rubble. The moon was waning, and the sky was studded with stars. So many stars, she thought.

"Ready for some soup?" Henry asked, distracting her. His bowl was empty already. She drizzled oil on her tomatoes and stuffed them into her mouth. The flavor burst against her tongue. She mopped up the last of the oil with a chunk of bread, then held up her bowl.

The benches beside them were all occupied now. Sue was there. Lucy was glad the girl hadn't been snatched. She couldn't be any older than eleven, but she was mothering a handful of grimy urchins, breaking their bread into small pieces and picking the basil off their tomatoes. Lucy looked around for Grammalie Rose and found her a couple of tables down, warming her swollen fingers before the fire. Lucy checked and saw that she had food. Aidan was nowhere to be seen. She pictured him glowering in the shadows somewhere, breaking sticks or punching walls, or something equally useless. When Henry came back holding a bowl in each hand, she gave him her biggest smile. He stepped backward as if he had lost his balance. Soup sloshed over the edge of the dish.

He sat down, carefully setting her meal in front of her. "Hey," he said, grinning like an idiot.

"Hey," Lucy said, bending her head over her bowl. The soup was thick with chunks of potatoes, onions, and carrots. Droplets of oil swirled on the top with a scattering of fresh herbs. A few skinny rabbits between thirty people didn't go far, but she figured she had at least a couple of pieces floating in there somewhere. The whole time she was eating, she felt Henry's eyes on her. It made her feel uncomfortable and embarrassed, but good, too, in a way.

She smoothed her hair back, tugging her fingers through the tangles. It fell in wild ringlets around her face. She gave up trying to push it behind her ears, letting it flop. Lucy leaned back in her seat. Her stomach was full. She toyed with another piece of bread, letting the chatter flow over her. The kids were half-in, half-out of their chairs now, wrestling and tagging one another, overtired but full of energy. She was reminded of her brother, Rob, who'd get so wound up at the end of the day, shortly before he crashed. She watched the children run in circles, weaving among the tables, dodging people carrying bowls of soup, ignoring the hands that reached out to grab them or give them a warning shake. And then they were playing in the narrow passages, a complicated game that combined hide-and-seek with tag. One of the boys was blindfolded; the others hooted and catcalled, tossing pebbles around his feet.

The frightening events of the past few days were fading for them already. A couple of the really little kids nestled together, clutching blankets and sucking on their thumbs, already half-asleep.

She figured about a third of the camp dwellers were under the age of thirteen. The rest of them were split equally between young adults and senior citizens. It was weird to be in an environment where she was one of the adults, where her opinion might actually count for something. Of course, she thought irritably, it already sounded like no one would be taking her side.

Lucy watched as a large group of people joined Grammalie Rose's table. She wondered if after all there would be some kind of a meeting this evening. For the most part the people at the table were older, stooped, and gray-haired, but without the fierce strength that radiated through Grammalie Rose. Three of the figures were hooded in thick cloaks. Lucy couldn't stop her nerves from jumping. She caught the flash of Sammy's white mask. The others were masked, too. One was like a cat with huge tufted ears, the other painted blue with silver flourishes. And then she saw that Aidan was there with them, in his bright red sweatshirt, his sun-streaked hair catching the light. He leaned in and slung his arm around Sammy's shoulders. *His brother,* Lucy remembered.

She watched Aidan despite herself, noticing his quick smile, the light rumble of his voice, his graceful movements. She wondered if he was going to come over or if he was still mad. She was sorry, suddenly, that they had argued. But that didn't mean she was going to walk across the square to him. Lucy tore her piece of bread into little scraps and tossed them onto the table. She turned on the bench so she was looking in the opposite direction.

"Your eyes are the same shade as a stormy sky," Henry said, breaking into her thoughts. He leaned his chin on his steepled hands.

She was just able to keep herself from rolling those eyes. "My sister used to say they were the color of dirty window-panes," she said, trying to laugh it off.

"Oh no," he said, "they're exactly like—"

Lucy interrupted and changed the subject. "So what's going on tomorrow?"

Henry blinked. He looked a little bit like a frog with his big, round eyes. She fought a giggle.

"Tomorrow?" he said.

"Yeah. I was thinking I'd like to go out to the woods and the plateau. Maybe learn how to use a slingshot. Can you show me that?"

He gulped. "Normally we have a rotating schedule every week and people are assigned different chores. So it's the fields one week, and the next, rebuilding or hunting. With everything that's happened lately, we've sort of lost track of who's doing what."

"Great," she said. She grinned at him. "So what do you think?"

"Doesn't Grammalie Rose usually tell you what she needs you to do each morning?" he asked.

Lucy scowled. It was like she'd been drafted.

Henry hurried to say, "But you can already handle a knife, so maybe Aidan will give you some weapons training."

She sat up. "I thought he wasn't much of a fighter?"

"Since Leo and Del are gone, he's the best we've got. He's pretty good with a bow and arrow, and a slingshot. He's on hunting duty more than anyone. You'll have to ask him, though."

She frowned again. Aidan probably didn't want to hear anything she had to say. He was still over there with the S'ans, and he hadn't looked in her direction once.

"Listen, are you mad about something or just hungry?" Henry asked. "Do you want more soup?"

She forced herself to smile at him. "No, I'm fine. Just tired."

Henry got to his feet. He stacked their dishes.

"Okay. I've got to organize the dishwashers, but that'll only take about ten minutes. You'll be here?"

"Sure."

Lucy stretched out her legs and wiggled her toes. Then she leaned forward and cradled her head on her folded arms. The fire smoke tickled her eyeballs. She felt a huge yawn coming.

"Tired, *wilcze*?" Grammalie Rose said in her rough voice. The old lady sat down with a creak and a sigh. "Thank you for all your hard work these past few days."

Lucy straightened her back. “Sure,” she said, surprised.

“I see you have befriended Henry, our resident lothario,” Grammalie Rose continued. “Has he told you how beautiful you are yet?”

Lucy coughed. “Not exactly.”

“He will. He’s an eternal optimist.”

The old woman beckoned to Connor and Scout, who were walking by with linked hands. “They were responsible for our rabbits today,” she informed Lucy. “Did you two have to go out far?”

“A few miles out on the plateau,” Connor replied.

Scout frowned. “It took hours. They were really skittish.”

“Any trouble?” the old woman asked.

Connor shook his head.

Lucy couldn’t help but notice how their fingers clasped and unclasped but never let go, and how they leaned together, as if an invisible string were pulling on them. They walked on, Connor’s head bent to hear something that Scout whispered to him. The back of his neck glowed bright red.

“So will there be some kind of meeting tonight?” Lucy asked.

“Not tonight,” Grammalie Rose said. She pulled a box from a pocket and opened it. Inside were six or seven of the brown cigarettes and a crumpled book of matches. She lit one, blowing the smoke into the air in a long stream. “Tempers are still too hot tonight.” She picked a dried leaf of tobacco from her lip. "Sammy wanted to storm the hospital." She uttered one of her dry laughs. "He is as foolhardy as his brother."

Lucy was surprised the—Sammy had been thinking along the same lines as she had.

"Aidan doesn't want to go. He wants us to hide here," she said.

"Really? Perhaps he has finally learned to be cautious." Grammalie Rose squashed her cigarette on the sole of her clogs and put the butt into the box, which disappeared again into a pocket. She turned to look at Lucy. "You think Sammy is right, eh?" She patted her on the shoulder and got heavily to her feet. "You wear your emotions on your face, *wilcze*. I understand what you are feeling, but it will help no one if more of us are captured. We need time to plan."

She moved away.

Lucy looked around. The two little kids who'd been at the end of her bench were gone. She imagined them bundled in their blankets under tent cover, a tumble of bodies like drowsy puppies.

Others had pushed their benches closer to the fire pit. From behind her she heard the clatter of dishes and the chime of silverware. Water sloshed into tubs and people talked in low voices. Teams of four and six picked up the long tables and moved them back under the awnings. From the group by the fire she heard the strumming of a guitar, the chords spilling out in a stream of formless music. Someone clapped their hands, keeping time, and others stamped their feet against the tarmac as the guitar wove around the simple beat. And then a violin came in, a single, sustained note that seemed to climb into the air and hang there, anchoring the guitar. Lucy had never had much time for her parents' classical music. She'd thought it cold and clean and rigid, much like her parents and their friends, and she'd always thought that violins sounded like cats being sawed in half. But this was different. Lucy felt the melody in her chest, as if her heart would explode with fullness. It was the saddest, happiest, wildest, and most human sound she'd ever heard, as if all the yearning in the world had been bottled up and then released in a pure shot of energy. She held her breath, suddenly afraid that she was about to burst into tears.

And then the guitar switched tempo to a folkie reel, speeding up and playing a rippling series of notes wrapped around a repetitive verse and chorus, and the player's hand slapped the body of the guitar at the end of each sequence, speeding up the momentum. The violin came in again and wove around the tune so it seemed as though the two instruments were chasing each other like a dog after a cat. And everyone was clapping in time and stamping their feet.

The younger kids ran around the fire, lit up like little savages. Soon others were up out of their seats and linking hands and dancing. A conga line wound between the benches. It was so corny, Lucy could only squirm. Sue swept by with her pigtails bouncing, followed by a dozen people whirling in circles. Connor and Scout stood wrapped around each other, barely moving. Kids she hadn't seen before danced together in groups or couples. Grammalie Rose, her unmistakable hawklike profile turned toward Lucy, sat near the fire, nodding her head and tapping her toes.

Lucy was wondering how long the musicians could keep playing when someone tapped her on the shoulder. Her stomach flipped.

Oh no! She turned, expecting to see Henry's eager face. It was Aidan.

"Truce?" he said, holding out his hand.

"Sure," she said, shaking it. He didn't let go. His fingers tightened their grip on her own. He pulled her to her feet. She looked up into his face. His green eyes glinted.

"You can't just sit there like a miserable lump."

"I'm not miserable. I was thinking."

"Well, think later." Aidan drew her toward him.

"Oh no, you're kidding!" She dug her heels in.

"Come on. Come with me!"

"I can't dance. I failed dancing in ninth grade. My partner couldn't walk for two weeks afterward."

"I think I can survive it."

"I practically hamstrung the poor guy."

"This isn't really dancing. This is just moving around with another person. You can pretend we're sparring. I'm wearing my motorcycle boots," he added, pointing to his feet.

Lucy hesitated. She could tell that her face was red, but she hoped it was dark enough to disguise the fact.

"Maybe I'll let you take a swing at me later," Aidan said.

She relaxed and let him pull her into the crowd.

The guitarist was playing even faster, a galloping tune, a wild jumble of chords, and the violin soared above it, a high, sweet note. Aidan took both her hands in his and whirled her around, swinging her until it seemed her feet left the ground. Then he brought her closer, one hand clasping her own and the other around her waist. She put her hand on his shoulder, lightly, but she could feel the heat of his body, and they were moving together in a line, up one side of the fire and down the other, and her feet stumbled, but it didn't matter because he was holding her up. Lucy stared at the neck of his sweatshirt, too shy to raise her eyes any higher, conscious of the tickle of her hair against the wet nape of her neck and the sweat sticking her T-shirt to her back, and the drum of his heart. She was out of breath and she couldn't stop laughing.

They whirled and turned, and people's faces came out of the shadows, lit by flickering firelight and tinted by red flames. She caught glimpses as she spun by. The masked S'ans at their table painted a surreal picture, like a photograph of a

Venetian carnival Lucy remembered seeing once long ago. The kids were hysterical, exaggerated in their every movement, heads thrown back, bursting with the giggles. Lucy closed her eyes, feeling giddy. Aidan bent his head to her ear. She felt his warm breath against her cheek. "Lucy," he murmured, "you are so—"

The music stilled. It was abrupt and jolting; the last upstroke of bow on violin sounded harsh and grating. Aidan stopped moving. His hands let go. Lucy stood trying to catch her breath, scraping back the curls clinging to her sweaty face, unsteady on her feet now that the earth had stopped spinning.

From the direction of the road, a figure appeared out of the shadows.

Her face fell into the narrow shaft of light thrown by a lantern.

Lucy recognized the sleek black hair and the silver bangles on tanned arms.

It was Del.

CHAPTER THIRTEEN
BUNNY HUNTING

The tough stalks of grass tickled Lucy's chin. She shifted, earning herself a glare from Aidan. He put a finger to his lips. She scowled back. *I get it! Be silent!* But they'd been lying there on the ridge for over an hour watching the clearing, and nothing had moved in all that time. Her neck was cramped from holding her head at an awkward angle, she had to pee, and the ground was hard and still damp from the morning rain. Plus, she was lying on her knife and it dug into her hip bone.

The sun beat down. Del lay between them, head lowered, her long black hair tied back in a thick ponytail. She'd taken off the silver bangles she normally wore five inches deep on both arms. No jangling allowed. Lucy studied Del under the cover of her eyelashes. She looked like she was brooding. Even now, three days after she had appeared out of the darkness, she still seemed shaken up and not really present. She didn't say much about what had happened, just a few words at the supper meeting called for the day after the dance. She told them that she'd managed to break out of the waiting room the Sweepers had put her in, but she hadn't been able to provide much detail. The room had been white-walled and stark, and the maze of corridors leading to it were dark and lit only by bare bulbs. A long spiraling stairway rose up the middle of the tower. Del had somehow found a door to the outside, and then, after hours of stumbling around in the pitch-black, she'd been able to orient herself and make her way off the island. She didn't have any idea what had happened to Leo and the others. She'd been separated from them early on, but she did know that Leo had still been unconscious. The Sweepers had had to drag him from the van. At this point she'd started sobbing, and Grammalie Rose had ended the discussion, folded Del in her arms, and taken her from the square.

Aidan had even tried to ask her privately, hoping she could offer some details about the tower, the hospital, ways on and off the island, but she just shook her head and pressed her lips together. "It was dark. I was scared," she'd said, rubbing at her wrists. And the next day, when a bunch of them had been put to work in the pouring rain, shoring up the dikes along the canals with bags full of rubble and old masonry, Del had been even quieter. She'd responded to Aidan's questions and to Henry's flirtation with silence and the smallest of smiles. Only when she'd glanced at Lucy did something flit across her face. It had almost looked like fear.

Lucy had taken her cues from Aidan, and he was definitely concerned. He could barely take his eyes off Del. Lucy thought back to how he'd dropped her hand during the dance and stepped away abruptly. How stricken his face had been, as if he'd woken up and discovered that the girl he'd been dreaming about was not the girl he was with. She got the sense that there was a history between Aidan and Del, but she couldn't figure out if it went beyond friendship.

"The dynamic duo," Henry called them. "Inseparable." Lucy hadn't been completely successful in squashing a twinge of jealousy. She wondered again what Aidan had been about to say to her during the dance. "Lucy, you are so—" he'd whispered.

So what? So strange-looking? So awkward? So annoying? Or maybe, so amazing? It was conceivable, but it didn't seem likely.

And Del hadn't helped matters, either. She'd been distracted, even less friendly than usual (if that was possible), and full of mean looks. Like early this morning, when they were out picking tomatoes and snap peas for their lunch she'd barely said a word, but she seemed annoyed that they were all together again. Lucy had decided to ignore her and focus on her first hunting experience.

Now something stirred in the large thorny bush in front of her. She raised her bow. Aidan's bow, actually. A crescent of smooth red oak rubbed with olive oil until it shone. Aidan put up his hand.

Bird, he mouthed, and motioned downward. That's right. She wasn't to draw on a bird. They were too hard to hit, many of them were sickly, and they couldn't afford to lose arrows. Same went for deer if they were lucky enough to spot one. Just the thought of a whole deer made Lucy's mouth water. She cradled her chin on her arm and watched a column of ants carry tiny white eggs from one hole to another. She stifled a yawn.

When they had first hiked up to the ridge, Aidan had sat beside her on the grass. He'd strung the bow for her, shown her how to check the straightness of her arrows. She had eight slender lengths of springy ash, the tips needle-sharp and hardened in fire, the fletching cut from pliable plastic containers. Lucy had enjoyed Aidan's closeness, liked watching his deft brown fingers and the slight frown that ruffled his forehead as he explained something to her. There was a lot of physics involved in shooting a bow, apparently.

"So is the wind coming from a good direction?" she'd asked.

Aidan had nodded. "From behind, so we won't be shooting into cross drafts."

Del had snickered. Her hand had swooped down and plucked the arrow from Lucy's grasp. She'd turned it over in her hand, hefting the weight.

"You aim, you point, you fire," she'd said, sitting down between them. There was no room, but she had squeezed in, anyway. She'd flashed Lucy a triumphant look and Lucy had moved over to the right. She wasn't in competition for Aidan. She didn't exactly know how she felt about him. Del had made it pretty obvious what her feelings were, and since then, Lucy had been almost hyperaware of the girl.

Lucy couldn't help noticing that Del's body was right up against Aidan's now. Del's thigh pressed along the length of his leg, her tanned arm inches from his own. She had a purple bruise along one cheekbone and stripes of raw flesh where the Sweepers had fastened her wrists with plastic cuffs, but she was otherwise unhurt. Lucy wondered how she'd gotten away from the Sweepers when no one else ever had. She opened her mouth to ask the question, but stopped when Del leaned forward to whisper something in Aidan's ear. The tip of her ponytail swept across his face and he reached out and moved it away, his fingers tangled in the shiny black locks. Del laughed, casting a glance over her shoulder at Lucy. Lucy looked in the other direction.

She went over the instructions for shooting an arrow in her head, trying to remember everything Aidan had told and shown her. Months of training were squeezed into a few short hours in between the other work that needed to be done. At first she hadn't been able to hit anything. Just holding the string back without letting her hands shake was harder than it looked. And her fingers always seemed to be in the way when she released, sending her arrow into a wobbly, crooked trajectory that, nine times out of ten, landed it in a bush or the dirt. She'd also had to pretend she felt nothing when Aidan guided her arm or stood behind her with his hands on her fingers and his chest leaning into her back, while Del watched his every move with a glacial stare on her face. Lucy had bitten the inside of her cheek so hard that it bled, but she'd finally made a shot. At least, her arrow had struck the tree the target hung on and had quivered there for a few seconds before falling to the ground with a plop.

"Great!" Aidan had said. "How did it feel?"

"Good." She'd lowered her eyes. Not as good as having his arms around her shoulders, but she thought her fingers were getting used to the cramping grip on the arrow and the pressure of the bowstring and the quick, fluid motion she needed to master to send the arrow off on a straight path.

Now she raised herself on her elbows, positioned an arrow against the bow, and tracked across the glade from left to right, ignoring the soreness in her muscles. Her fingers sweated in the stiff leather glove she had to wear to keep the thin nylon cord from flaying her skin. She had her jacket on to protect the inside of her arm, and the leather was uncomfortably hot in the sun. But at least it wasn't raining. What did they used to call it before the climate went all haywire? *An Indian summer.* They were getting an odd respite from the usual constant heavy storms of the Long Wet. Unfortunately, it seemed as if every flying insect in the world had decided to take advantage of the weather, and they were mating up a storm. Midges, blackflies, and mosquitoes hovered in black clouds. Lucy's legs were clad in cutoff jean shorts, and she'd already counted fifteen bites in rings around her ankles. She squirmed, trying to rub the itches against the stubbly grass, and Del kicked her, then pointed.

Something moved on the sunny slope just beyond the shadows thrown by the spindly trees. It was buff-colored and small. Its pointed head came up and Lucy saw the long ears lying flat against its body. Del looked hard at Lucy with her blazing blue eyes, made sure that she had seen the rabbit, too, and then mimed the action of loosing an arrow. She touched her index finger to a spot just below her shoulder blade to remind Lucy where to aim. The arrow would travel directly to the heart. Death would be quick.

Suddenly, Lucy's fingers felt thick and inflexible. The arrow shaft was slippery and weighted wrong, and she couldn't focus her vision. She pulled the bowstring back. The rabbit's head came up again. It stopped in the middle of chewing a mouthful of grass. Wisps hung from its mouth like a straggly green beard. Lucy felt the scrape of the plastic fletching against her cheek. Her fingers were numb and sweat dribbled into her eyes. She couldn't let go.

Del exhaled, raised her own bow, took aim, and shot. The arrow thrummed, flying straight and true, and hit the rabbit with a force that spun the animal into the air. She was up on her feet and racing toward it before Lucy had lowered her bow. She stared at the ground. She'd caught rabbits, squirrels, and woodchucks before, but in snares. Traps tripped while she wasn't there. This was different, and it was nothing like aiming at a piece of wood.

Aidan touched her arm. "Hey, I puked the first time," he said in a low voice. "Del's always been better at killing things than I am."

Lucy felt her mouth twist. "It just wasn't the same."

"I know. You can try to imagine that it's a tin can or whatever, but it never works. All I can say is try to do it fast and try to do it right."

Del stalked back to them. The bunny swung from her gloved hand. Lucy looked away from the limp head, the eyes like foggy blackberries. A small red hole bloomed on its back.

Del wiped her arrow against a patch of grass and stowed it with the rest in the quiver she wore slung from her shoulders. She hunched down next to Aidan. She danced her fingers up and down his arm.

"If we're lucky," she said, "the other rabbits won't be alerted and we can get a few more. They come out in force just before sunset."

Lucy squinted up at the sky. The sun was behind them now. She rolled over to look at the clouds drifting.

Sure enough, as the sun lowered in the sky, more and more rabbits poked out their quivering noses. They nibbled grass and chased one another, innocent and carefree, reminding Lucy of the camp kids playing kick-the-can.

They're food, she told herself, but it was no good.

She heard the soft whicker as Del notched an arrow.

Lucy watched as Del shot four rabbits in quick succession before finally missing one. Instantly the animal darted to the top of a hillock and drummed the ground with its back foot. The other rabbits vanished into their holes. There was a curious light in the girl's eyes. It wasn't pleasure, but a glint of *something*. Like she was paying the rabbits back for an insult. Lucy was happy that she had finally missed.

"I'll get them," she said, clambering to her feet. She was stiff. The rabbits were hard to find in the long grass. Their soft, brown bodies splayed in awkward positions. They were smaller than she expected. Lucy picked them up, holding them by their velvet ears, feeling the uncomfortable heavy, boneless quality about them. They were still warm, and they flopped like stuffed toys. One remained lost in the undergrowth despite careful searching.

When she walked back to the others with the dead animals, Del exploded. "I shot four. Where's the other one? Do you think it's easy?"

"Obviously not, seeing as how I couldn't do it," Lucy said. Her cheeks burned, but she met Del's eyes. What was *with* this girl? "I looked for the fourth one. I couldn't find it."

Del snorted. She stripped off her glove and flexed her hand. The abrasions on her wrists looked raw. Again Lucy wondered how she'd escaped the plastic handcuffs by herself.

She unslung her bow and thrust it at Lucy. "Hold this."

She strode off, swishing her quiver back and forth across the long grass, ducking below the branches of a tree that swept the ground.

Lucy held the bow between fingers that didn't seem attached to her hand. The rabbits were cold now and their eyes had filmed over. She felt angry and a little sick.

"Give them to me," Aidan said, standing up and stretching. She looked away from the lean length of him and handed them over. He opened the neck of the canvas bag they'd brought and shoved the bodies in.

"Listen," he said. "She doesn't mean anything by it. That's

just Del. She always says what she thinks. She's been through a lot. . . ." His voice trailed off. He looked uncomfortable.

The kind note in his voice set her eyes prickling. She focused on the scuffed toes of her boots.

"Hey," he said softly. His hand reached out to her arm, fell short, and sort of brushed the air between them. She felt it against her skin, anyway. She took a step toward him.

Aidan pinched her chin and raised her face to his. She'd never seen his eyes so close. They were a deep green with specks of gold. She could smell the sun on his clothes. He smiled and leaned in farther. Lucy felt her head swim. She swore she felt a crackle of electricity. He was going to kiss her. They were going to kiss. His lips looked so soft.

"Crap!" Del yelled. Aidan froze, and Lucy stepped backward so quickly, she tripped over her own feet. Del was a few yards away. She swung a bunny from one hand. She was keeping the weight off of her left foot. "I think I turned my ankle in a rabbit hole." She winced, but Lucy couldn't help noting that the grimace was replaced by a smile as soon as Aidan hurried forward. She slung her arm across his shoulder, hobbled over, and handed Lucy the last rabbit and her quiver. Lucy followed behind, carrying the bag, the bows, and the arrows. She saw how Del clung to Aidan, her sleek head tucked against his chest. Her hand lay over his heart. Lucy quickened her pace until she was ahead of them, and then practically ran back to the camp.

CHAPTER FOURTEEN
MOVING MOUNTAINS

Henry was a whistler. Jaunty little tunes, like that one about working on the railroad, and the other about the hole in the bucket, which totally got on Lucy's nerves after the first hour. If she'd known, she probably wouldn't have requested to be on his team, but the alternatives were even worse: work with Connor and Scout, who were welded together so closely, you couldn't get a thin dime between them, or with

Del and Aidan. Aidan had been in a strange, quiet mood ever since yesterday afternoon. He wouldn't even look at her. And Del had been radiating anger, although Lucy noticed that her sprained ankle was miraculously better. They were working at the other end of the field, over where Sammy and the other two S'ans were raking over the soil. Lucy had discovered that their names were Beth and Ralph, and she was finally able to talk to them without shuddering. Visibly, at least. Inside, she still felt a clench of fear, wondering if some day she would wake up with her skin cracked and oozing and the disease rampaging through her body. She had noticed that they always kept themselves apart from the rest of the scavengers, and that made her feel slightly ashamed of herself.

Henry was all right. He reminded her of her brother, Rob—sort of cute and funny, like a cartoon character—but she'd also found out that he had basically one thing on his mind, with a relentlessness that was almost scary. He was so busy flirting that he had slowed his work to a snail's pace. She looked at the huge pile of stones and chunks of blacktop Henry had yet to load into the wheelbarrow and decided to take a break. They'd already filled the barrow four times and wheeled it out to where the big road entered the camp. Each load seemed pathetically small when they dumped it out. Aidan had been right that it would take time to block it completely, she admitted, but at least they were doing *something.* She wiped sweat from her forehead. Her back was aching, and she was pretty sure she had some major blisters under her leather gloves.

"The S'ans," Lucy said, leaning on her pickax. "I mean, Sammy, Beth, and Ralph . . ."

Henry looked up and threw down his spade. He stretched with both arms over his head and froze for a minute so she could admire his wiry torso as his T-shirt rode up. She suppressed a laugh. He'd taken every opportunity to show off his biceps. She pointed to the heap and then to the wheelbarrow, and, with a huge dramatic sigh, he began shoveling in the rocks.

Before he could start whistling about the chain gang, Lucy continued. "Are they totally healthy now?"

"Yeah. I mean, their bodies fought off the disease. Normally hemorrhagic smallpox kills in about seventy-two hours."

"And will their skin and their eyes go back to normal?"

He paused. "Hmm. Since there are no documented cases of survivors, I don't know. I mean, the burnt look and the bloody eyeballs are due to bleeding under the skin. I guess it makes sense that eventually the wasted cells will be washed away in the bloodstream, cleansed by the kidneys, and then flushed." Henry frowned and rubbed his nose with his glove, leaving a smudge of dirt. Finally, he said, "Seems likely. Who knows what's going on under those masks? The skin has an amazing ability to rebuild cells." His serious expression was replaced by his usual grin. "You know, I can tell that Beth might be really pretty. I think she's got those melting brown eyes like dark chocolate and a tight—"

Lucy aimed a punch at him, but he jumped backward and held up his hands in surrender. She lowered her fists, but neglected to tell him about the muddy smear across his face.

"So how'd you get on Lady Del's bad side so fast?" Henry said, pushing the heavy wheelbarrow up a few feet. Lucy glanced over to where Del was working next to Aidan at the other end of the field, and threw a chunk of masonry into the barrow. She pulled her sweatshirt hood forward. It was drizzling, and by the look of the black clouds massing overhead, they were in for a real downpour. The Indian summer was over. The weather matched her mood.

"How do you know it's not you she's throwing those mental daggers at? Maybe she knows you ate the last of those wild strawberries we found."

Henry grinned. "Not me. I'm her go-to man." He stomped on the edge of his shovel, pushing the blade into the iron-hard ground and breaking it into manageable chunks.

"Go-to for what?"

"For whatever she needs. She's Lady Del. Questions, answers, other more urgent needs. You know." His expression was smug. "She seems mightily interested in you, as a matter of fact."

Lucy wrinkled her forehead. "Me? I'm no one."

"That could be argued," he said with a wide grin. "Sometimes it's special favors she's looking for."

"Oh."

"I could be your go-to guy, too, if you like." He waggled his eyebrows.

"Umm, that's okay. I'm good." Lucy peeled her leather gloves from her hands and inspected the blisters across her palms. She looked at the small patch of ground they'd managed to clear. Even the youngest kids were helping—sort of: picking up one pebble every ten minutes and chasing one another around the rest of the time. Grammalie Rose was running lines of rope along what would be the furrows. Connor and Scout were wrestling with a clumsy wooden contraption shaped like a giant V, with two long handles and a thick plate of steel bolted to the underside. It was a plow, Lucy had been told, and it looked as if it would take ten of them to drag it through the ground once they'd gotten rid of as many of the stones as they could.

She eased the gloves back on, wincing as the rough material touched her tender skin. She squinted her eyes against the slanting rain.

"We all have roles. Sammy is her shoulder," Henry said as he piled a scant shovelful of rock into the wheelbarrow.

Lucy stopped in mid-swing. "What does that mean?" she asked. "What's with the high school nicknames?"

"When she needs someone to lean on, or to cry on. He's the shoulder. I'm pretty sure he'd like to be more," he said speculatively. "But for now, that's it."

Lucy turned to look at the small group across the field.

Aidan was talking to Sammy and Del now. Del shook her head at something Aidan was saying. Sammy put his hand on his brother's arm. Aidan shrugged it off and walked away. Lucy wondered what had happened. She saw Aidan hop a low wall and disappear into the jagged terrain left by the orchestrated bombing of what looked like at least three apartment blocks.

Del watched him, too, until Grammalie Rose barked at her. Then she turned around and looked right in Lucy's direction. It was like being targeted by a laser beam. Even from this distance—at least twenty yards—she could sense the anger in Del's deep blue eyes. Henry followed Lucy's gaze. He whistled. One low note.

"Ouch," he said. "You been trespassing on her property?"

"What's that supposed to mean?"

"She laid claim to Aidan a long time ago."

"Oh come on!"

"He's her O-O-H-A," he said.

"Enough already!" Lucy said.

"Object of her affection," Henry said hurriedly.

Lucy snorted. "That's so dumb."

Henry raised his eyebrows. "I've seen the way you look at

him. And he's always staring at you in a sly, undercover way. I bet Del has been scoping out the situation. You guys figured it out yet?"

Her cheeks burned.

"Do you really like him?" He watched her curiously, his voice serious all of a sudden.

She thought about it. "Yeah, I guess I do. But most of the time I'm so mad at him, I could spit."

"The path of love never runs smooth," Henry said, throwing out an arm as if he were declaiming poetry.

"No. I mean, we're friends but . . . nothing has happened. . . . No." Lucy stopped as the rest of what he'd said sunk in. She couldn't help the small smile that spread across her face. She bit the inside of her cheek and tried to look unconcerned. "You've seen him look at me?"

"Yeah. He pretends he's all cool and stuff, but . . ."

She turned her back and savored this information for a moment, and then spun on her heel to face him. "Wait a minute. What business is this of Del's? Doesn't he get any say in this? He's not a trophy, and he's not some pet she can put on a leash."

"I never said he was," Henry said with a roguish grin. "He plays it really well."

"Excuse me?"

Henry put down his shovel. "All I'm saying is, *I* wouldn't mind being caught in the middle of you two."

She whacked him on the arm hard enough that she felt the sting in her fingers. He stood there rubbing the spot, but the grin never wavered. She gritted her teeth.

"Don't be stupid!"

He had the grace to look embarrassed. "I'm just kidding. . . ."

"Well, don't." Lucy grabbed the pickax and hefted it, ignoring the worried look on his face. She worked off some of her annoyance by attacking the ground. After a while, she said, "So are they together?"

"Listen. I shouldn't have shot my mouth off. It's none of my business."

His tone was no longer teasing. She met his gaze. No smirk, no mocking light in his eyes. He looked chastened.

"There aren't too many secrets in camp. I mean, everyone knew Connor was gaga for Scout months before he made his move. But I can tell you honestly, I think it's all on Del's side. Why Aidan would pass up a gorgeous girl like that, I don't know, but that's the truth." He stopped talking all of a sudden. Lucy turned. Grammalie Rose stood behind her. Her clothes were covered in dust. The black leather of her clogs was barely discernible under a thick coating of dirt. Lucy wondered again at the strength of the old woman.

"Is this one talking your ear off, *wilcze*?"

"No, we were just chatting," Lucy said, wiping the sweat out of her eyes.

The old woman glanced at the square they'd cleared, the

half-filled wheelbarrow, the pile of rocks Lucy had collected, and Henry's freckled face, dry and unreddened by exertion.

"Too bad you exercise your tongue more than those strong arms of yours," she said, fixing Henry with a baleful stare. "A couple more hours and some of us can break for lunch. Beth and Ralph found puffball mushrooms in the field this morning."

"Some of us?" Henry asked. He kept the shovel in motion, exaggerating his breathing. He jerked his head at the pile of rubble.

"I believe that Lucy is responsible for that," Grammalie Rose said. She turned so only Lucy saw the way her lips twisted in the beginnings of a smile. "However, if you continue at the pace you are setting now, I think you will be one of the luncheon party."

"Why did Aidan get to slack off?" Henry asked, digging with more enthusiasm than he'd shown all morning.

Grammalie shot him a look. "He works harder than anyone else here. He was in the fields at four A.M. when you were still rolled up in your sleeping bag with those magazines you think I don't know about."

Henry mumbled something and turned away. The tips of his ears were an almost fluorescent red.

"Two hours more, I think," she said, resting her calloused hand for a moment on Lucy's arm. "At least the rain is stopping." The old woman walked away in the direction of the camp. As soon as she was out of sight, Henry put down his shovel. "Man," he said, rubbing his hand along his ribs. "I think I pulled a muscle." He turned to Lucy. "Think you could check it out for me?"

Lucy barely acknowledged him. Del and Sammy were shouting at each other across the field. Del tossed her pickax aside and threw up her hands. She pushed Sammy away from her. Her hair, loosened from its ponytail, swirled around her face. And then she turned.

With a start, Lucy realized the girl was heading toward her. Fast.

"Uh-oh," said Henry. "Lady Del's in a fury." He picked up his shovel again and moved closer to Lucy. She was oddly touched.

Lucy's hand stole to her waist. Her fingers found the comfort of her sheathed knife and then fell away. She was hardly going to stab Del, annoying as she might be.

She took a deep breath and stood her ground as Del stormed up. For a moment, neither of them spoke, and then Lucy said, in as mild a tone as she could muster, "Something going on?"

"Hey, Lady Del," Henry said in a determinedly light voice. "How's the digging going? Your boy Aidan bailed out early, huh? What a slacker!"

Del's deep blue eyes flicked over him and then returned to Lucy's face. Lucy forced herself to stay calm, but it was difficult. She tried to decipher Del's body language. It was as if she was barely keeping control. And she seemed on the edge of tears.

They had an audience now, too. Beth and Ralph leaned on their rakes. She saw Scout and Connor lower the plow to the ground. Only the youngsters and the older folk seemed unaware of what was going on. Lucy chewed the inside of her cheek, remembering the one and only fight she'd had in grade school, when Gracie Foster had accused her of stealing her heart-shaped pencil eraser. They'd ended up rolling in the dust of the playground with a bunch of kids egging them on. And when Lucy went home that afternoon, she'd had bloody scratches up and down her arms, and her scalp hurt. Gracie Foster had been her best friend after that, all the way up until eighth grade, when they'd gone to different schools. She wondered if Gracie was still alive.

Del got right in her face. "It's all your fault," she snapped. Her hands were clenched in fists. Lucy planted her feet. She felt a surge of anger, and it gave her confidence.

"What are you talking about?"

Del snorted. She paced back and forth, her hair streaming over her shoulders. Her silver bracelets jangled, and she pushed them up her arms impatiently.

"Aidan," she said. Her hand rubbed at her nose, and Lucy saw tears in her flashing eyes.

"What? I didn't . . . What?"

"I think he's either gone to the Wilds or he's trying to find Leo. Either way, you're to blame, Lucy Holloway." She practically spat the words out. Her finger came up and jabbed Lucy in the chest. Lucy slapped her hand away. She didn't understand this at all. She'd thought Del was going to give her grief over almost kissing Aidan, but instead it was these riddles.

"You're crazy!"

Henry moved forward to stand between them. They both glared at him and he stepped back.

"He likes to climb trees in the Wilds. It has nothing to do with me. And he said he wouldn't go after anyone who'd been kidnapped by the Sweepers." *Not even you,* she thought to herself. "He said we weren't prepared." Her toe scuffed the dirt. "And he was right. I get that now. We can't just storm in there with no idea of what to expect."

Del frowned and the accusatory finger rose again. "But that's not what you told him, is it, Lucy Holloway? You said that if he really cared about his friends, he would go anyway, right?"

"I didn't tell him to go anywhere. I just said that, if it were me, I wouldn't wait around for the next bad thing to happen. And besides, I was mad and I was just shooting my mouth off."

Del's shoulders slumped. The anger seemed to drain out of her. She shook her head. "Don't you get it? He can't stand that you think of him that way. Like he's some kind of a coward. God, don't you know anything about boys?!"

Lucy cleared her throat. She couldn't remember what she'd said to Aidan. She'd yelled. He'd yelled. She tended not to watch her mouth when she was angry. "Are you sure that's where he's gone?" Her voice was hoarse. She grabbed Del's arm. Del stared at her fingers, but she didn't brush them off.

After a moment, Del said impatiently, "No, I don't know. I *think* he's headed to the lake. I hope that's where he's gone. It's where he always goes when he needs space. He won't let me go with him, and he'd never say what he was doing." She looked down at her boots. "I followed him once." Her chin came up, as if she was daring Lucy to say something about it.

"He liked to climb to the top of the elm tree and look north," Lucy said, dropping her hand. "He said he wanted to travel up there one day."

"Yeah, that's what he said." Del sighed. "He probably just needed time to think, but he talked about the argument with you, and Leo and the kids, and then I got so mad at you for picking on him that I wasn't really paying attention to what he was saying." She raised her eyes to Lucy's face. They weren't snapping with fire anymore, but there was still something hard in them.

"Aidan can look after himself," Henry said. "He's been running wild since he was thirteen, right?"

Del drew a deep breath. She glanced at Lucy again. "Why did you have to come here?" she said. Her tone was strange. It seemed less angry and more tired. She rubbed her hand over her face and eyes, leaving smeary wet trails mixed with dirt. Her mouth twisted. "We're not friends, Lucy Holloway," she said in a voice that was no more than a whisper.

"Hey now, Lady Del," Henry said softly. He slung an arm around her shoulders. For a moment she collapsed into him, and then, with another shake of her head, she pushed him away.

She strode off. Lucy stared after her. She didn't understand Del at all. One minute she was spitting like an angry cat; the next, she was as emotionless as a robot.

"That was intense," Henry said. "Why'd she keep saying your name in that weird way? It was like she was putting a curse on you or something." He laughed nervously and wiggled his fingers in her face. "Voodoo magic."

Lucy shook her head. How could Del hate her so much?

"Maybe she got too much sun?" Henry said. He rubbed his chin with his gloved hand, staring in the direction Del had taken. "I've got to say, though, all that passion she's bottling up sure makes me wonder. I mean, it's got to find an outlet, right?"

"Oh, for God's sakes, Henry," Lucy said, trying not to laugh.

Sammy tapped her on the shoulder. She turned to face him. His hood was pulled forward, and he was wearing a different mask. This one was painted a glossy red with a broad, upturned smiling mouth and little red horns. Holes were cut out for his mouth and eyes. His red-tinged irises gleamed behind it. "He used to watch you and wonder about you. In your camp. He used to say you were the bravest person he knew."

Lucy raised surprised eyes to his face. "Me? Why?"

"Because you were alone and you were surviving," Sammy said. "Because you just did what needed to be done."

"Half the time I didn't know what I was doing."

"Yeah, but you kept on anyway."

She looked at Sammy properly for the first time. He was shorter than Aidan, probably a shade under six feet. His shoulders were broad, and his gloved hands were wide. He seemed a little clumsy, like he'd recently had a growth spurt. Under his hood she glimpsed a shock of the same dirty blond hair his brother had. And then the gruesome contrast of charred skin. It was smooth, though, not cracked and oozing as she had thought before. The surface was whole. It was underneath that great patches of black and red covered his body, like giant bruises. She thought she could see some hazel in his irises within the bloody whites, and the lobes of his ears were pink, like new skin after a bad sunburn. She thought about what Henry had said and wondered if he was right about the body fixing itself.

He returned her gaze. "You are brave," he said with the hint of a smile. She caught a flash of very white teeth. "Look at you right now. Not worried I'm going to crack your head like a walnut and eat your brains?"

She blushed. "That was so dumb. I just—"

"—believed the propaganda and the news reports." He nodded. "You're not the first." He shrugged. "They just didn't know what to do with us. Didn't know where to put us. It was like we were nonhumans or something just because we got sick. Ralphie still won't talk to anyone but me and Beth."

Lucy was trying to understand her fear. "I think it's because you survived. You're sort of like a living, walking reminder that there was a plague."

He shrugged. "Yeah, well, I can't do anything about that."

"Hey," said Henry. "Hate to break up the tête-à-tête, but I'm hungry, and if you guys don't help load and dump the rest of this, Grammalie Rose is going to personally see to it that I starve."

Lucy and Sammy exchanged a grin.

"Pretty please?" Henry said.

"With sugar on top?" Lucy said.

"I just can't resist a whiner," Sammy said.

Henry tossed a shovel at him. Sammy caught it.

"I'll give you a kiss," Henry said to Lucy, puckering his lips and opening his arms wide.

"Henry!" Grammalie Rose yelled from the camp.

Suddenly, a jumble of shouts and cries rose from the direction of the square. Something had happened. Lucy's heart started pounding.

"Henry!" And this time they all heard the shrill note of panic in Grammalie Rose's voice.

CHAPTER FIFTEEN
PLAGUE

The shrouded lump lying on the mound of bracken leaves and grasses was scarcely recognizable as human. And the sounds that came from it were more like that of a wounded animal. Lucy and Sammy followed Henry into the open space beneath the awnings. Grammalie Rose crouched at the head of the makeshift bed. A few of the youngest kids huddled together in the corner, and Aidan was there, too. He raised his head, meeting Lucy's eyes briefly. She was shocked at how pale and drawn his face was. He looked much older than seventeen. Henry dropped down to his knees opposite Grammalie and moved the covers aside. Lucy caught a glimpse of charred skin, a gasping mouth.

"Sue is boiling water for willow bark tea. Aidan soaked some sheets in water. He's bad," Grammalie Rose said. She looked at Sammy and beckoned him closer. "Get the children away," she said in a low voice.

Sammy nodded. He bent his head and pulled the white and gold mask from beneath his cape and switched it for the horned mask. Then he clapped his hands. "Strawberry hunt in two minutes!" The kids clustered about his legs, jabbering in excited voices, and he led them out into the square.

"He's burning up," Henry said, laying a hand on the man's forehead. "The willow bark tea won't bring his temperature down fast enough." He looked miserable. "What else do we have?"

"Elder flower, echinacea for the fever; but if the willow isn't doing any good . . ." Grammalie Rose's voice trailed off. "Valerian, black cohosh for the pain: There may be some motherwort left, but I used most of it when Lottie broke her arm. I have a tincture of rosemary for when he is calmer." Her hand brushed against the man's face for a moment. Then she pulled two small glass bottles from her pocket. One was filled with a gritty brown powder. The other glowed yellow-green.

"He'll probably die," said Henry. He bit his lip, as if ashamed of what he had said.

Grammalie Rose soaked a cloth in a pan of water and dabbed it over the man's face. She muttered under her breath. It sounded like a string of curses. Her eyebrows met in an angry frown over her hawklike nose. She glared at Henry.

"Then we will try to make him as comfortable as we can. Yes?"

Henry lowered his head.

Lucy watched the body writhing beneath the thin covers. She could see blackened skin covering a bald skull and spreading in splotches to the face. His eyes were half-open. The eyeballs were tinged an angry red. She couldn't distinguish his pupils at all. It was as if the sockets were filled with blood. He thrashed and threw off the sheets. Two thick gold hoops dangled from the charred earlobes, and under the skin of the muscular forearms she glimpsed swirls and bands of dark blue. Tattoos, she realized with a shudder of recognition, almost covered by the dusky hue of bleeding beneath the skin. It was Leo.

And now he was ill with the plague.

A feeling of hysteria rose in her throat, and she battled to keep herself under control.

Leo has the plague. She placed her hand over her mouth, ashamed of her weakness, and backed away.

Aidan was on his feet, pacing. The skin above his cheekbone was reddened and shiny. A new injury. Lucy moved around to join him.

"Did you find him?" she whispered.

"Yeah. I wasn't even looking for him. I was just wandering and there he was, on the big road a couple of miles up. I think they dumped him there." His hands clenched. "He didn't know me. He fought and I had to force him to come with me. He got a few good punches in." He rubbed his cheek. "Luckily he's weak; otherwise he'd have kicked my skull in."

Lucy put a comforting hand on Aidan's arm. He hardly seemed aware of it.

"He's been raving, slipping in and out of consciousness. God knows what he's seeing, or where he thinks he is." His shoulders slumped. "*Monsters.* He kept saying *monsters.* And he screamed like a little kid." Aidan ran trembling fingers through his hair.

"He'll be all right," Lucy said, trying to inject certainty into her voice. "Like Sammy."

"I don't know. Maybe." He swung around and stopped; his arms hung limply at his sides. "We don't have any medicine. Grammalie Rose has a few home remedies. Herbal teas and powders for headaches and minor injuries, but not for something like this!"

"I thought the plague was over," Lucy said. "How can it still be out there when everyone that's left has already survived it?"

"I don't think it will ever go away. It hides and it changes. We can't fight it." He groaned and kicked at the ground.

"Aidan and Lucy," Grammalie Rose said. "Come and hold him up. He is too heavy for me." Her raspy voice was calm. Her lips pressed together so firmly, they almost disappeared into the deep wrinkles of her face.

Lucy hesitated. Mentally she screamed at herself to move, but she couldn't. She dug her fingernails into her palms.

"Once the bleeding is visible, the risk of contagion has gone," Grammalie Rose said. "Two days ago he was perhaps a danger, but now he is only a man in pain."

Lucy swallowed her fear and went to the old woman's side.

Sue had returned holding a small steaming saucepan filled with a murky liquid. She held the metal handle with hands shrouded by the long sleeves of her sweater. She was chewing on the end of her pigtail, and her eyes were wet.

"Four heaping teaspoons in two cups of water, Sue?" Henry asked, taking the pot from her. The vapor rising from it smelled dank, like rotting wood.

"Yes," Sue said, taking her pigtail out of her mouth. She pulled her fingers through the wet end.

"Good, my *zabko,*" Grammalie said. "This will ease his pain. Go now."

Sue ran from the tent.

Grammalie held her hand up, the vial with the brown powder between her fingers. "Let me add valerian. It may help."

Her eyes gleamed like tar. She tipped the opened bottle, tapping in the last few clumps, and then nodded to Henry. Henry swooshed his finger around the liquid, testing the temperature. "We'll do it quickly," he told them. He spared a faint smile. "This stuff tastes like crap and he's not going to like it. He'll struggle."

Lucy took a deep breath and unclenched her fingers. She and Aidan got on either side of Leo and raised his head. Lucy cushioned it on her knees, and clutched his left shoulder and wrist in her hands. Aidan held him still on the other side. Leo screamed at the touch of their hands, as if his skin were being flayed. He bucked, trying to throw them off. His hands twisted and clawed as he attempted to free himself. His fingers were horribly swollen around the knuckles, and the nails were stained a deep purplish red.

Grammalie Rose pinned his legs under the weight of her body. Leo's head flailed from side to side. He tossed the covers off his body. His shirt was torn to shreds. Through it, Lucy saw the dusty blackness creeping across his chest. It was as if he had been beaten all over with steel rods. His eyes rolled back until it seemed like he stared at her through the top of his head. His mouth opened in a long, soundless scream. His tongue was black like a bird's.

"Hold him," Grammalie Rose said.

Henry poured the tea slowly down his throat. After each dose, he pinched Leo's nostrils closed and waited until he saw his throat swallow convulsively. It seemed cruel and heartless, but Lucy remembered having to give her dog medicine. She'd done it the same way, as quickly as possible and without thinking too much about it. She found herself stroking Leo's broad forehead and mumbling nonsense to him as though he were a baby.

Finally the last of the tea disappeared. They held him for five interminable minutes while Leo fought to free himself. Tears dripped from Lucy's eyes and fell onto his hands.

Eventually, he stopped straining against them and his breathing eased. He seemed to be asleep or unconscious. Henry sat back on his heels. The saucepan fell from his hand. The clanging thud was a signal to relax their hold on him. Aidan let go of his grip and flexed his cramped fingers. He stood abruptly and with his back to the group. Grammalie Rose took Leo's hand and enfolded it between her palms. The skin on either side of her mouth was deeply grooved and looked as delicate as cobwebs around her eyes. She took out the small vial of oil, uncapped it, and began smoothing it into Leo's twisted, lumpy knuckles. The smell was pungent, herbal. It reminded Lucy vividly of the Sunday roast beef dinners her mother had made after church. If she closed her eyes, she could almost see the starched white tablecloth, Rob's eager fingers dipping into the gravy boat, the mountain of buttery mashed potatoes, and the heat from the oven steaming up the windows.

Lucy moved back against the tarp wall and sat with her knees folded and her arms wrapped around her calves. She wanted to cover her head with a soft blanket and rock back and forth. It was something she'd done as a child whenever she was upset and needed to escape an unpleasant situation. She couldn't imagine the pain Leo was experiencing, but she felt she'd shared it somehow. Every spasm he had endured had rocketed through her body, jarred her bones, and made her grit her teeth so hard, the back of her neck was sore. And she was tired, as if she'd just outrun a tsunami again. Her hands shook and her legs felt like rubber. Lucy pulled her sweatshirt down over her knees.

Aidan came and sat next to her. His shoulder pressed against her arm. He was solid and warm. Without looking at him, she shifted slightly, and his hand reached out and found hers. Their fingers interlocked. Aidan watched Leo for a while. Aidan's body was tense, his grip on her fingers was almost painful, but finally his shoulders lowered and he relaxed.

"I was so scared of hurting him," Lucy said. "He screamed." She didn't think she'd ever heard a man scream like that.

"I doubt he knows what's going on. It's like he's trapped in a nightmare," Aidan said.

"He'll need another dose in about four hours," said Henry, wiping sweat from his forehead. His hair was soaking wet. His face was pale, but there was a stubborn slant to his mouth that Lucy had never seen. His crooked smile had vanished.

Lucy asked, "And all you gave him was the willow bark and the valerian?" She stumbled a little over the unfamiliar name.

"The local Superior Drugs is unfortunately closed for business. Looters took most of the medicine after the first wave. And then flooding took care of the rest. But it's the same stuff that's in aspirin." He nodded toward Grammalie Rose, who was hunched over Leo's still body. She crooned an odd song with guttural words in a different language. "She knows a lot about herbals. There's pretty much a natural alternative to most modern pharmaceuticals. Unfortunately for us, not many grow in New York State these days. There's too much rain."

"Will the tea really bring his fever down?"

"It should, but this disease is tenacious. If his temperature climbs above 103 degrees, it won't have an effect. We can keep him as cool as possible without sending his body into shock, but other than that . . ." He shrugged helplessly.

"Is there something stronger we can try?"

Henry exchanged a glance with Grammalie Rose.

"We have other remedies," she said heavily. "Nightshade. Foxglove."

"Great," Lucy said, and then noticed that everyone was looking grave.

"They're not cures," Aidan said, putting his hand on her shoulder. She reached up and clasped it.

"Not cures," she echoed.

"There are just ways to ease the inevitable," Grammalie Rose said. "They are remedies for the pain. Permanent."

"But Sammy, Beth, Ralph?" Lucy said. "They made it. And Leo, he survived until now."

"Sammy, Beth, and Ralph survived, but not because of any magic pill. Call it God's will, random selection. Luck. But this has gone too far," Grammalie Rose said, patting Leo's hand a final time and getting to her feet. Her hand went to her back as if it pained her. Today her legs were clothed in thick black tights and wrapped tightly at the ankles with bandages, and she wore her heavy woolen shawl tied close around her neck, as if she was cold.

Lucy persisted. "Shouldn't his immune system have kept him safe?"

"Maybe the disease has mutated," Aidan said. The words seemed to hang there.

Del appeared out of nowhere, exploding into the crowded space. Her knees were badly scratched, her boots crusted with mud, and her hair was loose and wild around her face. She dropped to her knees and grabbed Leo's hand.

"*Zabko,*" Grammalie Rose said, putting her arm around Del's shoulders and trying to lead her away. "*Zabko,* he is sleeping."

Del shrugged her arm off and leaned forward.

"Leo," she said, her mouth inches from his face. "Leo."

His eyes flickered open. A spasm snaked across his face. "Del," he gasped. His voice was raw and thickened, as if the words were being forced through a closed throat. "They let you go." He reached up and smoothed her hair.

"No. I escaped."

His forehead wrinkled. "How?"

Her fingers tightened on his. The knuckles showed white. He groaned.

"I got away from them," she said again. "Shhhh."

He shook his head. "Let me talk." He tried to rise from the ground but couldn't. "You're okay? They said they wouldn't hurt any of you."

"Oh, Leo." Del's eyes filled with tears. One splashed onto her hand. She rubbed her face against the sleeve of her sweatshirt.

"The kids? Lottie and Patrick. Were they with you?" she asked.

He shook his head. His tongue ran over his blackened lips. "They were kept in the tower. I was put in the hospital with the other adults."

"Hank?" Grammalie asked. "Walter and Olive from the sweep before?"

"I don't know. They were with me, but then—I didn't see them again."

"Why did they put you in the hospital?" Aidan asked.

Leo ran the tip of his tongue over his cracked lips. "Tests. Needles. Dr. Lessing said the secret was in the blood. But which blood . . . the dogs know."

He seemed to be raving again. The muscles along his jaw bulged and jumped. *Dr. Lessing,* Lucy thought to herself. The name was familiar for some reason. Not her family doctor. That had been dear old Dr. Ferguson, who handed out lollipops, and he was dead. Maybe an X-ray doctor at the hospital, though she didn't think that was it, either. But Leo was clearly out of his head. Maybe he was mixing up the past with the present.

"Let him sleep," Aidan said.

Del looked up at him briefly and then back down to Leo. "Did you get sick? Were they treating you?"

Leo's eyes rolled wildly. "Not treating. Infecting."

"What?" said Aidan. He dropped to his knees beside the man. "What did you say?"

Del shushed him. She watched Leo's face. His eyes darted from her to Aidan to Grammalie Rose, who stood behind them, clasping and unclasping her hands. Lucy wanted to leave, but her feet were rooted to the ground.

Leo took a deep breath. It whistled in his chest, as if he were sucking air through a blocked straw. Sweat broke out in huge droplets across his forehead, yet his teeth chattered. Grammalie covered him with the sheets, smoothing them under his chin as if he were a small child. Del stripped off her sweatshirt and carefully pushed it under his head for a pillow.

"They made me sick," he said between throttled gasps for air. "'Easy,' they said. They'd done it a hundred times. Then they injected me with different serums, vaccines. Looking for the secret in the blood. The blood." His chest rattled as he struggled to breathe. The flesh around his lips was as white as a fish's underbelly. Lucy found herself digging her nails into the palms of her hands. The healed knife wound itched. She remembered how gentle he had been when he bandaged it. She pulled off a loose strip of skin, wondering why it didn't hurt.

After a few torturous seconds, Leo continued. "It didn't work, so the Sweepers dumped me. They promised the kids would be safe if I cooperated. And you," he said, looking at Del.

Del sat up. Her fingers tightened around Leo's hand. "Did they lie about that?" she asked. "What happened to the kids?"

He drew another shuddering breath. His face purpled, visible even through the black blood. His chest seemed to be laboring with no effect. "I don't know. They weren't in the hospital. No one alive there now." His fingers tightened around her hand. "Del, she lied about everything."

CHAPTER SIXTEEN

GOING IN

Lucy stared at the mess of beans and overcooked rice on her plate. She pushed them around with her fork. She had tried to eat the food but it was tasteless, and just the sulfurous smell of it, the look of it, was making her stomach rebel. Across from her, Del was doing the same thing. Shoveling beans up into mountains and smashing them to mush, using her fork as a weapon. Her hair was a tangled mess. She'd gathered it back into a ponytail, but hanks of it fell forward over her face and trailed over the tabletop. And she'd chewed most of her fingernails off, one finger after another, spitting the half-moon curls into the air. One had ripped into a jagged edge, and a spot of blood welled next to the cuticle. She sat hunched in her seat as if her spine couldn't support her, and her eyes were shadowed and looked huge in her face. Lucy probably looked just as crappy. She knew her hair was one big frizzy knot, but she couldn't make herself care too much. She had the curious sensation that she wasn't really in her body. Beside her, Aidan turned a hunk of bread into a pile of crumbs.

Leo had died half an hour ago, first his breath becoming more and more labored, then the veins on his thick neck standing out like cables. He'd been unable to bear the touch of blankets or wet cloths against his skin. Grammalie Rose and Henry had talked, quietly, and then given him a glass of cloudy water to drink. Leo had gripped Henry's wrist and guided the edge of the glass to his lips. This time the big man hadn't struggled, although it seemed as if most of the liquid had dribbled out of his mouth and onto his chest. He'd kept his hand on Henry's wrist until the water was gone, and then he'd moved the hand to Henry's shoulder before letting it fall limply to his side.

At least, Lucy had *thought* it was water, but afterward Leo had sunk back against Del's pillowed sweatshirt and his eyes had closed. The lines of pain, the grooves between his blood-filled eyes, had smoothed, and it was only when Lucy had realized that she was holding her breath, waiting for his next breath, which did not come, that the truth became clear.

Now, she felt as if she'd hit her head. Her brain couldn't process everything that had happened in the last few hours, and simple things like eating and talking were beyond her capabilities. She could only sit and stare at the congealed heap of food on her plate. The only thing that felt real and alive to her was Aidan's hand wrapped around her own and the warmth his body gave off. Del had glanced at their interlaced hands and something had passed over her face, but it was so quickly replaced by a glazed expression that Lucy was convinced she had imagined it.

Del shivered now. Her bare arms were goose-pimpled. The wind had picked up, and she, Lucy, and Aidan sat at a far table, not wanting to be close to the people gathered by the fire. They'd made their way there by consensus, although it hadn't been spoken out loud. Lucy didn't think any of them had said more than two words in the last hour. Somehow, though, they had headed in the same direction, in a group, the three of them together.

Sammy had brought over the food. His white mask hung from his neck on a loop of string, his face bare for once. He'd put the plates down, a large bowl filled with beans and rice, bread, some water. He'd pulled Del into a hug. Surprisingly, she hadn't jerked away from his touch. Instead she'd nestled under his arm, her face turned against his shoulder. A few sobs had escaped from her mouth, and Sammy had stroked her head, murmuring words too faint to catch, before letting her go. And then, after a worried glance at Aidan's face and a nod to Lucy, he'd gone back to the huddled mass of people by the fire.

Lucy pulled her hoodie over her head and pushed it across the table, then shrugged back into her coat. Del glanced at her and put it on without a word. Afterward she went back to picking at her ragged fingernails.

Lucy looked over at the crowd. She thought that all the scavengers were grouped there, the young and the old. Henry was sitting close to Beth. She wore a pearly blue mask that glowed in the light of the flames and, instead of her usual black robes, a light sweater and a pair of jeans. Sammy was cross-legged on a bench. The kids sat in a circle on the ground, away from the flying embers, wrapped in blankets, and Lucy thought Sammy was telling them a story. He was clearly acting something out. She could see his extravagant gestures with his shadow leaping behind him on the hanging tarpaulins, the white mask catching the fire gleam, and she could hear the low hum of his voice. Every once in a while a child shrieked, but it was a joyful sound followed by squeals of laughter.

"Sammy knows how to scare them in just the right way," Aidan said.

Lucy searched for Grammalie Rose's unmistakable silhouette but didn't find her. "What will happen now?" she asked quietly. She couldn't tell if Del was listening or not. Her hands were pulled into the sleeves of Lucy's sweatshirt. She had her head down, the hood up. Her silver bracelets sparkled in a stack in front of her. She'd stripped them off as well as the large gold hoops she wore in both ears, pulling so hard she'd ripped the lobe, but Lucy didn't think she'd felt the pain.

"Connor and Scout are collecting wood," Aidan said. "Once dinner is over and the kids go to bed, they'll build up the fire." His voice cracked. "We have gasoline. No cars, but plenty of fuel."

Lucy felt the tears fill her eyes. She knew that was the way of it, but it filled her with horror. It brought back memories of the mattresses piled in the treelined street she had grown up on. She remembered the roar of orange flames and the surprising stink of burning fibers. The billowing black clouds that obliterated the sky like an eclipse.

"Does everyone know that he died of the plague?" Lucy asked.

"Not the littlest kids, but everyone else."

"I can't be here when they—" Del said.

Aidan cleared his throat. He squeezed Lucy's hand and then let it go. He reached over for Del's hand, but she just stared at his fingers until he withdrew them. Lucy noticed the hurt look that flashed across his face, and something in her belly hardened. Aidan cleared his throat again. "We won't be," he said. "We're going to the tower." He looked at each of them in turn. "Right?"

Lucy sat up. "Can we?"

"We know that the kids are in the tower, not the hospital. It probably won't be guarded as well. I mean, they're a bunch of kids, not one over eleven years old." He sounded excited and determined. He looked at Del. "You saw the tower. You remember the basic layout." She nodded slowly and sat up straight.

"I remember the way in. A big winding staircase with lots of rooms coming off it." She frowned. "There was a main entrance and a fire door around the side."

"We know the kids *were* in the tower," Lucy said. "They might not be there anymore."

"We need to try," he said. "Things have changed."

It went unsaid, but the words hung in the air: *They're killing people.*

He shifted on the bench. "We'll have to head west across the plateau and the Great Hill, and then south, and cross the mudflats. Find the bridge to Roosevelt Island."

"What about taking the big road? The way the vans came? Wouldn't it make more sense to go that way?"

Aidan shook his head. "Too exposed. There's nowhere to duck and cover if the vans are out. They could just scoop us up." He met her concerned look.

"I know," he said. "It's miles longer, and over uneven ground, but we have a better chance of getting there unseen."

Del stared steadily at the table, tension visible in the line of her shoulders.

"I've been thinking about it for a while," Aidan continued. "It'll be tough at the beginning, but once we're down on the low ground, it should be pretty straightforward."

"The mudflats are probably still dry enough," Lucy said, feeling a bubble of excitement. "Did you check them out earlier?"

He shook his head. "Not today, but last week. Leo was wandering around that gully where the Grand Canal crosses under the road." His voice roughened and he cleared it. "You'll have to lead us over the Wilds. It'll be dark and you know them better than anyone."

Lucy thought. They were still barely into the Long Wet. When she'd left her camp, the waters had been high, but no higher than the top of the toadstool on the Alice statue. Rainfall had been light and the tsunami had swept through over a week ago. "The ground shouldn't be too bad." She hesitated. "I can find my way around there pretty well, but the island bridge must be half a mile long, exposed, and we'll have to cross it. We'll be easy to spot if they post guards."

Del looked up. "There are no lights on the bridge. If we keep low, we should be okay. There's lighting inside the tower and the hospital. A generator. I could hear it." She swallowed.

A mixture of emotions ran over her face. Lucy had no trouble recognizing one of them. *Fear.* It was on all their faces.

"Good," Aidan said.

Lucy was suddenly nervous. "It could be pretty dangerous." She wasn't sure which was worse, heading in blind or, like Del, knowing what was waiting for them.

"We have to go," said Del. "Otherwise it won't ever stop." She pushed the hood back off her face. Her eyes glittered feverishly. There were dark shadows beneath them, and her face was pale and sick.

"We'll go and we'll bring the kids back home, no matter what," she said quietly.

Slowly the sun went down. The children went to their bedrolls. No one lit the lanterns this night. The light from the great fire and the scattered stars was enough, although there was no moon. Every stick of broken furniture, every scrap of timber gathered for the cold months ahead was thrown onto the blaze. The flames shot up higher and higher, transformed into tongues of orange and red by the gasoline Sammy sloshed everywhere. He had removed his mask again, as had Beth and silent Ralph. In the sporadic flashes of illumination, their features looked deeply etched, swarthy but normal.

From the shadows, Lucy watched the flames climb. It seemed impossible that Leo was dead. She remembered his strength and gentleness. She couldn't see Del's face, but sensed her overwhelming grief and anger. The girl held herself apart from the others, her gaze fixed ahead, unmoving except for her fingers, which continually worried the red scabs on her wrists. She'd grunted when Lucy told her how sorry she was, and turned her face away when Aidan tried to hold her.

"We should all eat something," Aidan said, after a time. He handed a loaf of bread around. Lucy tore off a hunk and dutifully chewed. Her mouth was dry. She swallowed with difficulty, taking the water bottle from Aidan and washing down the lump that had caught in her throat with a hefty swig. Del ate a tiny bit and shoved the rest into the pocket of Lucy's sweatshirt. She still shivered.

"Let's go now," she said. "I can't stand being here any longer."

"Are you going to be warm enough?" Aidan asked her.

"Once we're moving. Don't worry about me." She sprang up from the bench.

Lucy zipped her jacket and tucked the ends of her hair into the collar. Her legs, clad in cutoffs, were chilled, but she didn't want to change into her jeans in case they went through water. She checked the clasp on her backpack and shrugged the straps over her shoulders. Aidan and Del had retrieved their packs, too. They each carried a short bow and slingshots, and had stuffed their pockets full of sharp rocks. Lucy had her knife. She made sure the sheath was buckled securely at her hip. In her right hand she hefted a long spear. She'd whittled it out of ash yesterday, and it was similar to the frog spear she'd used at her camp. Five feet long with a three-inch point hardened in the flames of the campfire. She was far better with it than with a bow and arrow, and she had already impressed Aidan by hitting a target four out of five times. Del cast a snotty glance at it, but Lucy ignored her.

"Let's go," Aidan said, getting to his feet. "Slowly, as if we're hunting for rabbits."

Lucy rose from the bench and followed him. The weight of her bag chafed her sore muscles, but it felt good to be moving. Aidan and Del walked ahead, and she was content to let them lead. Maybe Aidan could calm Del down. She could hear the soft murmur of his voice. A short reply from Del—the tone of her voice so musical when she wasn't pissed off. He slung his arm over her shoulders, gave her a quick hug, and then let go.

Their forms were bulked out by the backpacks. Lucy wasn't worried their leaving would give rise to suspicion. Even if someone in the camp saw them, which didn't seem likely, pretty much everyone carried their personal possessions with them at all times. More so since the last Sweeper attack.

If they were lucky, they'd get to the tower before dawn broke.

Lucy concentrated on where she placed her feet, being especially careful while her eyes were adjusting to the dark. Thousands of stars lit up the sky, but the twisting alleys around the camp were still confusing to her, and they were treacherous, strewn with trash and rubble. She knew they were heading west at first, until they'd crossed the bridge out of the Hell Gate and reached the plateau. Then they would turn toward the south. The terror of her journey across the canal was still fresh in her mind, and she fought to control her breathing. *One foot in front of the other,* Lucy told herself, stubbornly determined not to let Del sense her fear.

Too soon they had reached the suspension bridge and the gorge. The winds seemed stronger here, whistling past like racing cars. A horrid thought occurred to Lucy, and she ran to catch up to the others.

"We're just going to cross one of these things, right?" she asked Aidan in a low voice, darting a glance at Del. She appeared to be distracted. She stood a few feet away, tearing at her raw thumbnail. Her sleek head came up when Lucy spoke.

"Scared?" she said mockingly.

Lucy felt her cheeks redden. She found herself missing the grieving, silent Del. "No." *Yes,* said the voice in her head. "I came this way already, remember?" she reminded the other girl. *Helped along by a tsunami at my back and too panic-stricken to really watch where I was going.*

"Hmm," said Del, like she didn't believe her.

Lucy itched to hit her.

"By herself," Aidan added, putting his arm around Lucy.

Del's face took on a sour expression. She pulled her hair back out of her face and secured it tightly with an elastic.

"Pretty windy tonight. It's going to rock and roll." She touched the thin ropes. They vibrated with the force of the wind.

It looked flimsier than before, Lucy thought, this slender device made of old, braided hemp and recycled planks, which hardly seemed capable of supporting a cat.

Del adjusted her bow and quiver across her back. Then, casting one of her arched-eyebrow, curved-lip smiles at Lucy, she walked out onto the bridge.

Walked wasn't really the correct word. She *danced* her way across before Lucy had even begun to summon up the courage to move forward. Quick, sure-footed, and agile.

Lucy told her feet to move. They ignored her.

In the end, it was Del who provided the impetus. She stood on the other side with her arms folded across her chest, the hood of Lucy's sweatshirt pushed back so that her triumphant face was visible. In another minute she would start prancing back across, just to show how easy it was. Lucy longed to strike Del across her smug mouth.

Lucy tightened her grip on the spear, shrugged her shoulders to center her backpack, and stepped out onto the first wooden slat. After she'd successfully negotiated the jagged hole that had almost killed her the first time, it was just a matter of moving forward. The darkness actually made it a little easier since she couldn't see the sharp rocks thirty feet below her, and Aidan's presence was comforting. Her breathing calmed, and the panic released her from its grip. She began to relax.

Halfway across, Lucy tripped over a protruding nail and would have fallen if not for Aidan's hand, which shot out and caught the collar of her leather jacket. He pulled her backward with a force that rattled her teeth and squashed her throat. She cracked her hip against a wooden support, bruising the bone against the hard metal knob of her knife as she clutched at the rope. The rough hemp burned her palm and she felt the old wound burst open again. The bridge swayed back and forth, shimmying. Twenty feet away on solid ground, Del watched, her mouth hanging open.

"Lucy!" Aidan yelled, transferring his grip to her arm.

She raised tear-filled eyes. "I'm okay. I just tripped. Bashed my hip. Stupid," she said.

"Didn't drop your spear, though," he said.

"There is that," she agreed. She kept her eyes fixed firmly on her feet for the rest of the way. Aidan's hand remained on her arm.

"Way to jack up the excitement, Lucy-loo," said Del with a sneer.

"It's an adventure, right?" said Lucy, feeling so much better for the hard earth beneath her boots. "It wouldn't be worth much without the terror-fraught moments."

Del laughed.

As soon as Lucy had caught her breath and unzipped her collar from the tender skin of her neck, she removed her knife and scabbard and slipped it into the inside pocket of her jacket. She pressed her fingers against her bruised hip and sucked in a breath. *Ouch!*

"Okay to go on?" Aidan asked her, passing around the water. He winced. Lucy noticed he held his left arm against his body. He must have hurt it when he stopped her from falling.

"Don't be a moron," she said sharply, trying to conceal her concern. His smile lit up his eyes, and the crooked smirk was back, curling his lips. She wondered what it would be like to kiss it off his mouth. *Snap out of it, Lucy!* she told herself. *Stupid notions like this are why you almost took a header off a bridge a moment ago.*

"Is your arm okay?" she asked as they crossed the plateau, moving faster now that the going was relatively easy.

"A little sore," he admitted. "You could come over and make it better."

Del frowned.

Lucy turned away from his grin and checked out the terrain ahead of them.

She walked to the edge of the plateau, using the end of her spear to test how crumbly the ground was. The rain and the unusual heat of the last few weeks seemed to have solidified it into hard clay. It would get rockier and looser the farther down they climbed. She tried to remember how many gorges she'd crossed on the way here. It had seemed like dozens.

Aidan pointed a few degrees to the right. "That's the easiest way. The way I go." She considered. Easiest but it would take them pretty far out of their way. She could see the thin grove of trees at the crown of the hill where she had first rested beyond the reach of the giant wave. Just out of sight was the meandering rough path the deer used to go down to the water. Before that, though, were several miles of treacherous ground split by crevasses. Slabs of gray granite glimmered in the starlight among deep pockets of shadow where the earth had sunk or cracked. Lucy took a long breath. It would be better once they were in it. The vertigo that seized her at the top of a tree or on a swaying bridge didn't affect her when she was climbing, using her fingers to pull herself up a sharp slope or to steady herself down a hill.

"We going to move, then?" said Del impatiently. She toyed with her slingshot. The pouch of Lucy's sweatshirt gaped with the weight of the pebbles that filled it. Del's face looked even paler in the dim light, and there was a faint sheen of sweat on her forehead.

"Just figuring out the fastest way down," Lucy said easily, wondering why Del looked so sick and nervous now, when she'd been almost giddy just a few minutes before.

Aidan peered down the slope and whistled softly. "Faster. Definitely."

Del pushed her hair back and looked over her right shoulder, away from what was left of the city, away from the scree-covered slopes, and Roosevelt Island. *North.* Lucy wondered if the sky was bigger there. It looked bigger, and the stars clustered more thickly, bleaching a wide ribbon of sky that wreathed above the mountaintops.

"Don't you ever just feel like saying 'forget it'?" Del said. "There's just too much . . . responsibility," she said finally. Her mouth clenched around the word. She looked at Lucy, then at Aidan. Her eyes gleamed. "I mean, we're teenagers, right? Aren't we supposed to be getting ourselves into trouble? Having a good time? Sex and drugs and rock 'n' roll! Isn't that what it's supposed to be like?" Her voice lowered and softened until she sounded like a little girl. Wistful and sad.

Del stared across the Wilds with such an expression of rage on her face that it stopped Lucy's breath in her throat. She yelled—it was more of a howl, really—throwing her head back. A clatter of stones rolled beneath her feet and bounced over the rim.

Aidan reached out his hand. "You're standing too close to the edge."

She looked at him. "Isn't that my MO?" Del kicked at the ground viciously with her blunt-toed boots and sent another torrent of rock over. "Let's go. This way, right?" she asked, throwing a backward glance at Lucy.

For the next few hours, no one could spare the energy for conversation. Lucy went first, followed by Del, and then Aidan. She used her spear for added balance and to prod the earth on the steeper slopes. It seemed that every step caused a mini avalanche. Sometimes Del crowded her, her forward momentum throwing her against Lucy's heels, and Lucy angrily gestured the girl back. Slowly, they made it past the upheaval of old highways and the chunks of tarmac. There was no sound but the crunch of rock, the patter of crumbling soil, and their breathing. Del was oddly quiet except for the occasional cry as she slipped or stumbled. Lucy couldn't help noticing that she wasn't as agile on the uneven ground as she'd been on the bridge. Rocks rolled under her boots; chunks of dirt slid away, shooting past Lucy; and her balance was off. She was stiff and didn't seem to know what to do with her arms.

Lucy paused on a granite outcrop, as if to catch her breath. Aidan had stopped some way back to retie his boot laces. Without looking at Del, she said in a low voice, "Don't stare down at your feet. Look just ahead so your brain can note the slopes and the changes in the ground. Use your hands to grip and for balance. And bend your knees a little."

There was silence.

Out of the corner of her eye, she saw Del bite her lip. She braced herself for the volley of swear words that was sure to come.

"Thanks," Del said finally. She leaned against the cliff wall and pushed her ponytail into the collar of her sweatshirt. She wiped the sweat from her forehead. "I like being up in the air. But all these sheer walls and deep crevices make me feel like I'm being crushed alive."

"Really?" said Lucy. "I feel safer. There are things to grab hold of, to dig my heels into."

Del scanned her face. "We're so different."

"Yeah, we are."

Del paused. "Where is Aidan?" she said in one of her lightning-quick changes of mood.

Lucy looked around. Aidan was still behind a short distance, crouched down and hunched over something. It was too far to see what he was doing. She shrugged. "We're not going anywhere for a minute or two. Catch your breath."

"So, which way next?"

Lucy pointed with her spear. "See the big patches of gray up ahead? It's the beginning of the next plateau. Granite, grass, and earth, and no more of this crumbling cement and blacktop. It'll be easier."

She spun on her heel, considering the best path down. She'd come straight up the hill through the grove, which lay a few hundred yards to their right. It was a narrow, twisting, ankle-jarring deer track filled with ruts and rocks, and at the end of its sinuous length it would leave them a couple miles out of their way. Lucy dropped to her belly and hunched over to the steepest edge of the escarpment. It dropped about fifty feet at a sharp, almost 45 degree angle. The granite face was wind-roughened and scraped her fingers like sandpaper. She sat up and crossed her legs, considering their options. Her boots were chafing her ankle bones. She untied them and pulled her slouchy socks back up, retied the long laces, and double-knotted them.

"What are you thinking?" Del asked. She was unable to keep the nervousness out of her voice. She picked at the raw skin around her thumbnail, and Lucy wanted to slap her hand away as if she were a little kid with her fingers in her mouth. "A little payback for teasing you on the bridge?" Her chin came up and she looked mulish.

Lucy couldn't get the image of a little kid out of her head. It fit Del perfectly. Her mood swings, her temper, her wanting the whole cake for herself. Lucy disregarded the last statement, noting the frown that appeared when Del didn't get her fight. That was the trick: Ignore the most outlandish remarks. Refuse to play the game. Lucy felt pleased with herself. It would probably drive Del crazy!

"I'm trying to figure out the fastest way. We want to get to the tower while it's still dark, right? Here there are lots of tree roots to grab on to and the slope is gentler after about twenty yards, although if you fall it'll take some skin off. It's the quickest. So follow me. But not too closely, okay?"

Del nodded.

Aidan jogged up. "Thirsty?" he asked, uncapping the bottle of water. He took a sip and passed it to Del, who drank as if she was parched.

When she'd finished drinking, she held the bottle up to Lucy, who shook her head. "No thanks," she said politely.

"Where to next?" Aidan asked.

"Down," Lucy replied. He immediately sat. She giggled, ignoring Del's over-the-top eye-rolling.

"No, I mean we're going that way." She pointed down the hill.

He peered over the edge. "Looks doable." He shot a glance at Del and then a questioning look at Lucy, who quickly nodded her head.

Del wiped her mouth on her sleeve. "What were you up to?" she asked.

He took his hand out of his sweatshirt pouch. His fist was full of small- and medium-size gray and white pebbles. "Making trail markers. So when we come back it'll be easier to find our way."

"I thought you were just lagging, couldn't keep up." Del had pulled her boots off. Her socks were even worse than Lucy's. The heels were riddled with holes. Del peeled them away from her feet. She had two good blisters going. The skin was rubbed raw, and bubbles were forming. "Eww," she muttered, digging in her pack for a spare pair of socks.

Lucy felt a sympathetic twinge and turned her attention back to Aidan.

"So, a trail of bread crumbs?" she said.

"A little more permanent." He kneeled down by the edge of the slope and carefully piled two stones, one on top of the other. Lucy sat beside him.

"This identifies a trail." He placed another stone to the right of the pile. "This means turn to the right." He placed a third stone on top of the heap. "And this would be a warning."

"Pretty cool." She bent forward over the stones. "Where'd you learn it?"

"When I was a kid, Sammy and I used to leave each other messages on the road between the foster home and school. But we used tin cans and empty cigarette packs and stuff like that instead of rocks and sticks." Lucy danced her fingers over to where his hand lay. She held her breath.

He brushed her hair away from her cheek and lingered there, and she looked up at him.

Del groaned. Her head was down, her fingers tightening the ties of her backpack with what seemed to be unnecessary force. It might have been the blisters, or it might have been her way of expressing her opinion. In any case, Lucy and Aidan broke apart.

Aidan's eyes twinkled at her as he shouldered his bow.

Casting a quick glance to make sure Del looked ready, Lucy set off down the hill. For a while she was able to step down on a diagonal, zigzagging back and forth. When she reached the sharpest point of the incline, she carefully tossed her spear ahead, flipping it lengthwise and aiming for a patch of grass so as not to blunt the point. She turned to face the pitted rock wall. There were plenty of crannies to fit her fingers into, and the stone was rough enough for her boot soles to grip. The rock face was still warm from the day's sun, and she leaned into it, feeling the heat seep through her clothes. She hadn't realized how chilled she was. The night was not cold, but it was damp and it sank into her bones.

"I don't like this," Del said, just above her. Her boots scrabbled for a hold. A fine spray of dirt was knocked loose and floated into Lucy's eyes. She scrubbed the grit away. Del's limbs were extended like a starfish. She was frozen in place, holding on by determination alone. Aidan was about ten feet above her, but Lucy signaled to him to stay where he was.

The last thing Lucy needed was Del landing on her head. She forced her voice to be calm. "Tree root just past your right foot. If you feel dizzy, press against the wall for two or three breaths, but don't stop moving."

Del inched her foot sideways.

"Okay. Move your hands over, feel that bulge in the rock. You can hold on to that. Now reach down with your left foot. There's a ledge about two feet below you. Good. Grab the tree root. Now below the ledge is a thick patch of ivy. It's like climbing a rope ladder. You're doing great."

Lucy watched to make sure Del followed her instructions, and then climbed down the last twenty feet. From below she directed the other girl until she stood beside her on the grass. Del collapsed onto her back, her chest heaving, her fingers clutching the ground as if she would never let go.

"I feel like I just got my butt royally kicked," she groaned.

"It's easier going up," Lucy promised, watching Aidan.

Del rolled over onto her stomach. "Oh no. I'm not going back that way. Plus, we'll have the kids with us. We'll go the long way around." She raised her head. "The kids are the important thing." She said this with force.

"Of course," said Lucy, a bit surprised.

Aidan jumped down, brushing his hands on his jeans.

Lucy picked up her spear, checked to make sure the point hadn't been damaged in the fall. It was still sharp enough to draw blood from the pad of her thumb. Then she walked a dozen feet to where the next part of the hill sloped down gently. She caught her breath. Her shortcut had taken them in a straighter line than she'd expected.

Below them and only a mile away was what had once been Lucy's home. If she hadn't known exactly where she was—the southern face of the Great Hill with the giant stone needle, tilted now, and pointing at them like an accusatory finger—she wouldn't have recognized it. Mud was what it was mostly. An ocean of dry mud, strangely smooth and sculpted into drifts by wind and water. Edged with a white salt crust, like the frosting on a birthday cake. And in places were great troughs and gouges in the earth, where trees had been hurled like javelins by the wall of water. Broken limbs and bushes were tumbled together into rough fences, marking the highest points of the wave. There was an overpowering smell of brine and the stink of organic matter rotting in the sun.

Lake Harlem gleamed in the distance, and on the other side, flanking the land, pressing up against it, the Hudson Sea. Lucy shivered and drew her jacket close. She had never been scared of the water before. She'd loved it. It had fed her and it had offered her protection on two sides, but now she knew it was a huge living thing, and it could be merciless and unpredictable.

She was hardly aware of Aidan and Del as she made her way quickly down the long slope. Stumbling a little, bracing herself with her spear, she slid on the silted, sandy soil unfamiliar to her feet because it was fresh-laid, rootless, and as smooth as a cotton sheet. She stepped over a sodden mess of leaves, disturbing a cloud of small blackflies. This was where her doorway had stood. Two of Lucy's trees had been uprooted and flung far away. Of the two remaining, one leaned over almost flush with the ground, still alive, though, with fresh green growth along the horizontal length of the branch. And miraculously, the calendar tree was still standing. Its bark was blackened and scoured. The small crown of leaves at the top was curled and shriveled. She ran her fingers over the notches carved in the trunk, counting them silently. Thirteen. It had seemed much longer. Caught in the exposed roots and the drifts of earth she found a few of her pots and pans, dented and crushed.

"Smells like dead fish," Del said, kicking a saucepan lid.

Aidan shushed her.

"What?" she said, then followed his gaze to Lucy. "Oh."

Lucy took one more look around, patted the tree trunk, and faced the lake. They moved faster now, and no longer in single file but spread out. Their boots crunched through the crusty mud and the dried leaves. A low-lying mist wreathed their feet. The hulk of the Alice statue looked black under the stars. The water lapped just below the stiff bronze lace of her petticoats. They skirted the grove of trees where Lucy had first met Aidan. The only indication that the sea had reached this far was the curving tide line of pine needles and the residue of salt. A few of the smaller saplings lay tumbled like pick-up sticks. Lucy felt a chill run up her spine and realized she was braced for the sound of dogs howling, the quick thud of their paws. But it was quiet except for the skittering of small animals in the brush and the constant sound of water. They began the long trek across the mudflats.

Aidan spoke in a whisper. "I can see the tower light." He pointed. The red beam seemed to flicker through the tracery of clouds against the paling sky.

"If we head for that, we should end up at the bridge," Del said.

"You lead," Lucy said.

Del gnawed the tip of her thumb. "Last chance to back out," she said, and then laughed. It wasn't a happy sound, but forced. She adjusted her quiver so it hung within reach of her hand and tapped the string of her bow until it twanged. Feeling suddenly breathless, Lucy unzipped her jacket and felt inside, assuring herself that her knife was still in her pocket. Her grip on her spear was clammy. Her boots felt as if they were filled with concrete. The ground cover was almost nonexistent here. They'd be in the open. Dawn was coming, and the fog was starting to disperse. The red light blinked like the eye she'd imagined it to be. They should be crawling along the ground, not walking three abreast like this, as if they were on a Sunday stroll.

They reached the bridge. It joined up with the road to the left, and then rose out of the bank of mist and curved twenty feet above the lake at its highest point. That was where they would be the most visible even if they kept to the sides. It was wide enough for a vehicle, made of gray concrete with high steel guard rails and a box of welded steel at the end, which supported it. The fog made it appear as though it were a length of black silk unwinding in space. The three of them would look as if they were walking across the water, Lucy thought, peering ahead, and they would be highly visible.

The stone building, a low and squat block, and the tower, tall and angled, occupied most of the space on the island. A cistern dwarfed by the tower perched on the roof, and some thick pipes jutted out at the side. A whip of black smoke hung in the air. There were no trees, just vast half-moon parking lots in the front, completely empty of cars, and two narrow, rectangular lawns with a dozen park benches. Two or three tall streetlamps burned with a flickering orange light as if they were losing power. There were no lights on behind the windows. Lucy wondered where the white vans were kept. Maybe they were out on a sweep. She remembered the news footage from here. The hospital, with its gleaming floors, bright lights, hordes of doctors in white coats, and smiling nurses, had looked so different from the hospital her family had died in. That had been ill-lit, with gurneys crowded in the halls or pushed into alcoves, the smells of vomit and blood seeping into her nostrils, the floors filthy with soiled bedclothes and pillows piled in heaps in the corners, and rarely a doctor to be seen. Lucy had had to wander for hours searching for her parents, checking charts and toe tags, before grabbing a nurse and forcing her to help. The blood drummed in her head.

Del stepped onto the bridge first. "Let's go," she said. "We've got about an hour of dark left."

"Keep to the sides. Watch for headlights," Aidan said. "Once we're across, we'll make for the side entrance. Right, Del?"

She nodded. "That's the way I came out."

Lucy could hear the suppressed excitement in Aidan's voice. Was she the only one who was scared? She put her foot down hesitantly, as if she were afraid the bridge would crumble under her weight. She had never felt so terrified. They were on their way to a place where people disappeared without a trace. All except for Del, who'd managed to escape, and Leo, who'd basically been murdered. She tried to swallow past the dryness in her throat. Aidan glanced back at her and smiled. She hefted the spear to her left hand, and then switched it back.

Lucy forced herself to move, sliding her hand along the guardrail. She watched the mist swirl around her feet like a net. It reminded her of a nightmare, glue or quicksand trapping her as she tried to run. She looked back. The grove was in shadow. The salt-poisoned pines looked like skeletal fingers. The mudflats were as barren and pocked as the surface of the moon. And still she would rather have been back there than walking across this bridge, the sound of their boots muffled yet loud in the silence. There was a soft, strangling quality to the air. It felt heavy and dank, and it suffocated her like a tangle of blankets wrapped around her head.

Del had stopped at the point where the bridge began to arch down toward the island shore. When Lucy and Aidan were a couple of paces away she swiveled around to look at them, then turned back and narrowed her eyes. Her arms were wrapped around her body as though she was cold, or in pain. Her face was hidden.

"Why are you stopping?" Lucy whispered.

Del didn't answer her.

Lucy was conscious of an industrial hum coming from ahead. It throbbed, and she could feel it through the soles of her boots.

"Generator," said Del.

"Is the entrance to the left or right of the front door?" Aidan asked.

Del hunched her shoulders. She scrubbed one hand over her mouth. She was very pale. Before Lucy could say anything, she'd crossed to the rails opposite and leaned over the edge. They heard the sounds of her vomiting.

Aidan waited until the heaving had stopped and then walked over to her with the bottle of water in his hand. He held it out to her, standing silently while she drank and splashed her face with a little water. She took a deep breath.

"Are you all right?" Lucy started to say. Aidan shook his head.

"Right or left?" he asked Del again. She stared at him blankly, teeth gripping her bottom lip. Her hand was frozen against her face. Her fingers trembled.

"Right," she said, taking off so fast, her hood blew back.

Aidan and Lucy exchanged worried glances and followed.

Their steps echoed on the concrete. Del walked ahead with her head up, no attempt at concealment. She took a straight line across the parking lot, her shadow stretching ahead of her on the ground. Lucy reached into her jacket pocket and loosened the knife in its sheath. Her eyes darted everywhere looking for a flicker of movement, expecting at any moment to see the Sweepers in their white suits, and the dogs racing like specters toward them. She felt a clamminess grip the back of her neck. Only Aidan's presence by her side gave her the strength to continue.

Now they were crossing the lawn and all was silent again. Pools of darkness thrown by the sides of the building shrouded them. A caged light threw a feeble beam. Moths and mosquito hawks bumbled into it occasionally, combusting with tiny *pops* against the hot bulb. The door was directly beneath it, a plain steel door with a silver ball handle and a keyed lock above it. Del muttered something. Lucy watched as she reached out for the knob and twisted it. It clicked and the door swung open.

Inside there was a single light. A bare bulb, flickering and emitting an erratic hum like the rest of the lamps outside. A staircase wound upward like the inside of a conical seashell. Lucy smelled the tang of iodine and some kind of powerful cleaner.

"Three or four floors up," Del whispered, leading the way. Their steps echoed. The light behind them faded to a pinprick and then disappeared. Their breathing sounded as loud as the ocean. The dark, complete now, felt like a pulse against Lucy's skin, it was so thick and impenetrable. She walked with her hands in front of her face, as if she could push it away. They reached a landing, paused, unsure of which way to go. She felt Aidan on one side, Del on the other. She heard the click first, then the buzzing like a hundred angry bees. Powerful incandescent lights flashed on, blinding them.

CHAPTER SEVENTEEN
THE OCTAGON TOWER

"I'm sorry," Del said, and stepped away.

"Why—" Lucy started to ask.

More lights blazed, so bright and white they hurt Lucy's eyes. The generator grumbled and then hummed at full roar.

They stood on a large octagonal landing with doors leading off each of the sides. The stairway climbed on upward. At the very top was a skylight, and through it Lucy could see the last of the stars winking out in the dawn sky.

A woman in a white lab coat stepped through the door opposite them, followed by a troop of hazmat-suited Sweepers. Helmets shielded their faces, and they held Tasers pointed outward.

Aidan notched an arrow and trained it on the closest Sweeper. Lucy swung her spear into position. Del darted forward. Her bow came up and struck Lucy's spear so hard, she felt the vibration in her knuckles. The spear clattered to the ground. Lucy grabbed for it, crouching low, and Del's foot slammed down, crunching Lucy's wrist against the linoleum. With a cry, she pulled loose, ignoring the sting of chafed skin. Still on her knees, she lunged at Del, and the girl stepped back and to the side, easily evading her. Lucy stared up at her face. It was like a mask.

Two of the Sweepers moved closer, pinning Lucy against the stair railing. Blue flames surged and spat from the black boxes they held. One of them kicked her spear across the floor.

Aidan grunted. His bow swept from side to side as he tried to sight on a target and steadied at a point between a helmet visor and the collar of a man's suit. Lucy saw him blink as a drop of sweat trickled into his eye.

Del put her hand on his shoulder.

"It's not you they want. It's her." She faced the woman in the white coat.

"This is her, Dr. Lessing. This is Lucy Holloway."

Aidan moved in Lucy's direction.

Del gripped the hood of Aidan's sweatshirt and yanked him back toward her. He struggled to keep his bow steady. "What are you doing, Del?" he asked through clenched jaws.

"It's complicated," she told him. "But it's for a good reason, I swear. Please, Aidan." Her hands ran up and down his arms.

"No."

"She's just one girl. What does she matter?"

He shook her grip loose, shoved her backward with his shoulder. She hit the steel railing with a thud. Aidan's eyes were furious.

"I don't know you," he said.

A moan of pain escaped Del. She stood apart, rubbing her arm. She looked like she was on the verge of tears. With one last glance, she turned away from him.

"I brought her," she said to the woman. "Now, let the kids go. Like you promised!" She spat the last sentence out.

Dr. Lessing smiled and stepped forward. She swept her gaze over them. Her teeth were very even and small, her soft brown hair was pulled back in a neat bun, and her brown eyes seemed warm and friendly. She laughed. It was a merry sound, and it threw Lucy off balance. This woman reminded her of her favorite fourth-grade teacher.

"You're being overly dramatic, Delfina," she said. "As usual. The children are being well looked after. They've been awaiting your return, in fact." Her glance traveled from Aidan to Lucy. Del made an explosive sound of frustration.

"How quickly you've reverted to savages," the woman said in the same light tone. "There's an article in here somewhere. 'Primitive Response to Traumatic Stress Syndrome,' perhaps?" She sounded amused. "Your weapons are hardly necessary."

"What about the Tasers?" Aidan yelled. His arms were trembling with the effort of keeping his bowstring flexed. Beads of perspiration ran down his forehead.

Three of the Sweepers turned to face him. Dr. Lessing lifted her hand and looked toward the burly man standing to her left. His hands were bare. Lucy noticed the red hairs bristling from his knuckles and his chewed nails—small details that seemed magnified. She tried to see his face, but the visor was too dark. It was disorienting, like trying to see to the bottom of a murky pond. She could tell that the Sweeper standing on the other side was staring at her. A woman, she thought. Medium height, plump, the ends of her blond hair sticking out from under her helmet.

"Simmons," the doctor said. It sounded like an order, though she said no more than the man's name. The Sweeper with the red hair on his fingers jerked his head at the others. The other Sweepers stepped back, holding their semicircular formation.

"Better?" she asked. "Come, now. Surely we can be civilized? You haven't been living in the Wilds for so long?"

Lucy looked at Aidan. She was separated from him by twenty feet of gleaming marble tile floor. Two Sweepers still guarded her, their Tasers primed. They were so close, she could smell ozone frying. Del hovered next to the staircase leading down. Her bow was shouldered, the arrows stowed in her backpack. Lucy stared at her, willing the girl to meet her eyes. Del ducked her head. Her hair hung across her cheek. Tears tracked down her cheeks. Lucy felt no pity. She wondered how Aidan was feeling. One glance at his contorted expression was enough to tell her. He had gone red with anger, but as she watched him, his countenance whitened. She could see the muscles bunch in his jaw as he ground his teeth together.

She turned to face Dr. Lessing. Again the name stirred a memory. "What do you want with me?"

"I wanted to meet you. To talk with you."

"Why?"

Dr. Lessing smiled again. She smiled a lot. "There are things I'd like to ask you, but not here, standing in a foyer. Come to my office. I can make some coffee and we can chat."

Lucy glanced at Aidan, who had not lowered his weapon. "And what about them?"

"If they'd like to join us for coffee, that would be fine. Otherwise, Delfina can go."

"Aidan?"

"Aidan is supposed to come with me!" Del said.

"I'm not going anywhere with you." He cast her such a look of loathing that she backed up.

"We'd like to check Aidan. Make sure he's healthy. I can't help but notice he's favoring his left arm."

"Like you 'checked' Leo?" Lucy said.

Dr. Lessing spread her hands. "Leo was ill. He carried the plague, and it flared up. We tried to help him."

"That's crap and you know it!" Aidan said. "You attacked the camp!"

"We came to the camp to help you. We were attacked before we could explain."

"You brought weapons," Lucy pointed out.

"There are wild animals everywhere. You know that."

"People have been disappearing for months, and it all leads back to this place," Aidan said.

Dr. Lessing transferred her gaze to him. "Is this some kind of conspiracy theory?" she said gently. "Look at us. I am just one doctor. These people are here to keep the hospital and patients safe. Many of my staff lost loved ones. We help people; we don't harm them."

"Leo was healthy until he came here. He was the strongest person I knew."

"The disease lies dormant. In birds, in rats, in people. Sometimes for months. He was already too far gone. We tried to sedate him, but he fought, injured one of my men and got out of the building. He escaped into the Wilds, and we couldn't find him."

"He died," Lucy said. She had a sour taste in her mouth.

"I am sorrier than I can say," said Dr. Lessing.

"What about the dogs? You use dogs to hunt people," Aidan said. His grip on his bow faltered. With an effort he raised it up to his shoulder. The string pressed against his cheek, and Lucy saw the livid mark there, red against the whiteness around his lips.

"The dogs are a search-and-rescue team. They are trained to find people after a disaster. They track humans by the scent of their blood. It's quite amazing, really," she said with another wide smile. "They can detect the differences."

Lucy shook her head. She was too tired to figure out what was a lie and what was the truth. This woman had an answer for everything, and her voice was calm. She sounded concerned. She looked like someone you confided in.

"There really isn't much choice, Lucy. You're outnumbered, after all." She said this with another broad, white-toothed smile. She was teasing them.

"What'll happen to them if I go with you?"

"Delfina can go home right away. Aidan will be looked after, as I said before. We'll give him a thorough checkup. I'd hate to think the plague was incubating in your camp. There are all those children. Think what a tragedy it would be!"

Lucy hesitated. This rang true. Wasn't she worried that she might be a carrier herself?

Dr. Lessing nodded to Simmons. The Sweepers backed up even farther and lowered their Tasers.

"I just want to talk to you, Lucy," Dr. Lessing said. "You are a very special girl."

"Why do you say that?" Lucy said, suddenly nervous. Could they know that she hadn't been vaccinated?

"I know all about you," she said. "You're a survivor."

"Can I get the kids now?" Del demanded. Her nails were ragged horrors, the tender pads of her fingers torn and chewed.

"Of course," Dr. Lessing said. "You know the way, dear. Your friends will be right behind you. Emi and Jack are on the next floor down. They'll be so excited to see you. They've been ready since six o'clock this evening. So eager!" She laughed again. "Kelly, go with Delfina and help her, won't you?"

The blonde Sweeper stepped forward. She passed by quite close to Lucy, and once again she had the clear sense that the woman was staring at her from behind her dark visor.

Del muttered, "Del, not Delfina. You're not my friggin' mother." She cast one last, pleading look at Aidan, which he ignored, and ran down the stairs. They heard the intake of breath as she stumbled, the click of the door opening and then closing one floor down. Kelly followed at a slower pace.

Lucy didn't want to be separated from Aidan, but it seemed silly to insist on it after Dr. Lessing had shown them to two rooms adjoining each other. "Simmons is an EMT—one of two on my staff. Kelly is the other," she said, opening the closest door. Inside the small room was an examining table, an IV drip, cabinets, and an armchair. "He can check Aidan's arm. Or is it your ribs?"

"I just wrenched my shoulder," Aidan said. "Could have pulled a muscle," he admitted, opening and closing his fist. A flutter of pain crossed his face.

"He can make you more comfortable. Run a few tests." She looked into his eyes. "Does that sound feasible? It shouldn't take long, and then you can join us for coffee if you'd like. Or I'll send a cup in."

Aidan nodded.

"You can join us later," the doctor continued. "I'll leave the door to my office open."

Aidan shot Lucy a reassuring smile.

She reached out for his hand, moved closer, and spoke in a whisper. "This doesn't seem real. I feel like I'm dreaming. Can we trust her?"

"I'm not sure. See if you can get some answers."

Simmons had removed his helmet. He smoothed his hands over his bushy red hair and slipped his Taser into his pocket. He was younger than Lucy had expected. His face was pale and sweaty. The hazmat suit was zipped up tight under his chin, and the skin above it was red and angry-looking, as if he had heat rash. It was warm inside the building. She felt the lining of her jacket stick to her skin.

Simmons cleared his throat. "You can put your bow and your backpack just there on the chair, Aidan." And he waved him into the examining room.

"Come along, Lucy," Dr. Lessing said. Lucy entered a room furnished with a large wooden desk, a tall cabinet, and a couple of deep, upholstered armchairs. A thick carpet in rich hues of red and gold covered the floor. It was a comfortable room, but Lucy could smell the strong odor of cleaning fluid and other odors, antiseptic and medicinal. It seemed to permeate everything. And it was chilly, a shock after the humidity on the landing.

"Have a seat," Dr. Lessing said, propping the door open. Her gaze never left Lucy's face, and she frowned as if she were concentrating on a puzzle.

Lucy took the seat closest to the hallway so that she could keep an eye on the closed door of the examining room where Aidan was. She pushed her backpack under the chair. She looked around. The walls were bare and painted white. Floor to ceiling built-in shelves, also painted white, were filled with a collection of wide-spined books covered in red leather. Medical books, Lucy guessed. Off to the side, a door opened onto a closet-sized space with a narrow cot bed. Heavy curtains were drawn over the windows, which she guessed looked out on the parking lots and the bridge. The thought that Dr. Lessing could have been sitting here in the dark, watching them sneak across it made her feel jumpy.

The doctor seemed nice enough, though. Lucy watched her as she busied herself at the countertop behind her desk. An electric kettle whistled. The air conditioner rattled and wheezed. The air tasted metallic. The drone of the generator was just background noise now and hardly registered. Lucy tried to remember what it would be like to live with electricity, but failed. She wondered if the hospital staff listened to music, had dance parties on Saturday nights. It didn't seem likely.

The two desk lamps felt too bright to her. She was used to the small dancing flames of the lanterns and the steady orange glow of a campfire.

"It's only instant, I'm afraid," Dr. Lessing said and turned around with two steaming mugs. "Artificial creamer?"

Lucy shook her head and accepted the cup.

Dr. Lessing sat down behind her desk. "I miss cows, don't you?"

"I guess," said Lucy. She missed donuts and her family. Mostly her family. And feeling safe.

She took a sip of her drink. It was searingly hot and very sweet. The doctor had added sweetener without asking her. In the past she drank it black and unsweetened, but coffee, even this chalky, sugary mixture, was coffee. And it was comforting.

She blew on it, watching the woman from behind the rim of the cup.

Dr. Lessing put her cup down on a neatly folded square of tissue paper and opened a drawer to her right. She pulled out a thick folder. Lucy leaned forward. Coffee slopped over the edge of her mug, splashing onto her leg. She yelped. Dr. Lessing looked up momentarily. A little frown creased her forehead and then smoothed itself. Lucy recognized the folder. It was hers, from the nurse's office at school. And now she remembered Dr. Lessing's name from the reports inside. The school nurse, Mrs. Reynolds, had sent all the blood tests here.

"Why do you have that?" Lucy asked. The coffee wasn't waking her up. Just the opposite. She felt like curling up in this soft chair and taking a nap. She forced herself to sit straight. "Did the school send it to you? Why?" She peered at it. There were pages covered in small, precisely written words. It was much bulkier than before.

Dr. Lessing closed the folder and pressed her palms flat against it. She stroked it and smiled. "They did so many tests on you, Lucy. Did you know? A veritable plethora, looking for the usual things: heightened immunity, some kind of increased antibody production, excessive white blood cells, excessive red blood cells. And then they got creative with it. The most far-fetched possibilities were considered, but there was nothing." Her fingertips caressed the folder as if it were a cat. Her smile didn't waver. "They died without ever finding out. I can't imagine anything more frustrating." Her eyes lingered on Lucy's face. A spasm flickered across her eyelid.

Lucy swallowed the gulp of coffee she'd been holding in her mouth. She sputtered as it went down the wrong way. A tiny thread dribbled down her chin. Dr. Lessing handed her a tissue from the box on her desk.

"Am I sick?" Lucy asked in a whisper.

Dr. Lessing tapped her lip with a pen.

"Your parents didn't vaccinate you."

It sounded like an accusation.

"Yeah, I guess," Lucy said. "I had an older brother who died from an allergic reaction when he was a baby."

The doctor's mouth pursed. Her eyes narrowed. She seemed to be looking at something that was far off in the distance. Lucy shifted in her chair. She finished the rest of her coffee, so hungry she even drank the thick syrup at the bottom, and held the mug in her hands. "You didn't answer me," she finally said. "Am I sick?"

"I didn't believe it at first, but the tests corroborate it completely. You're an anomaly. You shouldn't exist." She slapped the folder so hard, it made Lucy jump. "But you do!"

"What does it mean?"

Dr. Lessing got to her feet in a quick, smooth motion. She walked to the window, pulled the curtain aside. The sun was coming up, flushing the concrete parking lot with pink and gold light. "It means," she said, "I've searched for you for a long time, Lucy Holloway. I almost got you at the Midtown shelter, but you vanished." She frowned. "And then Del mentioned your name while I was asking her a few general questions about the settlement. Such an unbelievable stroke of luck. I don't think she likes you much, by the way. It took some convincing, but she eventually saw that it was the right choice to bring you here."

"She didn't escape," Lucy said, suddenly sure of it. "You let her go."

"She's a capable girl, that one. A little vindictive, but trustworthy, and her heart's in the right place." She swung around. "She'd do anything for the little ones, you know. Quite motherly, although she doesn't look it."

"She's a rat."

Dr. Lessing laughed. "She was stuck between Charybdis and Scylla."

"Whatever."

Lucy didn't care much about Del anymore.

"I don't understand," she said. "The blood tests and all that, that's in the past."

"Somehow, within your body, within your blood, you have

the ability to withstand a disease that killed almost everyone on Earth. I'd say that's still relevant, wouldn't you?"

"Yes, but the plague is over." *But then what about Leo?* She shifted again, pressing her spine to the back of the chair. Her brain was so slow and her eyes felt gritty. She wanted to close them. "I mean, it won't ever come back like before. Will it?" She tried to sit up straighter, but her spine felt like a limp noodle.

"You're missing the point. The answer is what is important. A scientist can't rest until she has the answer."

Rest. That's what she needed. Just a little nap maybe, and then she'd get Aidan and they'd go home.

Dr. Lessing opened the cabinet. It had plain wooden doors on the outside and looked like it belonged in a kitchen to hold plates and dishes, but its interior was more like a refrigerator. Tubes and vials fitted into individual slots and racks. Some were filled with a clear liquid, others with red. There were hundreds of them. She picked up a tube and tilted it. The lamplight turned it into gooey paint.

"What are all those?" Lucy asked. She rubbed her eyes, stifled a yawn. Her eyelids fluttered and then opened again. She was so tired.

"Answers . . . questions . . ." Dr. Lessing murmured. She turned suddenly and stared at Lucy. Her smile was gone. "Every answer fits into a box, and that leads to the next question. That is what is so perfect about science. We can be methodical about it. Blood. Plasma. Serums. Vaccines. The answer is in the blood."

Lucy had heard that before. It was a creepy phrase and it had stuck in her head. She tried to remember who had said it. Her mind was sluggish. She gripped the arms of the chair, tried to clear the fog. *Leo!* Leo had said the same thing.

"Leo!" she said out loud.

Dr. Lessing was suddenly just above her, so close Lucy could see the large pores on her nose, could hear her breathing, heavy and quick, and smell mint candy. The doctor's soft brown eyes were now hard as pebbles.

"Everything fits, except for you," Dr. Lessing said. "You should want to help. With your blood, I can synthesize a vaccine. A synthetic duplicate. Even if the disease mutates, I'll be able to control it."

"I don't care. I don't want to be a lab rat. It's my choice, not yours."

"It's an opportunity to help so many people and to keep us safe in the future."

Her voice sounded like it was coming from far away.

"What did you put in the coffee?" Lucy said. It was difficult to push the words past her lips. Her tongue felt thick.

Her head snapped back, whacking against the chair. Her eyes flew open. Suddenly, she felt as if she were falling from a great height. She struggled to stay awake, but it was impossible. She was drowning, so heavy in her body that she couldn't help but be pulled under.

Just before her eyes closed for the last time, she heard Dr. Lessing call out to someone unseen: "Kelly, can you please take this cup of coffee to Aidan?"

CHAPTER EIGHTEEN
IN THE BOX

Lucy woke up. The inside of her mouth felt like it was stuffed with cotton, and her head pounded with a dull pain that started behind her eyes and continued to the base of her neck. She'd felt the same way after her wisdom teeth had been pulled. She pressed her thumbs into the flesh of her temples, and then rubbed her fingers over her forehead. The pain didn't lessen. Her hair felt like one matted clump on top of her head. Her legs and arms were heavy and almost impossible to move. With an effort, she rolled over and opened her eyes. The faint glow cast by a recessed light showed the white walls of a small room, the bed she was lying on, a small metal nightstand with a plastic pitcher and cup, and a tall bucket in the corner. There was a tiny window high up, and the door was closed.

She swung her legs around, put her feet to the linoleum floor. It was cold. Her arms felt stiff and they hurt. Lucy peeled back her shirtsleeves and stared at a trail of new puncture marks that ran up the undersides of both forearms. There were four or five on each arm, and every hole was circled by bruised skin.

Her head spun. She closed her eyes and bit down on her lip, hard enough to make her eyes tear. She would not faint. She would not vomit. She poured herself a glass of water. It was tepid and tasted unpleasant, but it soothed her dry throat. She stood up. The dizziness rushed back and then ebbed. Her bare feet slapped against the tiles as she walked to the door. She twisted the handle. It was locked from the outside. She pressed her hands against it. It was made of steel and was cold against her palms. She clenched her fists and hammered them against the unyielding metal.

Her boots stood against the wall, her socks balled neatly beside them.

She put on her socks and boots. She kicked the door. Finally she gave up. Her toes hurt, her wounded palm throbbed. It was then she noticed that it had been neatly bandaged. A square, flesh-colored adhesive.

"Dr. Lessing," she yelled. She kept yelling for a few minutes.

Lucy got down on the floor and tried to look underneath the door. It was flush with the linoleum. She ran her fingers along the crack in the doorjamb. She could see the tongue of the bolt lock. Maybe she could jimmy it open. She didn't have anything, but . . . her knife! Was her knife still inside her jacket pocket? She scrambled to her feet and went to the bed. She felt the lump from the outside of the jacket, pulled it out, and ran back to the door. She slid her knife in and eased it down until she felt the top of the bolt, then jiggled it gently. She thought it gave a little. She pushed down harder, wiggled the blade to the side. Metal slid on metal. She twisted and pushed at the same time. With a squeal the knife snapped. She was left with three inches of rough blade, a hilt-heavy thing that felt clumsy and unbalanced in her hand. Her father's knife.

The tears took her by surprise. Hot, they exploded out of her, ripping through her rib cage. When they ceased, she was exhausted. She lay down on the floor, her useless knife clasped between numb fingers. And the door—the door was closed as tightly as ever. The room seemed too small. It didn't have enough air in it, and her lungs couldn't get a full breath. She felt the walls pressing down on her.

The window. It was at least fifteen feet above her. She could tell that even by standing on the bed she wouldn't be able to reach it, even if she could somehow stack the side table onto the bed and then clamber up on top of it without breaking her neck. And it looked too small to squeeze her shoulders through, anyway.

She paced, feeling the frustration well up in her until she was sure she would explode with it. She sank down onto the bed. It felt weird being so far from the ground. She pulled the covers off and heaped them in the corner. She curled up on top of them, shrugged her arms into her leather jacket, and yanked a rough blanket up to her chin. She turned her knife over and over in her hands. The blade was toothed now, two spikes of metal with a sharp edge. Sooner or later Dr. Lessing would come, and she would jump on her and press the knife to her neck and get out of this box.

She slept fitfully, with her knees tucked in and her sore arms folded across her head. The blanket was scratchy and thin and smelled of detergent. She drifted in and out of sleep. The air conditioner was loud. The rattle of the generator, thrumming far below her as it surged and quieted again, kept her on the edge of wakefulness. And the electric light, weak though it was, shone down on her. She'd looked for a switch but the walls were bare. She worried about Aidan. What had they done with him? Was he still next door? She scratched at the wall with her fingernail, tapped out a sequence, wishing she knew Morse code or something. Aidan probably knew secret codes, like he knew about trail markers and how to make bows, but it was no good, anyway. Either he couldn't hear her or he wasn't there. She pressed her ear against the wall and slipped into unconsciousness again.

The fumbling noise at the door woke her. She dragged herself upright and then to her feet. Her right hand was behind her back, holding the knife ready. It was still dark outside. She moved forward and to the side of the door, where shadows offered some concealment. It opened outward, and she planned to rush whoever was coming through it, kicking and screaming, punching and stabbing, if that's what it took. The idea crossed her mind that it might be a Sweeper with a Taser. The thought of that bolt of electricity made her shudder with fear. She tightened her grip on her knife. Her eyes were glued to the door handle. She heard the click as the lock disengaged, the handle turned, and the door swung open slowly. Lucy balanced with her weight forward on her toes, ready to spring.

Someone stepped into the room. Her eyes registered black clothing and then she was on him, her weight knocking the person to the floor in the office beyond. They were in darkness except for a desk lamp. She brought her knife up, ready to plunge it down.

"Tell me what's going on," she said, "or I'll kill you."

The figure beneath her struggled. She pushed her weight down. Her left arm was pressed against what she thought was his neck. The clothes were voluminous, black, his face covered by a hood, and now, as she leaned in closer with the knife, she saw a weird smoothness, an emptiness where the face should be. His legs drummed against the floor. A strangled sputter erupted from his mouth. Never moving the knife, she relaxed her arm somewhat.

"Lucy," he gasped. "You're choking me."

"What?" she said, recognizing Sammy's voice. She rolled off of him, then held out her hand to help him up. "What are you doing prancing around in the dark?"

He pushed his black mask down so it hung around his neck. His red eyes blinked away tears. His hand massaged his throat.

She was so glad to see him, she threw her arms around him and gave him a big hug.

"I wasn't prancing," Sammy said over her shoulder. "Del and I came to rescue you."

Lucy jerked away. She felt the dull thud of anger again.

"Del!" she said. "Rescue us? She's the reason we're here. She led us into a trap."

He shook his head. "Me and Henry tried to follow you guys. It was pretty hard going until I spotted some of Aidan's trail markers. We met up with her by the Needle. She had Lottie and Patrick with her. Henry took them back to the camp, and we continued on. Del insisted on coming back even though she's so exhausted she can hardly walk."

Lucy closed her ears to the note of sympathy in his voice.

"Where is she now? How do you know she isn't raising the alarm?"

"I know her," he said. Oddly, it was the exact opposite of what Aidan had said on the stairs when they realized Del had tricked them.

"If she gets in my way, I'll hurt her," Lucy promised. "You bring weapons?"

He showed her a small knife and a hammer. He grinned. The knife had a curved blade and looked wickedly sharp.

"Nice tiny sickle," she said sarcastically. "You plan the whole look with the robes and the mask and everything?"

He pulled the mask up over his head and stowed it in a hidden pocket under his robes.

"Just working the plague victim–grim reaper angle. In case I run into anyone. You'd be amazed the effect a simple black cloak can have." A broad smile spread across his charred face. "It's a billhook, though. Sickles are those long cut-your-head-off tools. Wish I had one of those."

"All kidding aside. Are you prepared to use it?" she asked.

He looked serious. She saw his throat work and wondered if his mouth was as dry as her own.

"I guess so. You?"

"I will if I have to," she said, realizing it was true.

She slipped her knife into her pocket, then closed and locked the door to the sleeping chamber. The door out to the hallway was shut. Everything was quiet. Gray light leaked through the thick curtains.

"Do you have any idea what time it is?" she asked.

"About eleven thirty, midnight," he said.

"Of the day after we left?"

He nodded. "What's up with you? You seem kind of out of it."

No wonder she still felt groggy. She tried to do the math. The sleeping pills had put her out for about sixteen hours. "I'll be okay," she said. "I'm still lively enough to take you down."

"You jumped me from behind," he said, with a hurt expression.

"I don't think anyone's going to be playing fair here, so be prepared for some dirty fighting." She looked around the room. "See anyone on your way up?" she asked.

He shook his head. "All clear. The dogs were barking up a storm. Maybe they smelled me."

"They're locked up somewhere though, right?"

"Basement, I think. Del said something about kennels."

Lucy hurried over to the desk. Her backpack was still under the chair. She slipped the straps over her shoulders and looked around for her frog spear. It was nowhere to be seen. She remembered how Del had knocked it out of her hands and she knotted her fists.

Her medical folder was still centered carefully on the desktop. Behind it stood the refrigerated cabinet. Lucy stared at the papers—so much information gathered about her without her knowledge. It was weird. And there were probably at least eight new vials of her blood stored in the refrigerator. She felt sick. Although she'd told Dr. Lessing how she felt, the woman had still gone ahead with her plan. She had taken away Lucy's ability to choose. Lucy rubbed her arms, felt the prickle of new scabs.

"Del's getting the rest of the kids. Do you know where Aidan is?" Sammy asked.

"I'm hoping he's still next door. There may be someone with him. But give me a minute, will you? It's important."

Sammy cast a look around. "Listen," he said. "I didn't see anyone on the way up, but this place must have guards, right?"

"There aren't so many of them anymore. I think a few have bailed. Maybe ten total. They won't be expecting a rescue mission." She rested her hand on his arm. "This is seriously important."

He nodded. "Okay, but be quick. This place gives me the creeps."

She stood still, willing her brain to work. It wasn't fair. She wanted to have the choice to decide what to do with her life. But perhaps this was a gift, and it was bigger than she was? She thought of her parents, her sister and brother, of Leo and the terrible pain he had suffered. Maybe if a cure made from her blood had existed they would still be alive. Of course, she argued, if Dr. Lessing hadn't infected Leo in some mad experiment, he'd never have gotten sick. Figuring out the morality of the doctor's motivation was impossible. There was some single-minded craziness going on there, she was sure of it.

But Lucy *could* make a difference.

There were vials of her blood in the refrigerator, and she remembered the doctor saying something about a synthetic duplicate. The question was, what should Lucy do about it?

She moved around to the front of the desk. A white lab coat draped over the chair smelled of Mercurochrome and rubbing alcohol and evoked Dr. Lessing as clearly as if she were standing there. Lucy felt a flutter of fear. Looking increasingly nervous, Sammy followed her over to the desk. Lucy flipped open the front cover of the folder. There was the photo, beginning to fade now. Her hair longer. Her face younger. High school seemed centuries ago. Words jumped out at her.

"Subject shows natural resilience to the highest degree. Possible living source of Mother Vaccine. Risk of death to the subject from controlled blood extraction — 97.2%."

"God," Lucy said. Her hand started shaking.

"What's all this medical mumbo jumbo?" Sammy asked, poking his finger at the page.

"It's all about me, Sammy. My blood."

"Yeah, right," he said. "Why would they have a file like this on you? There must be a hundred pages. What's your blood made of? Twenty-four karat gold?"

She shook her head.

"We have to destroy this stuff." She picked up the folder. It was heavy; the papers spilled from it. She kneeled and picked them up. There was a report from when she'd sliced open her calf running through the glass door. There were even the results from the mandatory state physicals all students had to take. Her entire physical history, gathered in one place. *I'll take it with me*, she decided. She pulled opened the rest of the drawers. They slid easily on metal runners. More folders filed neatly. Unfamiliar names. She wondered if any were kids like her, before remembering that the doctor had called her an anomaly. Lucy ignored them, moving on to a thin stack of notebooks covered in Dr. Lessing's neat handwriting. She opened one, scanned the pages, filled with numbers and strange symbols, reams of medical language she couldn't begin to understand, and some diary-like entries, which seemed oddly personal. Lucy's name leapt off of the pages. Opening her backpack, she stashed them and her medical folder inside. Then she turned to the cabinet holding the samples. It stood as tall as she was. She opened the door and gazed at the rows of glass vials glistening like rubies. There were ten neatly labeled with her name.

She could destroy them; it would be easy. But she hesitated. Insane as Dr. Lessing seemed, she was trying to protect the human race.

"Whoa," said Sammy. He kept an eye on the door.

Lucy spared a glance for him. "This is evil stuff, Sammy. That's my blood in there, and who knows what else."

His teasing expression turned serious.

"Okay. Finish what you've got to do, and then let's find Aidan and get out of here."

Lucy debated. She picked up one of the tubes and held it in her hand. If a cure really did reside in her blood, then it would be wrong not to give that much at least. She tried to see past the emotional, the feeling that she had been violated, and the knowledge that she had been drugged against her will. With a sigh, she closed the cabinet door. Hardly knowing why, she decided to take one and leave the rest.

She opened her backpack and placed the vial inside her tinderbox, padding it with her spare socks. Then she shrugged her arms through the backpack straps and felt the cumbersome weight settle against her back.

"Come on," she whispered.

Lucy opened the door and peered into the hallway. It was empty and quiet except for the weird clicking noises the turned-off air conditioner made. She unlocked, then twisted the knob of the adjacent door. It opened with a creak that set her muscles jumping. The scent of antiseptic was very strong. The room was darker, but she could just make out the shrouded form on the gurney. Plastic IV bags hanging from the stand dripped a viscous liquid, and clear tubes snaked beneath the sheets.

Sammy, close at her heels, flipped on the light. The sudden blaze threw everything into stark relief. Lucy froze, her heart pounding. "God, can you stop doing stuff without warning!" she snapped. "We're supposed to be stealthy," she continued in a furious whisper. The figure on the bed groaned. Lucy sprang forward, tripping in her haste. Her boots squealed on the shiny floor. She caught Sammy's smirk and ignored it.

Aidan lay on his back. His T-shirt was damp with sweat. His eyes were open, but they were bleary. He blinked, shaking his head as if to clear it.

"Aidan," she said, bending over him. A tube ending in a needle ran into the small veins of his hand, another into the larger vein of his forearm. The liquid they carried was clear. They weren't bleeding him. They were doing something else. Lucy frowned. She couldn't think about it now. They would get him out first. She clawed at the covers. Someone had tucked him in tight.

"Here, let me," Sammy said, putting his arm around Aidan's shoulders and heaving him upright. The blankets fell to the floor. He was still wearing his jeans and socks. Lucy looked around quickly and located his boots and sweatshirt on the chair. His bow and quiver were gone.

Aidan blinked again. "Lucy. Sammy," he said in a rough voice. "I'm feeling a little sick." His head slumped forward. His breathing was labored.

Lucy ripped the needle out of his hand. He groaned again. A trickle of blood leaked from the wounds.

"You going to be sick?" Sammy asked him.

"No."

"Good."

Sammy slapped him across the face. The crack was shockingly loud.

"What are you doing?" Lucy said, trying to get her arms around Aidan. She could feel a bandage of some kind wrapped tightly around his shoulder and ribs.

"He's got to snap out of it," Sammy said, his fingers busy with the tape holding the second, thicker needle in his brother's vein. He ripped it off and slid the needle out.

Aidan's eyes were open now, and they did seem clearer. He swung his legs over the side of the gurney.

"Remind me I owe you one later," he told his brother with a grimace. "What the heck are you doing here, anyway? Didn't I tell you to stay at the camp?"

"Didn't you always tell me to question authority?" Sammy pulled his hood down lower. "Besides, if I hadn't shown up, you guys would still be locked up. So now that I have rescued you, why don't you get a move on so we can get out of here already? Or are you just going to lie around?"

Lucy glared at him. He grinned back at her.

"He's right. We should go. I'm okay," Aidan said to Lucy, squeezing her hand. "Just a little woozy."

"Are you sure?" she asked, smoothing his hair down.

"Yes."

"What were they injecting you with?"

He shrugged. "He took some blood first. After he checked my arm. Pulled muscle, maybe a cracked rib," he said in answer to his brother's querying look. "I think the small IV was a painkiller. The big one. I'm not sure."

Lucy gasped.

"I saw the bottles of medicine," he said. "They were legit. Sealed. Big pharmaceutical names. It could have been an anticoagulant, so I'd bleed quicker. The nurses always had a hard time getting blood out of me. They said my veins were buried too deep. Remind me to ask Henry when I see him next."

"You don't feel like you might be getting sick?" Lucy asked, pressing her hand against his forehead. It was clammy, but not warm. There was no air conditioner, and the room was humid.

"No. I remember drinking some really bad coffee. It must have had six spoonfuls of sugar in it. And then passing out." He rubbed the puncture in his arm. The wounds in Lucy's arm stung in sympathy.

"There were sleeping pills in the coffee," she said. "If you walk around a little you'll feel better."

He took a deep breath, and cautiously probed his ribs. Lucy didn't miss the grimace that flickered across his face.

"Are you sure you're okay?" she asked him again quietly.

With a brief nod, Aidan stood up. "That guy, Simmons, taped me up pretty good." He frowned. "It's weird. I mean, are they bad guys or good guys or what?"

"I vote bad," Lucy said. She brought his boots to him, pushed his fumbling hands away when he tried to lace them, and did it herself. While she was pulling them tight, Sammy brought him up to speed.

"Del came back?" Aidan asked, his face serious. Lucy couldn't read his expression.

"She's getting the other kids out," Sammy said. "Two floors down. Emi and Jack."

The kids who'd been taken in the first raid, Lucy remembered.

"So what's the plan?"

"The plan?" asked Sammy. He rubbed his chin. "To get out of here as fast as possible. Meet up if we can. We didn't have much time to come up with anything." He grinned. "This seems to be working pretty well so far."

"Weapons?"

"I've got my broken knife," Lucy said. "Sammy's got a bill-hook. And a hammer."

Aidan's green eyes opened wide. He looked more awake. His lip curled. "A hammer?"

"It's heavy. It's blunt. It's all we've got," Lucy said. She went to the door, put her ear against it, and listened.

Aidan made a face.

"Well, where's your bow, your slingshot?" Sammy asked him.

"They must have taken them."

"So a hammer doesn't seem like such a bad thing anymore, then, does it?"

"Not if we meet a loose nail or a hanging shutter."

"Stop bickering and get over here," Lucy hissed. "Sammy, give Aidan the hammer."

She flicked the light switch off and eased the door open. The foyer was empty.

"Quickest way out?" Aidan whispered.

"Side door?" Sammy said with a shrug. "That's how Del and I got in."

"Us, too."

"Four floors down," Lucy said.

"Guards?"

She shrugged.

"Likely, then."

She gripped her knife. "Quiet now."

The recessed lights high above them must have been on a dimmer switch. It took a minute for her eyes to adjust to the murk, but she could see the glimmer of the floor tile and the sheen of the metal handrail, which followed the curve of the spiral staircase. She felt Aidan behind her. Sammy, to her right, grumbled to himself, and she nudged him sharply. "Shhhh!"

"I turned the alarm off, but there's a number code for the door lock," a voice said. A shadow on the far side of the corridor peeled itself away and stepped toward them. Lucy froze.

CHAPTER NINETEEN

KELLY

Although the light was dim, Lucy recognized the form of the blonde Sweeper, Kelly. Dr. Lessing's second in command. Lucy sucked in a breath and curled her fingers around the hilt of her knife. Beside her, Sammy and Aidan tensed. Kelly walked forward and showed her hands. They were empty. No Taser. She was wearing regular clothes, a button-down blouse and jeans. Her hair was tucked behind one ear, and on the other side it hung loose, draping her face.

"Keep your hands where we can see them," Sammy said in a deeper voice than usual. He had the billhook out. His hand trembled.

"You can't stop us," Lucy said. "We'll . . . kill you if you try." She eyed the staircase. It was between them. She thought they could tackle Kelly before she could reach the first step. "If you make a sound, you'll be sorry." She pointed the ruined knife and ignored the small voice in her brain that wondered if she had enough blade left to stab someone—and the will to do it. Maybe Kelly would think the tremors shaking her hands were barely suppressed rage.

"Every door has a numeric locking code, and there's a building-wide security check done at midnight, so you won't be able to get back out again without help," the woman said. Somehow her voice was familiar to Lucy. It nagged at her memory. She cudgeled her brain, but her thoughts were still muddied by the drugged coffee.

"We want to leave," said Aidan. "You'll help us get out of here?"

"Yes."

"Why?"

"Lucy."

Lucy forced herself to take a couple of steps. She squinted

into the faint light, trying to see the woman. "Who are you?" she said.

Kelly turned toward them. Her right eye was surrounded by grafts of too-pink flesh, the tint of a pencil eraser. Lucy caught a gleam of a milky pupil and a cheek, cratered and pockmarked and covered in flesh-colored makeup.

The other half of Kelly's face was normal: skin pale and even, her left eye, bright blue. The round-collared cotton shirt she wore was as neat and white as the uniform Lucy had last seen her in; only the wreck of her face spoke of the months that had passed. Time seemed to shift backward. In her mind, Lucy could hear the nurse's measured tones warning of the pinch of the needle, feel the rubber tubing tied tight around her biceps, smell the pine-scented cleanser the school janitors used. Automatically she looked down at the woman's feet, expecting to see the standard issue white brogues, but they had been replaced by gray cross-trainers.

"Mrs. Reynolds!" Lucy said. "I don't understand. What happened to you?"

"Who is that?" asked Aidan, sidling up beside her. He wasn't too steady on his feet. Sammy, one step behind, gripped his elbow.

"The nurse from my high school."

The generator started up its slow grumble again. Frigid air blew from the vents. Lucy felt the skin on her arms rise up in goose pimples. *Equal parts chill and fear,* she thought.

Mrs. Reynolds had moved closer. Now she stood with her good eye facing them.

"What happened?" Unconsciously, Lucy's hand, the one not gripping her knife in a death hold, flew up to her cheek, felt the reassuring smoothness of her skin. Immediately she was embarrassed. The woman's scars were horrifying. In the light, she could see that the nurse's right eye was opaque with a bluish cast. Blind.

"The plague. The risk of nursing sick people."

Lucy's chest contracted in pity. It was awful, but she had to remember the circumstances. Mrs. Reynolds was in this place. Which made her an enemy. She flexed her fingers and tightened her grip on her knife.

"And what are you doing here?"

"I work here," Mrs. Reynolds said.

"For her?"

"It's complicated. Dr. Lessing is . . . she . . . she saved my life. Everyone here owes her a debt of some kind. The work she's doing is important."

"So are you here to convince me to just give up everything?" To her horror, Lucy found that she was crying. Seeing the nurse was a jarring reminder of her life before.

"No, I'm not. You'll have to trust me."

"Crap," Lucy mumbled, swiping her streaming nose against her sleeve. She looked up at Aidan. His face was shocked. She gave herself a mental shake and raised the knife.

"You all right?" he asked.

"Yeah." Lucy transferred her attention back to the nurse. "If that's true and you want to help us, get us out of here now."

Without a moment's hesitation, the nurse said, "Okay."

They crept down the stairs, their boots slapping against the hard marble. Mrs. Reynolds led them quickly, sure-footed in the gloom. Her sneakers were silent. Lucy glanced over the railing. The hallway far below was in complete darkness. It looked like a bottomless hole.

One floor down, then two. She could barely discern the outlines of doors leading to unknown rooms. No light gleamed from the cracks under the doors. She wondered if the other Sweepers were sleeping. The air conditioner had shut itself off again, and the generator was quiet. All was silent but for the puff of their breathing and the faint squeaks of rubber soles.

Slowly, Lucy's eyes adjusted to the dark. The steep stairs became more distinct. There were different grades of black, shades of gray. She quickened her pace, holding on to the railing in case she stumbled. Aidan and Sammy were right behind her.

Lucy could see the front door now. It was massive, steel, with a gleaming column of locks and bolts on one side and a heavy chain looped across it. They should have been suspicious when they'd come and found the place open, should have known it was a trick. People like this didn't leave their doors unlocked.

"Break to the right once you're outside," Mrs. Reynolds said in a low voice. "The floodlights only illuminate the immediate area around the front entrance. If you stick to the edges, you'll be practically invisible."

Lucy hesitated. She didn't know what to say.

"Just go. Once you're through the door, run as fast as you can."

Lucy hurried toward the door. Her hand reached up to pull the chain free and to click back the first of the deadbolts. The nurse, her shoulder pressed up against Lucy's, tapped a sequence of numbers into a keypad. A red light turned to green. Lucy tried not to stare at the ravaged cheek so closely. She fumbled with the heavy bolt. It was stiff and she needed both hands to pull it back. But what to do with her knife? She didn't dare put it down.

She felt the rush of cold air against her back first. An inner door had opened somewhere. Then the scuffle of heavy steps came out of the darkness behind them. She whirled around. Prepared for the suddenness of blinding lights, she pressed her free hand to her forehead and shielded her eyes. Even so, when the switches were thrown, the glare from the fluorescent tubes was dazzling. Lucy blinked furiously to sharpen her vision. Sammy had fallen back, his hood pulled over his black mask. Aidan braced himself. His eyes cut left and right looking for an escape route, but they were trapped.

At the corner of her field of vision, Lucy saw Mrs. Reynolds draw away from them. *So much for her help,* Lucy thought. *We should have threatened her. Taken her hostage.* She pressed up against the door, feeling the heavy bolts against her spine, searching for some way out. The foyer split into two corridors, which threaded around behind the steps. She didn't know if they linked up or meandered in opposite directions. She knew the facility was huge, complex.

"Why are you acting like this?" Dr. Lessing said in her calm voice. She rested her hand against the steel banister. Her hair was no longer contained in a neat bun. She had it tucked behind her ears. Her lab coat was unbuttoned as if she had just thrown it on, and she wore blue slippers on her feet.

"Guests don't sneak out like furtive thieves in the night," she continued. "I'm disappointed in you, Lucy and Aidan. I thought we were being honest with one another." The cool gray-painted stone walls picked up her words and threw them back again. The echoes were disorientating. Her gaze lingered on Sammy's form, and a frown appeared momentarily on her forehead. His eyes glittered through the sockets of his mask.

"Who is that?"

"My brother," said Aidan. "He thought he'd come and check up on us."

"At one o'clock in the morning?"

"He couldn't wait."

"And is the costume in keeping with the rest of the theatrics you all seem partial to?"

Sammy pulled his hood lower. Aidan said nothing.

Dr. Lessing broke out into a peal of laughter. It rang loudly. She was bent over double by the force of it. At first the laughter invited them to join in, but it went on for too long, and when she raised her head again, she looked exhausted. Lucy felt a thrill of fear.

Dr. Lessing caught her breath, smoothed her hair down, and buttoned her coat. She uttered a short order, and the figures behind her stepped forward.

"Who are they? Your secret police?" Sammy asked.

"They're here to keep us all safe," she said.

She was flanked by eight Sweepers. All helmeted. All armed.

"Do they sleep in that getup?" Sammy asked. The doctor ignored him.

Lucy recognized Simmons by his bulk and his red hair. *Doesn't he know his boss is crazy?* Lucy raised her knife, feeling foolish as she did so. A broken knife against a bolt of electricity. She wondered how it would feel. A burning sensation, or maybe just a jolt to the heart that stopped it dead? Her palms were instantly slick with sweat. Aidan tried to push her behind him, but she resisted. "You're still weak," she whispered. "I heard you behind me tripping all over your feet."

"Your knife is wrecked," he whispered back.

"It's still sharp."

Dr. Lessing's face softened. Her voice was pitched low. "Aidan, you shouldn't be out of bed. Simmons told me at best you'd torn a ligament in your shoulder. There's considerable tissue damage." She turned toward Lucy with her hands out. "And Lucy, you were so exhausted, you fell asleep in my office between one sentence and the next."

"You drugged us!" Lucy said. "Enough of these lies!"

Dr. Lessing laughed. "Instant coffee, a little stale, but the best that I could offer you. Hardly a drug."

"You know what you did," Lucy spat. "Who are you pretending for? Them? They just do what you tell them, right?" She waved her arm at the Sweepers.

Lines of concern etched themselves onto the woman's face. "You're confused. You must have had a nightmare of some kind." She beckoned to Lucy. "Come, back to your bed, and we'll talk about it in the morning."

Lucy took a shaking step forward. She felt Aidan's hand on her shoulder, and then it fell away. She stared at the doctor and saw nothing in her eyes but compassion and a wrinkle of worry. It appeared genuine enough. She hesitated.

The scene in front of her seemed too absurd to be real: the Sweepers, silent, invisible faces behind the reflective Plexiglas helmets, grasping their bristling black boxes; the doctor in her lab coat; three kids armed with an assortment of useless weapons. Even Sammy's curved blade was better suited for slicing off a handful of basil. Lucy's head felt scrambled. She wondered how long it would be before whatever sedatives Dr. Lessing had given them wore off completely. What was real? That was the question that was nagging at her. Dr. Lessing had an explanation for everything. How much of what Lucy was feeling was paranoia seeded in the early days of the plague? The Sweepers, the S'ans. She glanced at Sammy. She'd been totally wrong about the S'ans. What else was she wrong about? Was it true that these people were just trying to make everything better? Safer?

Dr. Lessing moved a step closer, Simmons at her heels, but she gestured him back. The Sweepers kept their positions. A slight smile curved her mouth.

"You're so tired, Lucy. It's been so hard for so long," she said. "But it doesn't have to be this grim struggle for survival, you know. We just want to look after you. And your friends." Her smile broadened. She waited, her eyes intent on Lucy's face.

Lucy shifted from one foot to the other. Her arms were sore. The hilt of her knife was slippery in her fingers. How long could they face off like this? Should they rush the Sweepers? She didn't think any of them was up to a fight.

"I can offer each of you a bath, a bed, and a good hot breakfast in the morning."

Lucy felt her resolve weaken. Her hands dropped a bit. Dr. Lessing came another foot closer. Close enough that Lucy could see a smear of face cream caught in the fold of skin by her nostril. It reminded Lucy of her mother. She glanced at Sammy, whose face was still masked. Then at Aidan. His expression only mirrored the confusion she felt.

She tried to apply the skills she'd learned living in the Wilds. The ability to judge possible danger, sense predators, and make a quick decision based on a gut feeling. Now, her instincts felt dull. All she could think about was how good a hot bath would feel and the genuine kindness in Dr. Lessing's eyes. And what about Aidan? Aidan was obviously in pain. They could look after him properly here. It was what the staff had been trained for.

"We can leave whenever we want? And no more medical tests without our consent?"

"Of course."

She lowered her knife. Dr. Lessing clapped her hands together.

"Yes?" she said. "I'm so glad."

"Wait a minute," Aidan said. He reached out for Lucy's arm. He pulled her in close, still holding the hammer ready in case of attack. "Are you sure?" he said. "Just like that?"

She couldn't help but notice how he winced as his arm was jarred. His elbow was pressed up against his ribs as if they might shake loose.

"I don't know. I can't tell anymore. It feels like she's telling the truth."

He nodded.

"You talked to her longer than anyone. And your gut reactions are usually pretty right on."

"Really?" She felt herself blushing.

He stroked her arm. "Well, maybe not always," he murmured. "Sometimes it takes you a while to get a clue."

Sammy took a couple of steps back toward them. They stood shoulder to shoulder now. His back was rigid, his knuckles so tight around the hilt of his billhook that the burned skin was white.

"You're not buying this, are you?" he asked. "She reminds me of a teacher I once had. Seemed nice and fair and ready to make a deal, but then as soon as you let down your guard, you'd be hauled into the principal's office."

"That was in second grade," Aidan said.

"Yeah, but she's the same type. If it walks like a duck and quacks like a duck . . . You're forgetting Leo. And, Lucy, she took your blood. And these guys . . . they're not exactly acting friendly, are they?"

He spoke without shifting his glance from the Sweepers. Lucy looked up and noticed that although they still stood in relaxed formation across the foyer, their Tasers were raised and switched on. Dr. Lessing might pretend that everything was safe and civilized, but she still relied on force.

"You're right."

Sammy pushed his way in front of them.

"What about Leo?" he called out. "He was sick when he got out of here. You made him that way. He had no reason to lie to us."

Something flickered across Dr. Lessing's face. The smile on her mouth smoothed away as if it had never been there. Lucy sensed a shift in energy. The Sweepers seemed to stand taller, the blue flames of their weapons leapt and crackled. The hairs on the back of Lucy's neck stood up.

She searched out Mrs. Reynolds. The nurse had made her way around to stand a few feet away from Dr. Lessing. She stared straight ahead, expressionless. Lucy's gaze was drawn to her fingers twisting together. *Run,* she'd said.

The Sweepers inched forward. There was nowhere to go. The main entrance, still locked, was at their backs. The side door they'd come in through was somewhere to the left. Lucy was sure that was locked now, too. The stairs in front of them were blocked by the line of Sweepers. She could see a dark hallway to the left, a few closed doors. She wondered where they led.

Out of the corner of her eye, she saw Dr. Lessing make a gesture.

One of the Sweepers, standing off to the side, suddenly lunged at Lucy. She ducked barely in time to avoid the Taser. She heard the *pop* and *crackle* as it swished past her face. The Sweeper's arm caught her across the skull and sent her reeling backward. Her ear felt instantly swollen and hot. "Not the

Tasers," Dr. Lessing shouted. The Sweeper hesitated, clearly confused, and Aidan aimed a vicious kick at the man's knee. His legs buckled and he fell. And then the others joined in. Lucy heard the dull thud of blows exchanged. She tasted blood at the back of her throat, felt a bruise rising along her jawbone. It was a messy fight. No one really seemed to know what they were doing. And they were packed too close to land a punch with any force. She dug in to a chest with her elbow, kicked out with her heavy boots. Someone's shoulder slammed against her. Lucy fell back. Shaking her head to clear it, she brought her knife up and cleared a little space in front of her. She wondered how long before they realized the blade was broken and charged in again. Beside her, Aidan swung his hammer and connected with a helmet, cracking the heavy plastic. Sammy, his heavy robes swirling around him, wielded his billhook in a broad arc. Around the edge of his mask, she could see the wild grin spread across his face. Through the mouth hole, his teeth were bared like a wolf. He was clearly enjoying himself.

The doctor's choked voice haulted the Sweepers in their tracks. She clawed at something around her throat. "Stop!" she gasped.

Then the Sweepers were falling back. And Lucy, Aidan, and Sammy found themselves in the middle of the floor, with empty space around them. They circled, keeping their tight huddle, wary.

CHAPTER TWENTY

LIGHTS OUT

Del constricted her arm around the woman's throat and stepped out from behind her. Two small kids, wrapped in blankets, shivered at the base of the stairs. Their faces were pinched and gray, like they'd been hungry for a long time. Lucy remembered all the other children who'd disappeared from the shelter, taken away in the white vans. Who knew what had happened to them and the older scavengers who'd been taken against their will? They'd probably all died here. Somehow she'd forgotten those truths.

Del transferred her grip to Dr. Lessing's arm and held it twisted behind her back. She stepped forward and the Sweepers fell back. Simmons raised his hand and they froze in formation. They were now clustered before the front door. Lucy narrowed her eyes. She was pretty sure there were even fewer of them than before. Had some fled during the night?

"We're all leaving," Del said.

"Delfina. You're safe here," Dr. Lessing pleaded. Her voice was strained and high. "If you go back out into the world, you'll be in danger. You can't do that to the children."

Del's arm jerked and tightened. Dr. Lessing's eyes bulged. "Just shut up," Del screamed. "Stop pretending! Don't act like you know me."

"But you understand the work we're doing here."

"You lied to me. You used me to bring my friends here. You murdered Leo." The tears were pouring down her face. Dr. Lessing writhed, but Del's grip was too strong.

"I'm a doctor," she said, "and a scientist." She looked at Lucy with a pleading expression. "It's your duty. You've been given this gift."

"You were going to bleed me until I died!" Lucy said. Finally her mind felt crystal clear. "I read your report." She stepped forward and lowered her knife. "Did you infect Leo with the plague?"

Dr. Lessing's face contorted with rage. She ripped at Del's hands with her nails, but Del held on with a fierce expression. The doctor whipped her head backward suddenly. Her skull caught Del across the mouth, mashing her lips against her teeth. Del fell backward, her arms pinwheeling as she tried to regain her balance. She dropped to her knees, and blood gushed from her mouth.

The children wailed and shrank against the banister.

Dr. Lessing staggered to her feet. Her lab coat was speckled with Del's blood.

Simmons looked from the doctor to Del. He seemed unsure of how to act. Behind him, the Sweepers shifted uneasily.

"Del!" Sammy shouted. He ran toward her. No one stopped him. He reached her, put his arm around her shoulders, and helped her up.

Uttering a wild scream, Dr. Lessing sprang at him. Her fingers were hooked like claws, her hair streamed over her shoulders. She looked nothing like the calm, composed person who had greeted them hours earlier. Her forward motion threw Sammy off balance and Del was knocked backward. Sammy's boots skidded on the polished floor. His legs gave way and he hit the ground hard. The billhook dropped from his hand and skittered across the floor out of reach. He rolled away, arms wrapped around his stomach.

Del was tearing at her sweatshirt pouch. She pulled her slingshot free, fitted a smooth pebble into the socket, and extended her arm. She tracked Dr. Lessing as the woman attacked Sammy again with a flurry of blows. Lucy could see the frown of concentration on her face. But Dr. Lessing and Sammy were struggling together, a jumble of arms and legs, and Del couldn't risk hitting Sammy instead.

The doctor's breath came in loud gasps. Sammy tried to protect himself, but Dr. Lessing struck out wildly with the length of her forearm. The savage blow rocked his head to the side. The mask was ripped loose and skidded across the floor. Lucy could hear the murmurs as the Sweepers caught sight of his charred face and flaming eyes, the trickle of blood seeping from a wound on his forehead.

In an instant, Simmons tackled the doctor, pinning her arms behind her body, and dragged her away from Sammy. She struggled, then abruptly went limp. He held her wrists in his broad hands.

Lucy forced herself to move toward her friends. The marble floor stretched ahead of her. Her attention was fixed on the drops of blood, some of which had fallen onto the polished stone of the stairs. She wondered if it was Sammy's or Del's. How badly were they hurt? Dr. Lessing was sprawled, half sitting, on the floor, with Mrs. Reynolds and Simmons bent over her. She seemed really out of it. And the Sweepers. *What were they waiting for?* she wondered.

Suddenly Aidan gripped her arm so hard it hurt, and she heard a *pop pop pop*, and they were plunged into darkness.

"Del shot the lights out with her slingshot," Aidan whispered. He was so close, his breath tickled her ear. "Get up against the wall. She's going to lay down covering fire." Before Lucy had time to ask what that was, something hard whizzed past, inches from her face. She couldn't see it, but she felt the movement of air, and she heard a yelp of pain from someone behind her.

Lucy remembered the small, neat holes Del had made in the rabbits. The speed with which she'd killed four of them. The girl was lethal. She squinted, but the dark was absolute. They could feel their way along the wall, but in what direction?

Aidan pressed her against the wall, shielding her with his body. He whistled, a low warbling sound that was barely audible over the yells of pain and the sharp sounds of impact as stone after stone hit helmet, walls, and, most often it seemed, human flesh. Simmons bellowed orders, but from what Lucy could tell, no one was listening. Someone ran by. She felt clothing brush against her arm.

A second later, Aidan's signal was answered by another whistle. This one more like a trill. "Keep left," Aidan murmured. "Move!"

Lucy could barely see, but Aidan was pushing her into a run toward a deeper darkness, away from the ruckus. She thought they were heading for the short hallway she'd glimpsed before. She stumbled on, and just ahead she could hear Del and Sammy and the kids. One of the little ones was weeping. Small, feeble cries, like he didn't have the strength to bawl. She ran into a solid body and stifled a gasp. Felt the drape of a cloak—*Sammy*—and heard the sound of him fumbling with a doorknob.

"Locked," he said.

Del's low voice came from farther up the hallway. "This one, too."

They moved as quickly as they could through the darkness. Lucy shuffled her feet, expecting irrationally to fall into a hole at any moment.

And then, a little way past where the corridor made an acute turn, there was a recessed light, and she could see again. She looked back in the direction of the foyer. "They'll be on us in a heartbeat," Aidan said.

"Mrs. Reynolds said the outer doors would all be locked," she said. "Or they'll be rooms with no exit."

"There's a door to the basement somewhere here," Del said. "I remember it from before. Here." She threw it open and groped for the light switch. A bare bulb was set in the sloped ceiling. Old wooden stairs led steeply down, releasing the eye-watering smell of must and mold.

"We're going down there?" Lucy said. She couldn't help thinking of all those old slasher flicks. What was the foremost rule? Don't go into the cellar. . . .

"No choice, right?" Del said.

Lucy reluctantly agreed.

"There's always a way out of a basement," Sammy said. "A window or a coal chute or storm doors—something most people don't think about it." He started going down the narrow steps.

Lucy put out her hand and grabbed hold of his cloak. She looked at the scared kids clinging to Del's fingers and put her lips to his ear so they couldn't hear her. "Aren't the dogs down there?"

She could hear whining, excited yaps. The barks echoed wildly.

"Yeah, I guess—but like Del said, no choice."

Still Lucy hesitated. They didn't know what to expect. It could be a dead end, and they had no way of protecting themselves except for her knife, Aidan's hammer, and Del's slingshot. Aidan pushed urgently against her back. "Hate to tell you, but the Sweepers are coming."

And now she heard hoarse shouts and the scuffling of boots on the hard floors.

She hurried onto the stairs, grabbing a wooden railing, which bent under her weight. Behind her, Aidan pulled the door closed.

"Lock?" Del asked.

"Bolt, but one good kick will break it," he said.

On the first step down, Lucy slipped. The railing pulled away from the wall with a screech of nails. Del's hand shot out and gripped her elbow, saving her from a nasty spill. As soon as Lucy had regained her footing, the girl released her arm.

"Thanks," Lucy said.

"Don't mention it." She held one kid firmly by the wrist. Lucy thought it was the girl, but she couldn't be sure. The other one stumbled ahead with his arms outstretched. Both of them wore baggy gray pajamas and slippers. Both badly needed their hair washed. *So much for the hot baths Dr. Lessing mentioned,* she thought.

The stairs were steep but short. They found themselves in a large, concrete-floored space. Thick drifts of dust lay on the floor, tracked over by countless footprints. Steel-encased wiring stretched out in a lattice across the low ceilings, as did rusty pipes as thick as Lucy's arm. She could hear the trickle of water pumped down from the cistern. Pink insulation puffed out of crumbling plaster board like masses of cotton candy. Stacks of soggy boxes lined the water-stained walls. It smelled of damp and mushrooms, and overwhelmingly of animals: mouse droppings, but also the close, thick smell of many dogs kept inside, the tang of urine and dander and fur.

Numerous corridors led off in different directions, each poorly lit and dusty. Lucy tried to orient herself, but she'd lost her sense of direction. She thought she could pinpoint where the dogs were kenneled, even though the echoing barks confused her.

"Any idea what's down here?" Sammy asked Del. He'd lifted the little girl onto his back. She clung to him, her hair straggling in her face. Her eyelids drooped.

Del shook her head. "Besides canned goods and bulk food items? The dogs. A bunch of old boxes. Stuff left over from before the plague, I guess."

Aidan, who had been hanging back near the stairs listening for the Sweepers, looked excited. "If they were getting big deliveries of food, then there's probably a loading dock or something down here. We should head in that direction."

Del shrugged helplessly. "Your guess is as good as mine. It's as big as a football field. I wandered down here for a couple of hours before Dr. Lessing—" She broke off, her cheeks reddening. *Before Dr. Lessing convinced you to rat me out,* Lucy thought, and then was a little ashamed of herself. They'd still be fighting a losing battle if it weren't for Del.

She cleared her throat. She hated to say it, but it seemed only rational. "If they trucked in mass amounts of dog food, then they probably stockpiled it near the dog kennels. We can follow the sound of their barks." She turned slowly, tracking the sound. They were subdued now, but in her mind she could see the dogs. She remembered the rottweiler leaping at her legs as she struggled to climb the tree, the thick froth of spit at the corners of its jaws. Three narrow halls stretched in front of her. They were lit with dim bulbs.

"Look down on the ground," Aidan said. A jumbled trail of muddy footsteps led down the central one. "The middle way gets used a lot." He squeezed Lucy's hand. She moved into the hollow of his arm. A series of sharp *thuds* jolted them apart. Someone was trying to kick in the cellar door.

Exchanging panicked glances, the group crept down the narrow hall, moving as quickly as possible. Del soothed the kids with soft murmurs. The air was very still and dank. The acrid odor of urine and sawdust grew stronger, and the yelps of the dogs increased in volume.

They hurried toward the sound. Sammy ran ahead. His cloaked shadow leapt across the walls. The kid was attached to his back like a monkey.

They'd come a few hundred yards down the passageway, and still Lucy could heard the sound of wood splintering behind them and the buzz of voices. How many were there? Three or four? All of them?

Another volley of barks, louder and more excited.

They can smell us, Lucy thought with a thrill of fear. And then her mouth suddenly turned dry. *They can smell me.*

"Nearly there," Aidan said.

The corridor twisted and then opened up. Wire cages lined one long wall. Dogs of every shape and size pressed against the mesh. Some threw their bodies against the doors or clawed frantically, hard enough to rip at their paws. The yelping was deafening.

"Can you see a door out?" Lucy yelled. She was transfixed by a large dog that was staring at her. She flicked her eyes away, trying not to challenge the animal. Its black lips lifted away from sharp white teeth and the dog began to howl. At once the rest of the dogs lifted up their snouts and began to howl, too.

Aidan pulled at her arm and she realized she'd been standing still. "Come on," he said.

She tore her eyes away from the dog and moved across the room as quickly as she could, keeping her gaze on the ground under her feet and ignoring the rumble of growls, the clanging of dogs pushing against their metal doors to get to her.

The space narrowed into two corridors. Sammy hurried down one and almost immediately doubled back. "Locked door," he said. They all ran down the other way. The passage was lined with stacks of cardboard boxes. The dogs had quieted again, except for a few excited yips. Lucy heard the dull thud of running feet against the concrete.

CHAPTER TWENTY-ONE

THE BASEMENT

She turned to see Simmons, Dr. Lessing, Mrs. Reynolds, and one other Sweeper who wore his faceguard down and held his Taser in front of him like a sword. Dr. Lessing was sweating and pale. Mrs. Reynolds grabbed her arm. The doctor roughly shook it loose. Lucy stopped, feeling more exhausted than she ever had before. Her hand could barely hold her knife. The generator hummed and then roared into life.

Lucy remembered how she'd thought the light on the roof resembled the gigantic eye of a beast. Now she felt as if she'd been swallowed alive.

Del raised her slingshot. Aidan wrapped an arm around Lucy's shoulders. They backed up as the doctor and Sweepers advanced.

Lucy snuck a look behind her. A shadowy hallway stretched back. More boxes were piled five feet high—rows and rows of them. They were marked with the names of ready-to-eat food, vegetables, precooked meat, and dog chow. There was no outlet that she could see.

"Don't let them force us into a dead end," she said. They spread out in a thin line across the corridor. She noticed that the air was fresher. The scent of dog mingled with something she realized was the smell of rain. Del ordered the two kids to get back as far as they could.

"There's got to be some kind of outside access around here," she said. "How else did they get all these crates in here?" She reached into an open box and pulled out a can of dog food. She tossed it to Aidan, who caught it with his free hand. "Weighty," he said, hefting it.

Sammy helped himself to a couple.

"Just grab the girl, Ross," Dr. Lessing shouted suddenly. "I don't care if the others get hurt."

The Sweeper came toward them at a run. He aimed himself at Lucy. Aidan pelted the can at him, but Ross ducked.

Sammy threw both of his at the same time. One hit the man with a sharp *crack*, fracturing the plastic visor. Mrs. Reynolds shouted out a warning. Attempting to avoid the man's weapon, Lucy threw herself backward so hard she hit the stack of boxes, knocking the topmost one to the ground. The column teetered and came crashing down, splitting the cardboard and spilling tin cans everywhere. Aidan tripped and fell. The Sweeper came on, his Taser dangerously close. He flung his arm out, and the black box skimmed the sleeve of Lucy's leather jacket. She felt a jolt, which seemed to stop her heart for a second, and then her legs turned to water. Her head smashed against the ground, and she felt a trickle of blood edge into her collar. Aidan swept his leg around, felling the Sweeper. He stomped on the man's wrist with his thick-soled boot. There was a *crunch* as the bone broke, and the black box flew from his fingers. Aidan pounced on it quickly.

"Sammy," he said, keeping his eyes on the Sweeper who was curled up, cradling his injured arm. "Help Lucy up, will you?" He stepped toward Simmons. The black box sent out its flickering prongs. Simmons held his hands open in front of him and shook his head. He took a few paces backward.

"Just let me check on Ross, okay?" he said. Aidan nodded. Simmons prodded Ross's wrist. "Broken in about three places," he muttered. He helped the Sweeper to his feet and propped him against the wall.

Lucy's legs still felt like limp noodles. Her heart was pounding, and her head buzzed. It was difficult to fill her lungs with air. She freed herself from Sammy's tight grip. "Where's Dr. Lessing?" she yelled, looking for the white lab coat. The woman was nowhere to be seen. The dogs had started up a crescendo of whining. Then she heard the sound of electronic bolts shooting open. The barking broke out and quickly became a cacophony. A single howl rose. The sound made the hairs on Lucy's arm rise, and she felt cold despite her leather jacket. Mrs. Reynolds's face blanched.

"She's letting the dogs out," she said. "They'll go mad when they scent you. The trainer left a few days ago. If they find you before Dr. Lessing does, they'll tear you apart."

Simmons stepped forward. He spoke hurriedly. "Down that hallway. Green-painted steel door about ten feet on. You can bust the lock. It leads to a dog run with an eight-foot chain-link fence."

"We'll hold them off as long as we can," Mrs. Reynolds said. She looked at Lucy. "Be careful out there. The plague is mutating. It may return. That much is true."

Simmons set his shoulder against a column of boxes and shoved. The heavy boxes came cascading down, partially blocking the narrow corridor. He moved to the next row and heaved. Some split open. Cans rolled underfoot. Slowly the pile grew and wedged against the opposite wall. Mrs. Reynolds joined him, tugging down crates, and heaping them higher until the lower half of the passage was impenetrable.

Lucy hesitated. The others were already at the door. Sammy was hammering against the lock with a dented tin can.

Mrs. Reynolds met her eyes. "Just run. Run, Lucy!" she said, staggering under the weight of another box. The scars were livid against her flushed skin. Behind the nurse and the growing pile of boxes, she caught sight of Dr. Lessing. She was completely surrounded by furry bodies. The dogs swarmed over one another as they hunted for a scent. Lucy hesitated.

"I took my folder, the notebooks," she said. "They belong to me and no one else. But I left the blood." She turned away, but not before she saw surprise in the nurse's eyes.

Lucy ran to join Aidan. His arm was pressed tight against his ribs again. She saw the pain in the lines of his forehead. Although her skull was still buzzing, she felt surprisingly clearheaded. Sammy threw the can away in disgust. The thin metal was crumpled. Some kind of red sauce leaked out, staining his robes. He pushed his hood back. His blackened forehead was dripping sweat. Aidan set his shoulder against the door and heaved. The lock was battered, but still it held. From behind them, they heard the baying of the dogs.

"They blocked most of the way, but there's still space for the dogs to get through," Lucy said.

She remembered how the animals had propelled themselves halfway up the tree trunk, maddened by her scent. She pushed Sammy out of the way and slid her knife blade between the lock and the door and slammed it down hard, the impact jarring the old wound on her palm. The lock tore open with an awful squeal, and her knife snapped again. Straight across. An inch from the hilt.

Lucy subdued a stab of grief, shoved it back into her pocket, and thrust the door open. Cool air flooded over her. The dog run was long and concrete, with shallow channels running down each side. It had rained recently, and the cement glistened. Through the links of the fence she could see the shore, and beyond, the stormy surface of Lake Harlem.

"Almost there," she yelled, turning back to grab Aidan's hand.

Two dogs crashed through the barricade of boxes and cans into the hallway. Lucy caught a glimpse of their yellow eyes, the gums pulled back in hideous grimaces. A rottweiler and a pit bull. They leapt, arrowing in at her from two sides. She threw up a defensive arm, and then Aidan pushed her away, yelling. She hit the ground and rolled against the wall, smacking it hard with her head. She shook her head to clear it, scarcely aware of the pain, and dug frantically for her knife before remembering it was useless. Screaming in anger, she threw it at the rottweiler attacking Aidan. The hilt struck it across the skull, but the dog didn't pause. Del stood in front of the door to the outside, shielding the terrified children with her body. Her slingshot was loaded. She raised it, looking for a clear shot, but everything was happening too fast. Aidan was thrown backward by the weight of the dog. He grappled with it, pushing against its muscular chest and throwing his head around wildly in an attempt to avoid its razor-sharp teeth. He hooked his fingers in the dog's collar and twisted the leather strap, trying to strangle it. The dog's tongue protruded and strands of saliva glistened as the jaws snapped inches from his face.

Sammy hurled himself forward, trying to reach his brother. The pit bull jumped him, seeking the flesh beneath the robes. It clamped down with its jaws and whipped its head from side to side. The heavy black robes tore as Sammy kicked out at the dog. His boot connected with the dog's midriff. Another wild kick, this blow landing on its snout. The dog yelped and released its jaws, falling heavily to the ground. Del took her shot, sending a stone into the meaty part of the dog's thigh. The dog howled and scrabbled at the floor, trying to reach the wound in its leg. Sammy kicked it again in the ribs and ran, panting, to Aidan, who was weakening. He grabbed the rottweiler's collar from behind and yanked it into the air. Scrambling to his feet, Aidan thrust his hand into his pocket, pulled out the Taser, and pressed it against the dog's side. The dog yelped and collapsed, shaking convulsively on the floor. Its pink tongue lolled from its mouth, and then it was still. Aidan limped over to the whining pit bull and Tasered it, too.

He stood looking at the dogs, his face pale and sick, and then he slid down the wall until he was sitting on the ground.

Lucy crawled over to him. His left arm hung loosely. She put out her hand, afraid that she might accidentally hurt him, and settled for stroking him on the cheek. "Are you all right?"

"Painkillers wore off," he said scowling. "I'm pretty sure now that I've pulled a muscle."

"Come on." She helped him stand. They hobbled out the door into the dog run where the others stood waiting.

"Might have brought the Taser out a little sooner," Sammy told his brother.

"Couldn't reach it. You may have noticed the hundred pounds of dog sitting on my chest?"

"Always with the excuses," Sammy said, pulling his shredded robe awkwardly over his head. His forearm was imprinted with four deep tooth marks gushing blood.

Del cursed. "Can you still use it?" She sounded angry.

Sammy looked disappointed. "Yeah, it hurts bad, but—"

"You can climb?" Del asked.

"Of course," he said, watching blood drip onto the floor. "I didn't mean to get mauled by a dog, you know."

Del pressed her lips together. "I know," she said in a softer tone. Stowing the slingshot in her back pocket, she ripped a length of cloth from the discarded robes and tied it tightly around his arm. He gasped.

Giving him a look, she gathered the children to her and faced the fence.

"You go first," she told Sammy. "I'll lift the kids up to you."

He pulled himself up, swung over, and jumped down. Once he was on the ground, he held his arms up for the first of the two children. As soon as they were safely on the other side, Del went up, then Lucy, and lastly Aidan, who favored his left arm and climbed one-handed. He had just reached the top when the fox terrier burst through the door, barking madly. Its toothbrush tail stuck straight up, and the fur on its back stood up in a ridge. It ran back and forth along the fence seeking a way out, and then began throwing itself repeatedly at the chain link as if it were made of rubber.

"Let's go before the poor thing kills itself," Aidan said from the top of the fence.

Lucy turned away.

And then a second dog hit the fence barely a foot below the top. Another rottweiler, even larger than the first. It catapulted itself upward, thick black claws pushing the chain link outward as it tried to find purchase and muscle its way over. Aidan jumped, making no attempt to land gracefully. He staggered and then regained his balance, pulling Lucy back from where she stood almost mesmerized by the animal's single-mindedness. The dog fixed its hot gaze on her and, growling terribly, made another impossible leap into the air, landing almost on top of the fence before falling heavily back to the concrete.

Aidan hurried her a safe distance away. "It'll be over that in a minute."

The dog was panting heavily, but still it paced and jumped and whined. Lucy's presence was driving it crazy.

"It's not going to stop hunting us," Lucy said. She looked at the exhausted children huddled together in Del's arms and at Sammy trying to smile. "It wants me." She shrugged her arms out of her backpack, carrying it by the strap, and walked toward the fence. The rottweiler's lips inched back from its incisors. Its ears flattened against the bony skull, and an awful snarling rumbled from the barrel chest. Muscles bunched in its back legs as it gathered itself to leap again.

"It can't have you," Aidan said, trying to haul her away. "Get away from the fence, Lucy!" She shook herself loose, jarring his arm. He winced with pain.

"It's okay."

Keeping her eyes on the dog, she opened her backpack and dug around in it, locating the tinderbox.

The dog kept up its continuous growl. "You want my blood?" Lucy shouted, pulling out the vial. She raised it above her head and threw it over the fence. The glass smashed against the concrete. Thick red blood spattered against the wall.

▮▮▮▮▮

They ran. It wasn't until they reached the parking lot that they paused, looking back at the dark hulk of the building. Lights blazed on the top floors. In an upper window behind heavy curtains, they could see human figures hurrying back and forth. Lucy might have imagined it, but she thought she could hear a single, shrieking note that seemed to go on and on.

"Think they'll follow us?" Aidan asked.

Lucy shook her head, thinking of Mrs. Reynolds. "No. They have what they need."

The sky opened and rain began to fall, a hard-driving shower that soaked them immediately but was as warm as a spring shower. Lucy looked up into the lightening sky and let the rain push her hair off her face. If more dogs did come, the rain would wash away most of their scent. The fog had dissipated and the air smelled fresh and clean. The dull pain in her head subsided to a thump. Sammy carried a kid on his back; Del had linked hands with the other one. Lucy heard her voice, low and soothing, as she urged them to move. It was weird to hear such kindness from the girl.

The empty parking lot glittered like an ice rink. They ran through the rain, slowing down again once they came to the bridge. Lucy looked back at the tower. The red light was dark.

Aidan slipped his arm around her waist. She leaned into him, careful of his wounded ribs and arm.

"Which way?" he said.

She looked ahead. Del and Sammy and the children were walking slowly. They'd reached the bridge. With the sleepy kids and the exhaustion that she was sure everyone was feeling, it would take them hours to get home. She scanned the horizon. The long bridge curved above the wind-whipped waves of Lake Harlem. Beyond that lay the Wilds, as familiar to her as the lines on her palm. Lucy could close her eyes and in her mind navigate over the flats, the grove, past the salt marsh and the blighted pines, the remains of her camp and the Great Hill. And then onward up the shifting terrain of the gorges and the escarpment and the suspension bridges swinging wildly with the slightest breath of wind. They'd have to carry the children, or haul them up the granite cliff face somehow. Aidan and Sammy were injured. Her own body hurt so much, everywhere, that it was almost funny.

Lucy turned away from the thicket of tall trees and the gleam of the restless sea she glimpsed between the black trunks, and toward the broad, solid road that snaked north for five miles before entering the Hell Gate. The road the Sweepers had taken. "That's simple," she said with a grin. "For once we'll take the easy way."

She held hands with Aidan as they crossed the bridge, walking into him when he suddenly stopped.

"What?" she said, startled. "Do you hear something?" He put his finger to her lips.

"Shh," he said. "C'mere." He pulled her to the side where the shadows concealed them. His voice sounded thick.

Del, Sammy, and the kids had almost reached the road.

Lucy moved closer.

Aidan traced his finger to her cheek and then to her chin. He tilted her face upward.

And then she was looking only at him, his bright eyes shadowed, the messy fall of his hair over his forehead, his wide mouth with that infuriating curl in the corner. His hand moved to the side of her face, he leaned forward, and, letting her breath leave her in a sigh, she rose onto her tiptoes to meet his lips. Her fingers tangled themselves in his hair and she pressed against him, feeling the warm solidity of his body, the crushing strength in his arm as he pulled her against him, and the doubt draining away from her, leaving nothing but happiness.

After a long minute, Aidan pulled back a little. Her lips felt bruised. She was flustered now, conscious of the tingling sensation left on her mouth, the need to keep touching him. Her mouth hardly felt as if it belonged to her anymore. He kissed the tip of her nose and, linking his hand with hers, drew her toward home.

EPILOGUE

ABOVE THE WORLD

"Do you think the rain will ever stop?" Lucy asked Aidan.

He shrugged and she gripped his arm more tightly. "Oww," he said. "You think you could relax that death grip?"

"Did I hurt you?" she asked.

"No, I'm healed."

"Well, you know I don't like being up so high," she said. Aidan shifted his back against the tree trunk.

"Come here, then," he said, prying Lucy's fingers from his arm and guiding her forward so that she was nestled against his shoulder. She still didn't understand how he could be twenty-five feet off the ground and act like he was lounging on a couch, but she settled into the crook of his arm and crossed her feet on top of his legs. "So," she said, "The rain?"

"It's been, what? About two weeks?"

She thought back. "Ever since . . . you know . . . that night." The night they'd escaped. The night they'd first kissed.

He yawned, stretching like a cat. Her hand tightened around his arm again. She pushed the drift of her hair away from her mouth. The canopy of this elm was so thick that the raindrops ran out of steam before they reached their branch.

"It'll clear up any minute," he said lazily. "Either that, or it'll go on for months."

She pressed her palm against his forehead. It was cool and smooth.

"I'm not sick."

"I know, I just have to check."

"Every day?"

"Just until I'm sure that Dr. Lessing didn't do something to you."

He exhaled deeply.

"Are you falling asleep?"

"Maybe. I was up at dawn hunting bunnies," he said. "Ever since Del and Sammy left, I've been the guy. At least until you learn to handle a bow as well as you handle a spear."

His lips hovered near her ear. She felt the soft shushing of his breath. A shudder went up her spine. She snuggled closer. She could hear the dull roar of the waves, the rustle of the wind. As long as she didn't think about the ground, it was nice being up high, cradled and surrounded by thick, green leaves.

Aidan had picked his favorite tree, the elm, and his favorite place in it. At the very top. When he stood up, he said he could see fifty miles in every direction. Lucy had to take his word for it, because there was no way she was going to balance on a branch that dipped up and down under her weight, with nothing to hold on to but whiplike stems. He liked to be here at dusk, when the bullfrogs started their nightly warblings and the broken string of beacon fires along the northern route became visible.

Del had left a week ago. She'd taken the Geo Wash Bridge west, before heading due north to find the settlement up there. And surprisingly, Sammy had opted to go with her. Actually, Lucy amended, not so surprisingly. They had spent a lot of time together after they'd gotten back from the island, and Lucy had seen something in Sammy's eyes. Del had kept herself apart from the jostle and bustle of the camp. She'd hunted, she'd helped shore up the dikes now that the canals were filled with roaring cascades of water, she'd harvested tomatoes and squash, she'd worked like she was possessed, but after the work was done, she'd disappeared to places only she knew about.

Lucy had been anxious. Mostly for Aidan. She knew what Del's friendship meant to him.

"We talked. It's cool," Aidan had said. "She made a mistake. And you know, maybe I . . ." He'd stopped and looked at her carefully then. "Maybe I wasn't straight with her. About you. How I felt about you. That was wrong of me."

Lucy had dropped her eyes, suddenly shy.

"You'll make it up to me, then?" she'd said, teasing to break the tension.

"Lucy, you know how I feel about you, right?" he whispered now.

She was breathless. "Why don't you tell me?"

He tilted her face up. "Why don't I show you?"

"How?" she said, fighting the urge to giggle. If she started laughing, she'd probably fall out of the tree.

"Like this," he said, kissing the lobe of her ear. She closed her eyes, looking at him through her lashes. Her hands tightened on the tree limb. She felt dizzy all of a sudden.

"This," he breathed, planting more kisses along her hairline. His fingers tangled with hers. She was holding on to nothing but him. He was kissing her eyelids now. Each movement of his lips made her shiver. Aidan murmured her name.

She was melting. She couldn't feel the hard bark against her hip. Nothing existed but his gentle hands and his warm lips.

"You smell like blackberries in the sun," he said. "You taste like honey."

He could do this for hours. Kiss every inch, every centimeter of her neck and face except for her mouth. It drove her crazy, made her want to scream *Enough!*

"Aidan. Aidan! I'm going to fall!"

"Hmmm," he said, against her neck. He opened his eyes. They were sleepy, but she saw the glint that hovered in them.

Lucy leaned back in his arms and rested her head against his shoulder. Rocked in the elm's broad branches, she felt safe. The fires weren't visible through the heavy screen of leaves, but up above where the branches thinned were the stars. Aidan had shown her the North Star, tracing its path from the handle of the Big Dipper, which was pretty much the only constellation she could identify with any certainty. It hung low, not the brightest star, but special now after so many nights of picking it out together, as though it somehow belonged to them. "Are you sorry you didn't go?"

He took a moment to reply. "Some day, when we're ready. If you want to," he said, drawing his eyebrows together. The crooked smile was still there, dancing in the corner of his mouth, but he looked serious.

Lucy followed his gaze northward.

ACKNOWLEDGMENTS

Writing a book is often a solitary endeavor but making it good takes many people.

A million heartfelt thanks to: Silvia Rajagopalan, Charise Isis, Alison Gaylin, Jennifer May, and Charity Valk, who were there at the beginning. Without all your enthusiasm and help it is very possible there never would have been a book.

My family and friends, in particular, Arnaldo Treggiari, the Rajagopalans, Gail Parris, Lesley Sawhill at the Woodstock, NY Children's Library, and all the kids who have workshopped with me.

I'm indebted to my agent, Garrett Hicks, who digs deep; my über-editor, Lisa Sandell, who knows her way around words and then some; and the Scholastic team, especially Jody Corbett, Starr Baer, and Elizabeth B. Parisi.

To Milo, who understands when Mommy has to shut herself away for a few months, and still thinks the whole author thing is cool.

As always, to my husband, Marcus, who gives good advice and delivers mega cappuccinos to order.

And special gratitude to my dearest, brave friend Sacha McVean, who tried to outrun a tsunami and inspired a heroine.